POETIC JUSTICE

BOOKS IN THIS SERIES

Poetic Justice: The Dawning
Poetic Justice: Oxford
Poetic Justice: Fame
Poetic Justice: The Inheritance
Poetic Justice: Intrusion
Poetic Justice: Tyro

TYRO

FRAN RAYA

The Book Guild Ltd

First published in Great Britain in 2023 by
The Book Guild Ltd
Unit E2 Airfield Business Park
Harrison Road, Market Harborough
Leicestershire, LE16 7UL
Freephone: 0800 999 2982
www.bookguild.co.uk
Email: info@bookguild.co.uk
Twitter: @bookguild

Typeset in Aldine401 BT

Printed and bound in Great Britain by CPI Group (UK) Ltd, Croydon, CR0 4YY

ISBN 978 1915603 906

British Library Cataloguing in Publication Data.
A catalogue record for this book is available from the British Library.

I wish to dedicate the sixth book in my Poetic Justice series to The Book Guild.

Without their faith in my work,
I would be in obscurity.

Thank you to all who have made it possible
and helped me every step of the way.

Randal Forbes calls his phenomenal telepathic powers 'the gift'.

In this sixth book of the series, he welcomes the new Millennium with his family and followers.

His 'chosen' daughter and inheritress, Roxanne, is still at his side, and just as powerful. His wife, Alison, and their children, Ryan and Amber, together with his lifelong protector, Clive Hargreaves, all remain steadfast in his life.

He has dealt with his formidable righteous rival, Carlton Flint, but when Tyrone Pendle arrives on the scene, with a similar level of dark power, it's up to Randal to either tutor or remove him.

Randal Forbes has a dark side so powerful that only someone with a similar 'gift' will be able to challenge him. Is Tyrone Pendle that adversary?

1

Randal Forbes looked up at the night sky through the window in his hotel suite. It was ablaze with a multiple rainbow explosion: a spectacular exhibition of festive fireworks to welcome the new Millennium. It merged magnificently with his forty-second birthday, both celebrations locked together in a majestic, jaw-dropping display. A brand-new century with more historic hills to climb.

January 1st 2000.

He pulled his wife, Alison, close to his side as they witnessed the London skyline alight in psychedelic illumination.

"Happy birthday, and here's to the next thousand years together." She giggled as she sipped another glass of red wine.

"For sure," he replied, his unusual eyes glinting in the subdued lamplight of their room. "I'd say that was more than likely."

"It's a very special occasion, so can I have a drink, Daddy?" asked Roxanne, as she walked gracefully through the door and into the room.

His strange gaze softened as he greeted her.

"Just one. I don't want my sixteen-year-old daughter drunk

and disorderly. Sobriety suits you better," he responded half in jest.

"And here's me thinking I've got the coolest dad on the planet. Don't you dare disappoint me. Just keep me on my toes but let me fly occasionally."

They smiled their special smiles at each other. It was a constant, silent understanding of kindred spiritship. A total, telepathic telegraphy, as they spoke to each other's minds.

You look so beautiful, pumpkin. Do you know how stunning you are?

I take after my father apparently.

There's no apparently about it. It's official.

Randal winked at her as she tossed back her luxurious mane of red hair in a never-ending dramatic fashion. Her slate-grey eyes glimmered with tiny, yellow glints, ready to ignite at the slightest stimulation or displeasure.

"Everyone's asking where you are. They want to wish you happy birthday, as well as a Happy New Millennium," she preened, looking at her reflection in the long mirror as she spoke, thoroughly approving of her unique and vibrant image.

"Roxanne's right. We shouldn't be up here. Let's go back down now and join the party; your party, Randal," slurred Alison slightly, as she planted a noisy kiss on his cheek.

"In a moment. We came up here for a reason," he reminded her.

He got hold of her hand and beckoned Roxanne to join them.

"I want this to be a private happening. It's a very special time, a momentous occasion, and I don't just mean my birthday. Let's enjoy it before we all come back down to earth," he instructed, knocking back the remains of his brandy in one.

He luxuriated in the explosion of colour as he pulled Alison and Roxanne towards him. They stood in a line, arms around each other, feeling the excitement in the smoke-filled air, listening to the roar of the crowd outside. A unique moment in history. Randal contemplated as he observed it all.

The year 2000! Where did the last forty-two go? Material time is no time at all. My firstborn, Ryan, was eighteen on Christmas Day. Eighteen! It's like looking at me in Oxford with a less intimidating gaze! That's where the similarity stops. He's as philanthropic as I'm disenchanted. The human race just doesn't float my boat. They still persist in an endless quest to nowhere. So inferior, so violent, so petty, but most of all, so uninformed.

Roxanne picked up on his thoughts, forever in tune with his opinions, and totally in agreement of his analogy. Her shapely lips made contact with her wine glass and she licked them as a tiny drop escaped into the corner of her mouth. The act looked provocative and did not go unnoticed as Ryan came into the room at exactly the same time.

He felt the usual heady sensation as his eyes trailed over her beautiful features and down the tight-fitting, green, satin dress, that clung to her tall, slim, but curvy frame. He frowned as he saw the chummy admiration society in front of him and felt hurt that he had not been included in this very special celebratory moment, but then neither had his sister, Amber, who was still downstairs looking after their little brother, Oscar.

"Dad, Clive's asking after you. He's got a birthday gift for you but wants to present it in front of everyone. He's a bit too plastered if you ask me; too much wine and God knows what else. He's never strayed more than a few feet away from the bar," explained Ryan, with a disapproving look on his handsome face.

"No change there then." Randal half-smiled. "OK, gang, we better split."

He checked himself in the large mirror, before he faced his ever-eager family and guests. He still smouldered: six foot two inches of overpowering charisma. His hair was its usual thick, coppery red but with the odd silver strand here and there. His facial features had hardly changed.

His timeless sensuality scorched everything and everyone around him. His body was slim, hard and toned, looking magnificent in his slick black suit, combined with a grey silk open-necked shirt. He was still a seductive specimen of masculinity, with an edge of androgyny: irresistible to all genders.

"You look good enough to eat," affirmed Alison, with a hiccup and a suggestive stance, also looking ridiculously sexy for a woman in her mid-forties.

"Doesn't he just?" agreed Roxanne, linking his arm.

Ryan frowned again. He felt the oh-so-familiar resentment at his father's effect on his mother and family. That emotion had stayed with him throughout the whole of his childhood and had followed him into adolescence. He doubted if it would ever be any different.

Mum always drops everything the second he appears, and Roxanne's even worse. Even Amber's feeling surplus to requirements these days. I wouldn't mind, but Roxanne's adopted. She's our sister on paper only. The way I feel about her it's just as well. She's mesmerising. I guess I've loved her from the minute we met as kids. I wish I didn't feel this way. God, it's so complicated because legally she's my sister but biologically she's not.

Randal heard every thought in Ryan's head and it stopped him in his tracks. His deep concern was on the rise.

Whoa! This is bad! Really, really tricky! I can't tell him that Roxanne's my blood daughter, his half-sister. He'd freak out and Alison would go ballistic and that would be the end of my family life. I should have seen this coming. He's always been enraptured by her, but I thought he'd grow out of it. He's kept his deepest emotions away from my psychic antennae. I've been too busy to keep a check on his spiralling obsession.

Roxanne also tuned in to her brother's feelings and felt a strange mixture of unease and laudation but was savvy enough to realise that his infatuation needed to be nipped in the escalating bud. She spoke to her father's mind.

Don't worry, Daddy. I'll make sure that Ryan falls for someone else. I don't wish to hurt him emotionally. He needs to know that I don't want a physical relationship. He'll smart for a while and his pride will take a bashing, but it's necessary. I love him because he's my half-brother, but I can't tell him. He's bound to feel rejected. Better that than devastated.

Randal nodded in silent agreement but felt uneasy as they made their way to the elevator. The door swished open and they stepped inside the relatively small space with several other people. Ryan's heartbeat quickened as he found himself squashed up against Roxanne. His body language spoke volumes, but she made light of the situation as she felt her father's wrath filtering through the airwaves.

"Now I know how a tinned sardine feels before it's spread on a piece of toast," she jested, and they all laughed, except Randal.

Ryan tried hard to hide his feelings, but his growing erection had a mind of its own.

They stepped out on the third floor where their banqueting hall was situated.

"Go on ahead with Ryan," instructed Randal to Alison. "I just need to talk to Roxanne for a minute before we all get lost in the noise of the crowd."

"Can't it wait, Dad?" complained Ryan, feeling uncomfortable in more ways than one. "You've been away from all our guests for a while. You didn't even let the New Year in with them, never mind your actual birthday."

"Just do as I say!" insisted Randal with a glazed, unnerving stare.

Ryan knew that look only too well. He had been bottle-fed on it and lived in fear of its demonic dazzle. It was usually reserved for 'the detractors', as Randal called them: for those who wished to discredit him or invade his privacy.

"Try not to be too long, please. Clive's waiting impatiently and Amber's not happy about being lumbered with looking after Oscar," braved Ryan.

"Lumbered with Oscar? He's her little brother!" admonished Alison.

"He's a seven-year-old imp who's constantly up to mischief, so she needs eyes in the back of her hormonal head. He drives her mad with his hyperactive ways," protested Ryan.

Randal felt annoyed at the whole situation.

Roxanne's mouth twitched with sardonic humour, but then she reined it in when she felt her father's growing impatience and rocketing displeasure.

"Just go!" barked Randal.

"We're going, we're going. See you both at the party," appeased Alison, who was far too merry to sense an unwholesome atmosphere.

Ryan put a protective arm around his mother's shoulder as he walked her along the corridor. Randal turned to Roxanne as soon as they were out of earshot.

"Now then, mini-minx! We need to talk quickly and openly about your older sibling. This is your fault entirely, you know. You've led him on in a dangerous power game since you were kids, and now, you're reaping the unwanted reward of his incestuous desire. So, I need to know exactly what you're going to do about it! Well?" he pressed, with luminous eyes.

Roxanne's stare mirrored Randal's. She was furious at his insulting insinuation.

"So says my father, who can't tell his besotted son that I'm really his half-sister! The secret sibling, born out of a dirty, one-night stand with his tragic starlet! The one called Maxine Hale, who broke her neck and died on stage, at the aforementioned father's telepathic behest!" she snapped, regretting her outburst instantly.

Randal's face crumpled as he hung his head to hide his pained expression.

"Oh, Daddy, I'm so sorry! I didn't mean it! I love you so much! Oh, I get so mad not being able to let the world know that I'm your true daughter, your special child. I've got to hide it and I just hate it! I hate it!" she cried, throwing her arms around him in deep remorse.

"Shh. It's OK. I didn't mean to accuse you either. We're both at fault here, so let's wipe the slate clean," he whispered into her glorious red hair.

A couple of people walked towards them inquisitively, so they stopped conversing momentarily.

"I'll sort it all out with Ryan. I really will," she assured him when they were alone again.

He lifted up her chin so that they stood face to face.

"I know you will. But the sooner the better, otherwise he'll have to be fully hypnotised to break the habit of a lifetime, so to speak. You do understand that, don't you? Hmm?"

"I do."

"Right, that's OK then. Now, we'll get back to the flock-mock, and let our identical red hair down," he jested.

"Daddy."

"Yes, pumpkin?"

"I'm a good girl, really."

He smiled at her childhood trademark phrase and wiped her tear-stained cheeks with his thumbs.

"You're *my* good girl. My most special daughter. That'll never change. You're the authentic recipient of 'the gift' and that's more important than mere human acknowledgement. You've been chosen to carry our spiritual banner. The sacrosanct slogan of our heritage. The absolute embodiment of our benefaction. You'll always be my favourite child. *Always!*" he stressed.

"Even more than Oscar? He came along after all of us: the result of your deep love for Mummy. Another son born out of real passion. I think he's got a watered-down version of 'the gift'. Ryan's right, though, he's totally over the top and unmanageable, but I think he's frustrated. His powers are neither here nor there. You seem closer to him than Ryan. Do you sense a blossoming force within him?"

"Fractionally."

"So how can I be your successor? In out-dated, traditional terms, the male of the species is first in line to the crown," she pouted.

"Oscar's so-called powers are compromised. They are ineffective and could even fizzle out before he matures. Time will tell. As for the inheritance, well, you've been chosen. You know that. It's non-negotiable. You are the one!"

"I am, aren't I?" she gloated, her features altering into an imperious expression: a pompous display of sheer self-importance.

"OK, let's show these lesser mortals how to grab the bull by its high-flying horns. Ready?"

"Ready. I love you, Daddy."

"Of course you do. I love you, too."

"Forever?"

"Forever."

They walked arm in arm towards the party, causing heads to turn. A father-and-daughter striking picture. A dual magnetic presence.

As they came into view, Clive came tottering over to greet them, his balance affected by his alcoholic intake.

"Where the hell have you two been? You've gone and spoiled my surprise!" he slurred, still managing to hold his brandy glass without spilling any of its contents.

"I'm astonished you even noticed in that state! Slow down, Clive. It's a celebration not a pub crawl," teased Randal, but the joke went right over his protector's woolly head.

Clive's silvering, ginger hair looked like a static, thatched halo at the top of his head, and his freckled face broke into a sardonic smile.

"Less of the laconic lip, maestro. Just watch! I've got something to show you, as a true measure of my undying adoration," insisted Clive.

"Now you've got me curious as well, Uncle Clive. Can I see it too?" requested Roxanne.

"Everyone can. That's the aim," he explained.

Randal had a mental flash of a succession of photographs, but he hid his psychic vision well, even from his ever-inquisitive daughter. Clive meandered unsteadily towards the front of the room towards a small stage. He stepped on to its platform and picked up a microphone, tapping it to make sure it was amplified.

"One two, one two, can everybody hear me? Attention, please! Our birthday boy has resurfaced and I've got a unique present for him, but I want us all to share it together. *Can you hear me out there!*" shouted Clive unnecessarily, as the vocal sound waves were transformed into electric signals that overpowered everyone's conversations.

"What's this, Edward?" asked Margaret Forbes excitedly. "Is it yet another accolade for our precious son?"

"Sounds like it, but everyone needs to be quiet. They're still talking in clusters," observed Randal's father disapprovingly. "Clive's words are falling on deaf ears in certain quarters."

Edward was about to give Clive a helping hand, but Randal was spotted by all, and a huge roar reverberated through the jam-packed room.

"Here he is at last! Our very own Randal Edward Forbes!" fawned Clive, with a drunken, besotted expression.

"Happy birthday, darling!" His Aunty Dottie beamed, planting a sugar-pink lipstick imprint on Randal's cheek with an inebriated kiss, standing on tiptoes to reach him and nearly falling over in the process.

"She's had far too much to drink, as you can see. There's too much blood in her alcohol stream," quipped Dean, at his mother's exuberant greeting.

"It's allowed," verified Randal to his favourite cousin.

"See, Dean! See! My beloved nephew doesn't adman… admen… admin… oh, what the hell's that word?" she faltered.

"*Admonish*, Mother! He doesn't *admonish* you," mocked Dean, winking at his Aunty Margaret, who looked disapprovingly at her youngest sister for behaving like some tipsy teenager.

"Yes! That! He doesn't ever do that!" she agreed, wagging her index finger in Dean's face.

"Anyway, Mum. Shush now! Clive's talking. Look, he's got a birthday surprise for Randal," reasoned Dean, turning her round to face the stage.

The furore settled down and all eyes were on Randal's protector.

"Have I got everyone's attention now?" asked Clive on wobbly legs.

"Yes!" they all replied.

"Get on with it!" shouted his father, Paul Hargreaves. "I'm going on holiday in June!"

Laughter rippled through the banqueting hall at his affectionate sarcasm, and Randal chuckled to himself at the whole gathering.

Look at them all. I've got family, friends and sycophants coming out of my ears. What would they say if I told them who I really am, and who I'll always be? Only Clive and Roxanne know the whole story. Would they be so worshipping if they had a ringside seat at my homicidal circus? If they read my sacrificial real-life scripts? My imaginative, murderous plots?

And now, here comes my beguiled Uncle Ashley. He thinks the sun rises and sets in my altruistic orbit. I'm extremely fond of him, but eight years on, he still doesn't have a clue about my part in his son's enforced plunge off that perfectly placed motorway bridge, into a line of impacted, colliding traffic. The classic ending for my incompatible cousin. Spencer the sneak, forward-slash, snake. I've no regrets about his removal. Uncle Ashley's feculent, farcical firstborn.

Ashley Forbes slapped Randal on his back, shook his hand firmly, and wished him a happy birthday and an equally good New Year.

"Be quiet," whispered Edward in his younger brother's ear. "Clive's got a surprise for Randal, so shush."

A screen appeared at the back of the stage out of nowhere, and someone dimmed the lights. Clive seemed suddenly sober in his eager quest as he spoke, feeling the usual deep emotions that were entrenched forever in his heart.

"Randal. Randal, my dearest, closest, wondrous friend. Here's my birthday gift to you. I thought long and hard about it because what do you buy for the man who has everything? So, I came up with this instead, and seeing it's my own birthday in a few days' time, I thought this a very fitting commemoration for us both."

Clive's mother, Rosemary Hargreaves, felt her eyes fill up with nostalgic tears as a recording of Alison's original musical composition, accompanied a photographic journey into her son's, and Randal's, past. Her husband, Paul, also became rather emotional at the images.

It began in 1965 at Redwood, the private school where they met as little boys, then worked its way slowly through their teenage years. Memories came flooding back to both sets of parents, and Margaret bit her lip at the poignancy.

It embraced their university life at Beaumont College in Oxford, and Alison laughed out loud at Randal's heavy stage make-up for his self-penned play *Telesthesia.*

"It looks more like boot polish than foundation." She giggled.

"It felt like it," cringed Randal.

Amber smiled weakly at her parents' comments, keeping her ever-watchful eye on her brother, Oscar, who was overtired and overwrought.

I've not relaxed or enjoyed myself tonight at all. Dad thinks more of

Uncle Clive than of me, or Ryan, for that matter. And, of course, there's Roxanne. It's always been the three of them. A trio of conjoined triplets. They're so close and so closed.

"I want some pop! Amber, I want some more pop!" demanded Oscar, showing her his empty glass.

"Not now! Uncle Clive's showing us pictures of him and Daddy, as a treat. Watch it with me, just for a while." she instructed.

Oscar pulled a face and looked like Randal at the age of seven when he was displeased with a situation.

"OK. I'll wait, but not too long." He glared with glittering eyes, which appeared as if they would ignite but remained as they were.

Randal felt his wrath but knew that his anger would stop right there. He was incapable of any further response. His tantrum was more human: a little boy's reaction to not getting his own way.

The photographic collage carried on, and when multiple pictures of Clarendon Hall popped up, everyone gasped at its resplendence.

"Randal still visits Lord and Lady Pennington in Banbury, even after all these years," whispered Margaret, in her sister June's ear.

June instantly informed her husband, Christopher, with pomposity by proxy. Their daughter, Heather, Randal's maternal cousin, raised her eyes to the ornate ceiling. Titles meant nothing to her. They were meaningless and she still preferred animals to people. Her husband, Larry, nodded his head in silent approval of her indifference.

There followed some actual film footage in the Aztec rubble, when they stayed in Mexico to work on Randal's first book *Fiesta*.

A ripple of amusement filtered through the crowd as a photograph of the pair of them appeared, sat on their hotel balcony with naked torsos and sombreros, surveying the scene below them. Clive's heartbeat doubled as he remembered their time there.

God, he looks so hot with that cheroot in between his lips. I couldn't keep my hands off him that day and he wasn't exactly rejecting my advances either!

Randal heard his saucy recollection and the corners of his mouth turned upwards in a secretive, seductive smile.

Just look at my parents. Pride brimming over; so much respect and affection for Clive too. What would they say if they saw us thrashing about in the nude? Concocting different ways of reaching the ultimate thrill? They'd combust! Sorry, folks, even after all these years I still need that same-sex fix. But you'd still explode with homophobic hysterics!

Roxanne picked up on her father's bisexuality, although she had always saw right through his tight-lipped, sexual sideline. It made her smile rather than wince.

I don't blame Uncle Clive wanting my beautiful father. Who wouldn't?

The photographic pilgrimage continued on its nostalgic way, but now they were in America, when Randal had his first shot at screenwriting in Los Angeles, while Clive accompanied him as his agent. Randal remembered the way he'd bewitched the director into letting him have full control of the adaptation of his blockbuster novel *Fiesta* for the silver screen. In one of the pictures, Randal's expression was arrogant and domineering, as Clive had looked on with obvious admiration at the way he'd manipulated the production team. Clive's heart fluttered as he observed the images.

And I'm still in complete awe of his genius after all these years. Eternally well versed with his domination and swamping presence, that takes my breath away and threatens to stop me breathing at all, that leaves me helpless and vulnerable at his command. It really shouldn't be allowed! It's immoral. He's immoral, not to mention decadent and highly sexed. A walking, talking erection. Oh my! That's a celebration in itself.

"Wasn't Randal stunning in these shots?" boasted Margaret to Dottie.

"What do you mean, *was*?" shot back Roxanne in a questioning manner. "Daddy doesn't do '*was*'. He only does '*is*'."

Margaret's expression hardened. She thoroughly objected to Roxanne's contradictory stance. In fact, she totally disapproved of her constant presence and perpetual hold over Randal's attention.

"Look, Mum, here's a great pic of me and Clive in New York when we flew out for my TV appearance on that chat show," interrupted Randal, diverting her attention away from the discord.

He knew that she utterly resented Roxanne's close proximity and had major issues with her taking preference over Ryan, Amber and now Oscar. The feigned attack worked momentarily as his mother went back into adoring mode. Randal spoke to Roxanne's mind.

Cool it, pumpkin. Try and tone down the attitude. Butter her up instead of bringing her down.

I can't help it. I know she doesn't like me one bit.

Then make her! You've got the ability to charm anyone, anytime, anywhere.

Hmm.

So, do it. For me?

For you, but not for her.

She's still your grandmother in human terms.

But I can never tell her that, can I? I'm a forever secret. The eternal orphan. Maxine's unwanted voodoo child and Saul's counterfeit daughter. We both killed them! What would she say to that?

Stop wallowing in lesser mortal weakness and self-pity. It's irrelevant. How many times do I have to tell you this? Your legacy totally outstrips your biological heredity.

They looked intently at each other as Randal nodded to affirm his opinion. Then he smiled his special smile and Roxanne's heart melted. She felt her pulse race as the importance of his words really hit home. She must simply learn to adapt and deceive in equal measure, in order to avoid any discourse or suspicion.

I'll try my best. It's hard but I'll get there, she said telepathically, and Randal kissed her cheek.

Alison's captivating piano piece continued in the background as numerous pictures still flashed on and off the screen of all the noteworthy events that Randal and Clive had attended over the years. Randal meditated as the never-ending pictorial collage continued.

We certainly are tied together eternally. Even I didn't realise how many shots there are of us. I must admit he's so much more than my protector. We unite on many levels. He's my same-sex soulmate: appointed officially through 'the gift' to shelter me from assumption, suspicion and human emotional baggage. I really would be quite bereft without his devotion. I must tell him that more often. How much he means to me – to Roxanne as well.

Ryan's angry voice interrupted Randal's contemplation.

"Oscar! Oscar, stop messing with Amber's dress! You've left chocolate stains on it and pulled it out of shape," he scolded, as his little brother tugged at the hem of the expensive garment with sticky fingers.

"I want some more pop! Nobody cares! I want, I want, I want!" he repeated, his frustration causing his facial features to crumple.

"Oscar! Behave!" berated Randal with an ominous glare in his annoyed gaze. "Come here and keep still."

Oscar looked at his father's glittering eyes and backed down immediately like a dog with its tail between its legs. He joined him, burying his head underneath Randal's suit jacket to curry favour.

"Don't! Just stand here in front of me so I can see you, and stop ruining this surprise that your Uncle Clive has put together for me!" stressed Randal.

"Don't scold him, Randal. You know he's gets tetchy easily. Come here, Oscar, and I'll get you some lemonade very soon," said Alison softly.

"You spoil him! He needs to know that he's not the boss. He'll just grow up expecting everyone to fall in with his demands," chided Randal.

"Then he'll have a lot in common with his father. Won't he?" she replied sarcastically with a knowing look.

Amber's mouth twitched into a wry smile at her mother's sardonic but accurate response.

Take that, Dad! You're a complete control freak. Just like Oscar. And while I'm thinking about it, let's throw Roxanne into the same mix. She rules the Randal-roost, far more than any of your other litter. The rest of us are relegated on an annual basis, while she permanently sits at the top of the premiership table.

One day soon I'm going to tell you how rejected and angry I really feel. That's if I pluck up the courage. When I can face that alien, glistening expression in your narrow gaze. The same one that Roxanne shows me when she's challenged. She copies everything you do or say. She always has.

Randal tuned in to Amber's negative vibrations and tormented thoughts. He felt her pain bubbling under the surface, below the brave exterior she displayed at all times.

Shit! Still waters run deep. How long has she felt like this? Oh, these human frailties. I do love her, though. She's also my very own, so I better start showing her just that. All this analysis is marring Clive's presentation and my mass adulation. Being a father is disrupting my real purpose. But I must keep them all happy and safe and steer them away from resentment. And so must Roxanne.

A thunderous applause spread across the room as Clive's unique and touching presentation concluded with a very last photograph of them both: once again as little boys at Dunloe Gap in Ireland.

"Absolutely bloody marvellous!" clapped Edward. "What a unique birthday gift. It's got to be his best one – just as moving as Alison's actual soundtrack, and that's saying something!"

"Speech! Speech!" commanded the crowd as they all looked at Randal.

He shook himself out of his reflections and weaved his way through the throng to reach the stage, all the while being slapped on the back with affectionate respect.

He joined Clive on the podium, hugged him and looked at him with misty eyes.

Randal took the microphone and cleared his throat before he spoke. The actor in him itched to perform and a sense of theatre enhanced his dramatic aura. The wild applause abated and the room embraced the sound of silence.

"Well, well, well. What can I possibly add to that incredible photographic journey through the last century? Yes, guys, the last century! A different era beckons, and here we all are, on my forty-second birthday, welcoming the new Millennium. How cool is that?"

"A cool birthday for the coolest dude!" shouted Dean.

"All right, don't worry, Dean. You'll get your New Year's pay rise, in line with inflation," joked Randal.

"I never thought for one minute that I wouldn't," quipped Dean, and Randal waited for the laughter to stop.

"Seriously, though. Regardless of any future goals that myself and my beautiful family may achieve, I have to thank this guy here. My perpetual partner in creative crime, for the most original and touching birthday gift that a prolific genius could ever have. This special person at my side who goes by the name of Clive. He's my most loyal, irreplaceable and treasured lifelong friend."

Clive struggled to breathe with the emotion of the moment.

Randal felt his devotion and looked at him lovingly.

"Let's be honest here. Quite frankly I'd be fifty per cent worse off without him. He's the Morecambe to my Wise. The Holmes to my Watson, and, at times, the undisputable Laurel to my Hardy. Don't laugh, everyone. It's true! I could write another bestseller on the crazy antics we've got up to, but I can't tell you in front of my children. You're laughing again, but some things are better left unsaid. He knows everything about me and still puts up with my moods, methods and madness. So please; please raise your glasses to Mr Clive Hargreaves. May his frizzy hair and freckles continue to amuse me, and his all-seeing hazel eyes profess to adore me. *To Clive!*" enthused Randal wholeheartedly.

"*To Clive!*" echoed the guests.

"*To both of you!*" shouted Roxanne, moving nearer to the stage, with a wide grin on her beautiful face.

Her toast was repeated by them all.

Oh, Daddy. I know you love Uncle Clive with your body as well as your heart. It's a powerful connection regardless of gender. And he adores you and has sacrificed his life for you. It's perfectly understandable because you're unique and just devastatingly attractive. But most of all he accepts and protects 'the gift'. Sometimes unwillingly, but in the end unquestionably.

"Now, everyone, carry on merry-making. Having said that, some of you look ready for bed. Either that, or you've over-indulged," remarked Randal affectionately, jumping off the stage and into the path of his mother's sister.

"We love you, Randal," slurred his Aunty Dottie, with bloodshot eyes.

"Whoa! Aunty Dot! I was just about to light up a cheroot, but don't come near the flame! How many glasses of wine have you had?"

"Too many!" Her husband, Neil, laughed. "But who's counting? This is a very special occasion!"

Dottie wobbled over to Dean.

"See! Neil's on my side."

"You'll be on your side soon, Mum! On the bloody floor!"

"Gravity is a fair-weather friend, eh, Aunty Dot?" teased Randal.

Then all of his paternal and maternal family approached him, and he was mobbed by well-wishers.

His sister, Patricia, who now lived in France, had flown over especially for the occasion. She still looked blonde and beautiful. Her husband, Paul Dupont, and their twelve-year-old twin sons, Henri and George, embraced Randal with warmth, affection and love.

Alison, Ryan, Amber and Oscar were pushed away in the crush, but Roxanne was first in the queue.

I love you, Daddy. All of these people want a piece of you, but you're mine. Let's welcome the year 2000 to our kingdom.

And the telepathic removals that lie ahead!

2

Dean Gibson swivelled his chair around in studio one of Astral TV. He still worked for Randal's company in the capacity of head programme controller, and had added a considerable classy touch to the already well-established channel with his various innovative projects over the years.

Presently, he was planning the format of a new family quiz show but could hardly concentrate on the job in hand. It was not the structure or the content of the latest broadcast that stopped him directing his creative mind solely on his aim. It was the love for his current girlfriend, and the deep emotion and compassion she aroused in his heart.

He was thirty-four, and totally ready to settle down after a string of relationships. He was very eligible – physically, mentally and financially – but none of his past affairs came close to the rapture he felt for this current romance. He ran his fingers through his thick, black hair and looked once more at the photograph of his latest flame. His bright blue gaze burned with passion as he admired her long blonde hair, pretty face and her own bluer-than-blue eyes.

She was the image of her deceased father, and here lay the huge problem that her arrival would undoubtedly create in his own family circle, specifically the first-class, emotional baggage that would travel with her. Her name alone had a taboo connection, a macabre ring to it, together with multiple unsavoury memories. Dean frowned as he thought about the deep, unbearable trauma she had endured. His beautiful wife-to-be, her name forever stigmatised.

Maddie Flint.

She was only seventeen when her deranged mother maimed her father, Carlton, and killed two family friends with a meat cleaver, eight years ago. I felt compelled to help both her and her sister, Zoe, come to terms with the horrendous reality of it all.

Carlton Flint was a remarkable man, a mesmerising astrologer, but mostly he was my good friend. I made him a TV celebrity, but his star did not shine for long. He was critically injured on his last show of Celestial Bodies *by that monstrous falling screen.*

He ended up in a coma, but he survived, only to be maimed again by his axe-wielding lunatic wife, Francine. Then, while recovering in hospital, an equally deranged nurse murdered him with a morphine overdose. Maddie and Zoe were two devastated teenagers and had been left with their extended family but mostly the horrific fallout of their mother's heinous crimes and their father's untimely death.

Dean shuddered at the enormity of the gory recollections. In the beginning he had helped them both as a family friend, but in the last year, his feelings for Maddie had changed from platonic commiseration to a full-blown fervour, and she felt the same magnetic pull.

Dean was completely in the dark about Randal and Roxanne's demonic part in Carlton's demise. In fact, he had been totally duped all his life by Randal's counterfeit benevolence towards his fellow man. He did not sense the tiniest flicker of falsehood and had never seen the evil, noxious, unwholesome side of his beloved cousin, who had always gone out of his scheming way to protect and nurture him.

Randal's not going to be happy about this. He's always wanted the very best for me. I know he wasn't keen on Carlton, although I could never understand why. He didn't want to get involved with his family after the murders. This is a tricky one. A very tricky one indeed.

Randal's obsession with Dean had caused him to call upon 'the gift' to commit a chain of telepathic murders in the name of his corrupt justice: that so-called poetic justice against Dean's real kith and kin, resulting in the unfeeling, callous removal of his birth father and half-brother.

Additionally, there was the five members of the Haynes family who had dared to gossip about Dean's birthright, causing untold pain to his mother, Randal's beloved Aunty Dottie. In Randal's mind they were all guilty of unforgivable betrayal and injustice.

Carlton Flint became Randal's unexpected, fiercest telepathic rival and had to be removed, regardless of Dean's affection for him. Randal's hatred of Carlton outshone any that of previous targeted victims. Together with Roxanne, he had created the whole tragedy in which Carlton, Dr Winston Ramsey and Stella Reid had succumbed to their murderous telepathic instructions. A sickening, violent bloodbath with the blame being laid at Francine Flint's innocent, hypnotised door.

But the fallout from the devastation, eight years ago, had created unanswered questions. Rewinding back to 1992, there had been a deluge of doubt and suspicion.

***

Carlton had survived the meat cleaver episode and was hospitalised only to be 'accidentally' killed by a nurse administering a morphine injection with six times the recommended pain relief in the syringe: a fully manipulated nurse under the strict instructions of Randal's powerful hypnosis. The police arrested the alleged culprit, who was utterly inconsolable and could not remember even dispensing the overdose.

"Officer, please! Please believe me! I can't recall anything and I don't remember even being in the room! It's as if my mind's a complete blank. I'm not a murderer! I'm a dedicated nurse and this unforgivable error has destroyed me! But I can't remember! I simply can't remember!" she sobbed uncontrollably.

"How long have you been a nurse, Miss Archer?"

"Fifteen years, and I've always done my job well. I care deeply about all my patients and I'd never do anything so negligent. You simply have to believe me!"

"According to your superior, you were worried about a chipped nail rather than the fact that Carlton Flint was flatlining. Is that the case?"

"I can't remember! I just can't! You're not listening to me!"

"This doesn't make any sense, Miss Archer. You do realise that, don't you?"

Detective Inspector Wayne Bredbury contemplated as he handcuffed her.

Hmm. Francine Flint said exactly the same thing when we charged her! Very strange!

Carlton Flint was adamant about his wife being hypnotised and not in control of her actions. He blamed Randal Forbes of all people!

He told me that Forbes was a psychotic psychic who raided heads and used his powers to kill people. He insisted that Forbes wanted to murder him and would still come after him regardless. Did he? He also mentioned that Forbes's daughter, Roxanne, had the same dark streak. He was very sure about this. He sounded quite coherent, but I thought he was as deranged as his wife. I wonder? Should I look into this a bit closer?

As a result of Nurse Archer's duplicate plea of innocence, Detective Bredbury had made it his business to check out Randal's track record. His discoveries were extremely daunting.

Through police records and newspaper reports, he determined that Randal had been questioned in numerous instances with regard to various fatalities. He had always figured in the vicinity of or been linked with the deceased. He noted that Randal had been hauled in by the Manchester, Cumbrian, Oxford and Weybridge constabularies for cross-examination. Even more alarming were the deaths of the police officers connected to two of the cases, and the bizarre, extreme circumstances in which they had perished.

This is so weird! Chief Inspector Leonard Galloway was killed in a stationary car on a level crossing, with his friend Dr Patrick Shaw. A train collided with them and the car exploded, so any evidence was hard to establish.

The train driver's statement is also very odd. He felt that it was an accident waiting to happen, as one of the victims was just sat in his seat, staring straight ahead. The passenger's head was slumped on his shoulder. There was no panic to get out of the way. How could that be?

He researched further and saw that Leonard had been chief inspector with the Manchester police at the time of his death, and that Dr Patrick Shaw was his close friend. He looked at the newspaper article again.

Just a minute! Now this is really strange. It states that 'Victoria Shaw and her two daughters, Mandy and Louise, are being comforted by family and friends, including the famous author and entrepreneur Randal Forbes'. So, he's connected to the Shaw family. Why would he want to harm the doctor? Or the inspector? Or anyone for that matter? This theory is over the top. Isn't it?

He backtracked even further to see why Randal had been questioned by the Manchester authorities.

He was the last person, along with his cousin Dean, to speak to the Haynes children, before they all drowned in January 1976! His statement is quite straightforward, but something, or someone, pushed Leonard Galloway to look further into his movements. Did he suspect anything else?

Inspector Bredbury made himself a strong coffee to accompany his increasing curiosity. He studied the Cumbrian report.

Robbie Sterling, a student from Beaumont College, Oxford, died after falling off a cliff in the Lakeland Fells in summer 1977. And guess who was with him? Randal and his close friend Clive Hargreaves! So, they only had their word as to what happened. What had Sterling done to possibly arouse Randal's so-called dark powers?

Just a minute again! It states that Robbie was the son of the late John Sterling who was murdered in a hotel in 1965 and his assassin was never found! It seems that Sterling was married and having an affair at the time with one Dottie Thornton who was pregnant with his baby. Whoa! Dottie Thornton! That's Randal's aunt and Dean is Randal's cousin! Dean was that baby and now works alongside Randal at Astral TV. This is getting creepy.

He took a large gulp of his coffee and shook his head.

Surely this is all coincidence?

The inspector saw there was another investigatory report from the Oxford constabulary concerning the last day of October 1977.

Marcus Pennington, son of Lord and Lady Pennington of Banbury, was declared insane and sent down for setting his grandfather's rectory on fire and killing him as a result. Also, he had tried to hang himself but failed.

The report states that he was homosexual and probably argued with his grandfather over his same-sex preference, which caused the crime that subsequently led to his suicide attempt. And guess what? Randal and Clive were both questioned as they were all close friends at Beaumont College, Oxford. Again!

I know for a fact that Randal's still close to the Penningtons. He's been pictured with Lady Pennington often. Hmm.

He slumped back in his chair and took a deep breath. There was more evidence to sift through and he needed to take his time. He berated himself for even suspecting there was something unusual going on because nothing had ever been proved. But he carried on regardless, his interest stimulated and totally aroused.

The small-time impresario Don Cannon was killed in a car bomb explosion on Christmas Day 1981. Randal was hauled in with his artist Saul Curtis for questioning. Apparently, Cannon was claiming that he was owed money by Curtis, who he felt was still contracted to him. He generated scandalous publicity maligning Curtis's character and was a nasty piece of work.

Now, who was the officer in charge of this case? Oh my God! This can't be! The late Detective Inspector Ronald Grey, who shot himself through the head in a cemetery, resulting in a mysterious, complicated murder investigation.

The hairs on the back of Wayne Bredbury's neck stood to military attention.

What the hell have we here? The original Don Cannon investigation was closed due to lack of evidence. Nine years later, Saul Curtis was murdered alongside Inspector Grey, together with Don Cannon's son, Trevor.

All of them near Maxine Hale's grave! The same Maxine Hale who had committed suicide while performing in Randal's show! When Randal was in the audience!

Randal was her manager and made Maxine and Saul huge stars. He was at their wedding. They were all intertwined.

Oh my word!

A shiver trailed down his spine, and his body felt cold and clammy at the same time.

Why on earth was Inspector Ronald Grey in the aforementioned graveyard alone, without other officers, and more so, why did he top himself? He had called his team urgently to join him as there were crucial developments in the Saul Curtis case. When they arrived, they saw him put the gun to his head and shoot himself. It was deliberate. Why? He was the most methodical, level-headed officer I'd ever met!

He got involved with the case because Saul was being threatened. Who threatened him? Cannon's son? According to Ronald Grey it wasn't. He'd ruled him out. But it could have been. Why did they all go to the cemetery at the same time? And end up together in one ditch! Butchered and shot!

The room felt cold, so he put on his jacket. He was beginning to wish that he smoked to calm his nerves. Then the most important realisation smacked him in the face.

Oh my days! Randal, and his wife, Alison, adopted Maxine and Saul's daughter, Roxanne! I remember reading about it and thinking how much she looked like Randal. I need to check this fact out because alarm bells are more than ringing! They're positively Big Benning! And it's not tinnitus!

His hands began to tremble as he meditated some more.

What's up with me? It's probably a reaction to all this gloom-ridden supposition. Calm down, deep breaths and carry-on researching. Let's go back to Inspector Ronald Grey's report where he first interviewed Randal in 1981 when Don Cannon was blown to bits in his car.

His expression became more startled by the second as he read Ronald Grey's handwritten report, word for word. It was mind-blowing and made shocking reading.

After interrogating Forbes, I suspect he's hiding something. I was struck dumb by the chilling statement in his piercing eyes, especially when I dug a lot deeper into his past association with various individuals in unsolved homicidal crimes.

I was alerted beforehand to it all by Chief Inspector Leonard Galloway of the Manchester Constabulary, who had compiled a list of alleged victims, all connected to Forbes, in an ongoing investigation. Galloway said he was expecting Forbes to retaliate after Cannon's character assassination of Saul Curtis in the newspapers.

Galloway also touched upon the subject of paranormal activity. According to an unnamed medical associate of his, they felt that Forbes was actually fiercely telepathic and could invade minds, causing each victim to dance to his tune, so to speak.

I find this particular theory hard to believe, but I have to admit that I felt my head was being poached by Forbes, as if he was reading my thoughts.

I still want to meet up with Galloway because I do feel that Forbes is malevolent. His charismatic public persona did not correspond with the dark, brooding, forbidding and menacing aura that he displayed under investigation. Serial killers hide their movements well. I cannot ignore any possible involvement.

However, there is still no positive proof of this speculation, as it is just my personal opinion, but I have to note the possibility.

Report by Detective Inspector Ronald Grey –
27th December 1981.

Wayne Bredbury felt his head begin to pound with overwhelming swirling theories.

Who was the unknown medical associate of Galloway who suspected Randal's supernatural leanings? It's got to be Dr Patrick Shaw! And they were both killed in their car on a level crossing!

The Weybridge Constabulary have kept this on file but not in order to continue investigating Randal. It's mainly to show that Inspector Ronald Grey was unstable in his assumptions. They think that it was the start of his mental illness and that it may have contributed to his depressive state and subsequent suicide, albeit nine years later. Saul Curtis had approached him to report he was being stalked and threatened. So, Grey reopened the case.

Let's have a closer look at the newspaper write-up after Ronald Grey shot himself in the head.

He perused the harrowing article and then another name jumped out of the page at him, and he almost jerked his chair backwards with yet even more suspicion and alarm.

What! I can't believe this! It mentions that Ronald Grey was friendly with the barrister Spencer Forbes, and they had worked together on several court cases, but Spencer refused to comment when Ronald died and had actively distanced himself from the whole homicidal mess.

Spencer is Randal's cousin, for Christ's sake! Oh, hell, he was!

Because I remember he also topped himself by jumping off a motorway bridge into moving traffic, not long after Ronald's death.

What the fuck's going on here? I need a stiff drink. This whole thing throws a completely different perspective on Francine Flint's insane denial of murder in the first degree!

His research was interrupted by his second in command.

"Sir, are you coming with us for lunch? Travis is treating us all. He's had a win on the football pools and is feeling generous for once," he jested.

"What? No, no, you go ahead. I'm busy. I might join, you but I doubt it," he replied distractedly.

"Another homicide?"

"No, the Francine Flint case."

"But she's been convicted and sent down."

"I know, but something's bothering me, and I need to do some more research."

"Oh?"

"Just let me get on with it. If I've anything to report I'll let you all know."

He went back to his findings and meditated some more. He supped his cup of coffee, which was now stone cold, but he did not notice.

What did Carlton Flint say to me before he was morphined to death? He was adamant that his wife was being used. That she was under Randal's hypnotic control and not responsible for her actions.

He told me he had the same telepathic powers as Randal, but he used his to help people, not to kill them. He explained that Randal entered their heads through a photographic image behind closed doors. That he was a psychotic psychic and used his powers to remove them when under threat. Oh my days!

***

On the strength of his harrowing discoveries, Detective Wayne

Bredbury had decided to visit Francine Flint in prison. She had been unanimously found guilty of double murder in the first degree. She was serving two life sentences and would never be released.

There was also the little matter of Nurse Archer, who had pleaded diminished responsibility over her part in Carlton's death and had similarly been sent down for life regardless.

While he was driving on his way to the prison, another unsavoury avalanche of information came into his head. His mind was now totally focused on the life and times of Randal Forbes.

I remember that damning article in The Announcer *about his whole career being corrupt. It was slanderous. The journalist who wrote it was found dead in a river not long afterwards, yet again in mysterious circumstances.*

"Watch where you're going!" shouted another driver through his window at him.

Wayne nearly scraped his car as he overtook him.

Oh hell, concentrate, man, on the road, as well as on the case in hand. Multitask while you're contemplating! Now, where was I? Oh, yes, the drowned journalist. I remember the editor of The Announcer *publishing a full-page apology and retraction about the article damning Randal, hailing him as a paragon of virtue and an unparalleled genius.*

Fuck! The editor was strangled by his freelance photographer in the grounds of a psychiatric hospital. The very same cameraman who had taken ill in Randal's house when they interviewed him and was hospitalised as a result of an epileptic fit. And wasn't there some tragedy with his wife? She died in a hospital corridor, also from a fit after kicking up a fuss. This is unreal. Totally, unbelievingly unreal.

He took deep breaths because his heart was pumping at three times its normal speed. He had never felt so professionally compromised. By the time he reached the prison and saw Francine Flint, he had managed to get his lawful act together.

He was shown into a cold, stark room with a police warden

for company. He did not recognise her when she joined them. She had lost a great deal of weight and looked gaunt and haunted. Her cheeks were sunken in, and the dark shadows under her baggy eyes added years to her actual age. Her hair was a complete tangled mess. She was a total wreck and she did not seem to care two hoots over the fact.

He cleared his throat before he spoke. He was not sure how to begin, so he played it by ear.

"Hello, Francine. My name's Detective Inspector Wayne Bredbury," he heard himself say unnecessarily, because they already knew each other.

She looked at him with a blank expression and dead eyes.

"What do you want of me now?" she replied in a flat voice.

"I'm here to ask you a few more questions. I assure you that they may be to your benefit, so don't be alarmed by them."

"Questions?"

"Yes. About your statement. About your memory loss on the night of the murders."

The colour drained out of her once-pretty face.

"I don't want to talk about it. I can't remember anything. I didn't do it and yet... and yet... I must have because... because... because I was covered in blood. *Their* blood. But I can't remember anything," she repeated with a catch in her voice.

"I believe you. I believe you can't remember."

"You do?"

"Yes, I do. I've discovered there's a lot more to this case than meets the eye and it's nowhere near as cut and dry as I thought it was," he admitted.

Francine's eyes widened in response to his words.

"Not as cut and dry?"

"Now tell me Francine, how well did you know Randal Forbes? I'm aware that his channel televised *Celestial Bodies* and Carlton became a great success as a result. But did you actually meet him?"

"Randal? Yes, I met him briefly at his parents' house one Christmas, and also when he came to dinner with his wife, Alison, but I didn't know him well. He was there when... when Carlton was injured on live television. His cousin, Dean, was friendlier with Carlton... with both of us. Randal was more of an acquaintance," she said, swallowing hard.

"What did you think of him? Was he ever prickly with you both?"

"Prickly?"

"Let me rephrase. Was he as charming off-camera as he was on it?"

"Well... yes. He's very attractive and was attentive towards me. Carlton didn't care for the way he flirted but... but it was harmless fun. I guess," she recollected.

"Did he ever mention the Scarlet Pimpernel to you? Even in passing?"

"Why are you raking up that name again? You were witness to me admitting that he made me kill them all, even though I don't remember saying it!" she flinched.

"I know how hard this is for you, Francine, but try to think back. You say you don't remember. Was there any sensation in your head that felt different? That felt invasive? Take your time because I'm on your side," he coaxed.

She frowned deeply. Then quite suddenly a submerged memory flashed into her brain: a mental picture of her standing in the garage where Dr Winston Ramsey and Stella Reid were already dead with their heads split wide open.

She could see Carlton struggling badly and swearing at some invisible source. At that particular time Randal's hypnotic hold over her was diminishing because all of his powers were levelled at Carlton, as they both vied violently for telepathic victory.

Francine gasped and covered her mouth with her hand as she recalled the sight of the meat cleaver flying through the air towards Carlton's back.

"What is it? What have you remembered?" urged the inspector.

"I'm not... I'm not sure. I don't know if it's true. The psychiatrist said I'm seriously ill. He... he told me I'm withdrawn from reality. That I'm a danger to myself, and others. So... so I could be imagining it."

"Imagining what? Let me decide. Just tell me what you thought you saw. Please?"

"I saw... I saw Winston and Stella with their heads trashed. I... I remember Carlton looking very strange. His eyes were... they were flashing... bright blue lights... really glowing. He was livid and worked up with something, or someone. He came out with swear words, and he never swore as a rule. Oh, God! I remember him falling forwards with the cleaver in his back. It moved on its own and tried to... tried to kill him. It wasn't me! It wasn't me! It wasn't me!" she repeated, sobbing uncontrollably.

"It's all right, Francine. It's all right. Now calm down and take deep breaths. I'm not blaming you anymore. I'm just trying to help you remember. You're quite safe. I'm your friend, not your interrogator," he reassured her.

She stopped crying and looked up, blinking repeatedly as she spoke.

"Can I have a cup of tea, please? My mouth's so dry... so very dry."

Inspector Bredbury nodded to the warden in attendance, who in turn raised his eyes to the ceiling, tapping his finger against his temple in a mocking gesture to show that he thought she was crazy.

"I'll have some tea as well. This is thirsty work," the inspector said to the warden, who then left the room in the direction of the staff kitchen.

"Now, Francine. Are you feeling calmer? I can wait until you are."

She pulled herself together and looked at him directly.

"Am I mad, Inspector Bredbury? Am I out of my mind like they say? What I just remembered, was it real? Did it happen? Why has it taken me so long to recall it?"

"I don't think you're mad. I think that something prompted you to do what you did."

"You mean my psychosis?"

"No. No you had no history of mental illness until this incident. You did not have a police record and your sanity was totally intact."

"So why did I do it? I loved my husband dearly, and my best friend Stella. I had the utmost respect for Dr Ramsey. He helped Carlton every step of the way when he was in that coma. I would never harm them. Never!" she choked.

Wayne Bredbury looked at the intense, candid expression on her newly lined face.

She hasn't got the eyes of a murderer. She's as much in the dark about her actions as I am. I need to understand this latest recollection.

"Francine, what do you mean that Carlton's eyes were glowing?"

"They looked like blue floodlights. I can't explain it. They seemed to radiate."

"Was that the only time you witnessed it?"

"Yes."

"Have you ever seen a similar reaction in Randal Forbes?"

"Randal?"

"Yes, him."

"No, although… oh, nothing."

"Although?"

"Well, there was that time when he came to dinner with his wife, Alison. He and Carlton went into the conservatory to discuss *Celestial Bodies.* It was at the beginning of the project and they didn't hit it off, so Randal and Alison left early. I thought that Randal looked peculiar."

"In what way?"

"His eyes... they looked weird. Almost luminous with strange yellow glints."

"What did Carlton say after they left?"

"Oh, just that they had disagreed about the format."

"But it was enough to make Randal leave. Did Carlton see him again after that?"

"He tried to, but he could never pin him down."

"I see."

"I don't think it was too bad, though, or else Randal's Uncle Ashley would never have visited Carlton, asking him for help and advice," she added.

"His Uncle Ashley?"

"Yes, Spencer Forbes's father. He was bereft after his son committed suicide and he spent a whole afternoon at our house with Carlton and Dr Ramsey."

"Why did he need help?"

"Bereavement counselling, I guess. My husband was a caring man and helped many people who were grieving."

"Why was Dr Ramsey there as well?"

"He'd come down from London to give a lecture to some students at our local hospital. Carlton invited him to stay over with us, rather than at a hotel."

"How did Ashley Forbes look to you?"

"He was devastated and inconsolable."

"Did you hear any of the conversation?"

"Just the tail end of some of it. Dr Ramsey arrived in the middle, and when we walked into the room, I heard Ashley say the words, 'How could she be so oblivious to all that?' Then Carlton replied, 'You were, Ashley, and you've known him far longer than Alison has.' I presumed it was something to do with Spencer's suicide."

Wayne Bredbury felt instinctively that they were referring to Randal and that Ashley Forbes had somehow found out that

Randal was responsible for his son's death. And yet Randal's uncle was still alive. Why had Randal spared him?

Francine looked so very tired. Her features were strained and she was wringing her hands in agitation with all the reminders of her repressed, twilight-zone crimes.

"OK, we'll leave it there," said Inspector Bredbury, when he saw her anguished expression. "I might come back and see you again if I need to, but don't worry, there's no pressure."

"Come back? Why? What are you trying to do? I've been found guilty as charged."

"There's some inconsistency in the evidence and I want to tie up those loose ends. I don't want to give you false hope, but until I can determine whether it's relevant, then I'll have to look more closely at the whole case."

"But I'm guilty, even though I can't remember. My own daughters… my lovely girls have abandoned me. They don't come to see me anymore. You see, they hate me, and you know what? I hate myself," she croaked.

"Let me carry on with my post-verdict enquiries. In the meantime, you can console yourself with the fact that I truly believe you don't remember anything and because of that conclusion, I have to follow my hunch."

"Hunch?"

"The nurse who overdosed your husband in the hospital, causing his demise, well, she said exactly the same thing. She could not remember. In fact, it was practically a similar word-for-word plea. As a result, I need to investigate the coincidence. I need to convince myself that you are the real culprit."

"The real culprit? Do you think someone else is involved in all this, Inspector Bredbury?"

"Possibly, but it's far from certain at this stage."

Francine's tortured brain clicked into some kind of logical place.

"Why do you keep asking me questions about Randal Forbes? Is he something to do with it?"

"Let's call it a day for now, Francine. I'll be in touch if I need to," he concluded as the shutters came purposefully down.

The warden came back into the room with two cups of tea as the inspector got up to leave.

"You took your bloody time, didn't you? I've got to go now."

"Couldn't find the milk, sir. It was in the wrong place."

"Just give Mrs Flint hers. You can have mine if you want it," he offered, and the warden nodded as Wayne Bredbury departed.

I don't know about the bloody milk. If anyone's in the wrong place it's Randal Forbes. He's free but should be banged up instead of Francine Flint. I just feel it in my bones.

***

Ashley Forbes had just finished his breakfast when the telephone rang. His wife, Julia, answered the call.

"Hello, can I help you?"

"Mrs Forbes? My name's Detective Inspector Wayne Bredbury. I hope I'm not disturbing you, but I'd like a word with your husband if he's around. It won't take too long."

"Oh. Just a minute, I'll get him for you."

Julia's brow furrowed as she told Ashley who the caller was.

"A detective inspector, you say? I hope everything's OK." Ashley frowned, as he picked up the handset.

"Yes, hello? Ashley Forbes here. What's all this about, please?"

"Good morning, Mr Forbes. I'm sorry to intrude, but I need to ask you some very important questions, if you would be so kind to help me out."

"About what?" replied Ashley, feeling anxious.

"The late Carlton Flint. I believe you knew him quite well."

"Carlton Flint? I knew of him, but I only met him fleetingly at my brother's house one Christmas."

"Only the once? Didn't you go round to his home one afternoon, when Dr Winston Ramsey was there?"

"Who? I've never been invited to his home. Look, Inspector, what's this all about?"

"I've reason to believe that you were there after your son's tragic death. Mrs Flint told me that you were counselled by her husband, and that he helped you overcome your grief."

"What! She's crazy! I've never spoken to the Flints about… about Spencer's death. I don't even know her."

"Are you quite sure?"

"Look here, I would remember with great clarity if I had been there. I assure you that you're barking up the wrong tree. She's completely insane."

"What about your nephew, Randal? Was he close with the Flints, or was there any hostility between them?"

"Hostility! Randal gave Carlton Flint his big break. Now if anybody counselled me after Spencer passed away it was Randal! Without his loving care, my wife and I would be basket cases. He's been like a surrogate son to us. He even came down all the way from Weybridge to be with us for a while to help us sort out the legalities of Spencer's will. We were devastated and he was a blessing. We love him. Dearly."

"Spencer had drawn up a will? He was very young to have done that. It's unusual."

"My son was ill and we didn't realise just how desperate he was. He must have prepared it in advance. Randal said he planned it all in a disturbed frame of mind, that he had every intention of doing what he did to himself."

"I'm truly sorry for your loss, but I have to ask you this. Was there any ill feeling between your son and nephew? I read that Spencer was taken off the case when he wanted to sue Astral TV on behalf of Techscreen. Why would he want to represent the people who were prosecuting Randal's company?"

Ashley sighed deeply as the painful memories washed over him.

"I was the one who reported my own son to his law firm for being unstable. As a result, he was dismissed. I have to live with that guilt all the time: the guilt of not realising how damaged he was."

"What caused his depression, Mr Forbes? I know this is very painful, but I wouldn't ask if it wasn't important."

"What's all this got to do with Carlton Flint?"

"It's part of a wider, extensive examination. I can't reveal the real reason, but we need to know in an investigatory capacity. So, any information will help us."

Ashley sighed again but complied.

"It pains me to say this, but my son and Randal never saw eye to eye. There was discord. My brother, Edward, Randal's father, was very upset by it. We all were. Spencer suffered with some kind of psychosis in the end. He got it into his head that Randal was... how can I put this... that Randal was evil. That he was disingenuous and fooling us all. His claims were utterly ridiculous. They were the ramblings of a disturbed mind."

"What sort of claims?"

"I really don't want to discuss this. Spencer was very ill at the time and his notions were undermined."

"Can you give me one example? I understand that you don't wish to elaborate."

"Like I said, it's so absurd. He accused Randal of murder, of having some kind of satanic disposition and other wild allegations. That's all I'm going to say, Inspector. Now if you don't mind, I want to end this call because it's disturbing me. I've not come to terms yet with my son's death. I doubt if I ever will."

"I understand. I apologise for any upset I may have caused you and I appreciate your co-operation. I'm truly sorry for your loss and I wish you well."

They said their goodbyes and Wayne Bredbury sagged back into his chair.

Dear God. Spencer knew. So did Inspector Ronald Gray. They must have put their heads together on this. And Randal had to kill them. One by one.

He tried to work out why Francine Flint would lie about Ashley Forbes consulting Carlton. She had no need to fabricate about that particular incident.

She said that Ashley was inconsolable. She even heard the tail end of their conversation. Something prompted Ashley to go around to Carlton's that particular day. What? And why didn't he remember the meeting?

Aha! He didn't remember! Of course! That's the whole key. That's not to say that it didn't happen! Did Carlton hypnotise him to forget out of kindness? And to keep him safe? Away from Randal's wrath?

He thought again about Spencer's will. Why did Randal make a special journey to sort it all out for them? Was there something in it that he did not want revealed? Was there some kind of message or note implicating him? Did he have to check?

Let's think hard about this one. If Spencer was on to Randal, then he would want people to know. Perhaps he worked alongside Inspector Ronald Grey and they'd compiled a list of possible victims together. Where's that list now? Is it still in Ronald's past files? I'm going to have another look in the old filing cabinets.

He rummaged through the drawers and pulled out several faded folders. One hour later he was still looking and his fingers were cramping up from the effort. As he searched his thoughts were ticking over.

Why would Ashley want to consult Carlton Flint of all people? Did Carlton make contact with him after Spencer died? Did he have proof of Randal's involvement? It must have been something very convincing if Ashley looked so devastated that day.

It was a miracle that Carlton came out of his coma in the first place, with all his senses intact. I remember Carlton told me that he healed himself with the help of the now deceased Dr Ramsey, and that Randal knew this and wanted to kill them before they revealed the full extent of his crimes. I thought he was crazy. Not anymore!

His brain was working overtime with all possible theories. He never thought that he could ever believe in such an outlandish hypothesis, but everything was pointing in Randal's demonic direction.

The more I think about it, it's highly likely that Spencer compiled a comprehensive list of victims. Perhaps that was to be opened together with his will. If Ashley Forbes had read that list, he would have been out of his mind.

But that still doesn't tell me why Carlton was involved. Unless… unless he had already discussed it all with Spencer and they had also compared notes. Knowing Carlton's benevolence, he possibly wanted to help Spencer overcome his fear of Randal. Maybe Spencer instructed his father to consult Carlton. Who knows?

As he was contemplating and flicking through endless reams of paper, some sheets fell out of a seemingly haphazard portfolio. They fluttered to the floor, practically stuck together from lack of use. He picked them up and straightened them out.

There were only three pages, but their contents were devastating.

Oh, dear God! Here it is! Inspector Ronald Grey's top-secret research, hiding away from disbelieving eyes. The heinous, hideous list. It's all here in black and white!

Randal was only a child when he saw off his headmistress. It goes right the way back and ends with Maxine Hale's induced suicide. And there it stops.

Because his next victim was Ronald Grey himself!

May all their desecrated souls rest in peace. God help me bring this fiend to justice and save us all from his monstrous wrath.

***

Fast forwarding to the year 2000, Dean checked his new suit in the mirror. He wanted to look his very best on this special date, because tonight, he was going to propose to Maddie Flint.

He had not even mentioned her to his mother, let alone Randal, and the rest of the family. Firstly, Maddie had to accept, but he felt confident that she would. Secondly, she had been in and out of different sanatoriums on a regular basis, ever since she had witnessed her mother's violent crimes on that unforgettable night. That nocturnal mayhem of murder.

Neither Maddie nor her sister, Zoe, could bring themselves to visit their mother in prison, because they were far too traumatised and bereft by her psychotic actions.

Then, when their father appeared to have survived the vicious attack, his life had been snuffed out by a crazy nurse and her deadly hypodermic syringe. The double blow was shattering.

Dean stayed loyal to Carlton's memory and had visited the sisters when they both went to live with their paternal relations. Their lives had been decimated and the ugly, intrusive media coverage was endless. Just as they were coming to terms with their past, another event wrecked what little acceptance they had struggled to achieve.

Detective Inspector Wayne Bredbury, who had been trying to reopen the case to exonerate their mother, flung himself off a platform, into the path of an express train. The next day, Francine Flint had taken her own life in prison by jumping out of an upstairs window.

Dean shuddered as he remembered the additional devastation that both sisters had to deal with. At the time he had informed Randal of the catastrophe.

"Francine Flint has just topped herself! As if her daughters haven't suffered enough!"

Randal had frowned deeply.

"She was guilt-ridden and insane. Look, Dean, I'm not at all happy about your ongoing association with that family. I want you to sever all connection. They're cursed and completely blighted."

"It's not their fault! They need compassion. I can't desert them. It's too tragic."

Randal had forced himself to accept his wishes. However, Randal's Uncle Ashley had told him beforehand about Inspector Wayne Bredbury's phone call and his line of questioning. Randal had smelt a big, fat rat.

As a result, he'd entered the inspector's head, and had plucked the whole dangerous scenario out of his brain, specifically his quest to somehow get Francine's verdict overturned, due to the late Ronald Grey's list of Randal's alleged victims. That gut-wrenching, written 'evidence', albeit telepathic crime.

Randal's revenge was faster than the speed of light. He had removed the double threat promptly but not before he had hypnotised the inspector to dispose of any written proof. He did not blame his uncle Ashley. He blamed Spencer for alerting him to 'the list'.

He knew instinctively that Carlton had wiped Ashley's memory banks clean to save his life and sanity, to protect him from any repercussions.

Now I know why Uncle Ashley did not suspect me that day I went to visit him. I could not sense or read anything in his head, because he'd literally just returned from Carlton's and had been hypnotised to forget.

In some ways I'm glad that he did that for him, or else I might have caused my dear uncle harm. But oh, you other meddlesome, lesser mortals!

You'll never unmask me!

You're just pathetic putty in my healing hands, except I'd never revive you. I'll always displace you, destroy you, extinguish you, demoralise you, and I'll demolish and dismantle any evidence that would render me culpable, in order to protect my legacy.

'The gift' will always triumph! And the detractors will always die!

3

Randal and Alison were having lunch at a local high-end restaurant, when his mother, Margaret, phoned him on his mobile.

"Hi, Mum. Everything OK?"

"Yes, darling. Have you heard the news yet?"

"News? What news?"

"I thought you hadn't or else you would have called me. It's Dean. He's getting married in the summer, or so your Aunty Dottie said."

"Married! I didn't even know he was seriously dating!" exclaimed Randal.

"None of us did. It's totally out of the blue, but apparently, he's proposed and she's accepted."

"Who is she?"

"We don't know that either, but he's bringing her to Chester to meet Dottie, Neil and Shannon at their house. We're all invited apparently."

"Are we now? Well, isn't he the dark horse with blue eyes? He kept this one right under the radar. Maybe she's got two heads."

"Oh, Randal, don't be silly. He probably just had to make sure. Your Aunty Dot's delighted but puzzled at the same time."

"What's her name?"

"I haven't got a clue. Dean just wants everyone to be there to meet her."

"Does he now? And when will she have the obvious pleasure of our company?" asked Randal sardonically, totally miffed at learning the news second-hand.

"This Sunday afternoon. Are you free?"

"I am now."

"Well then, see you there and we'll chat some more. Got to go, your father's taking me into town."

"An earthbound meteorite wouldn't keep me away," he drawled.

Randal's expression was totally disgruntled as he ended the call.

"What was that all about?" asked Alison, when she saw the gathering molten hue in his slate-grey gaze.

"That was all about my furtive cousin's proposal of marriage to a mysterious woman who's clipped his wings."

"Which furtive cousin?"

"Dean. Dean's getting hitched apparently and wants us all to meet his secretive choice at Aunty Dot's house this Sunday."

"Oh, that's fantastic! I'm so pleased for him! He's such a great guy. She's a very lucky girl. Who is she?" exclaimed Alison with genuine delight.

"Fuck knows."

"Hasn't he mentioned her to you at all? Is that why you're put out? Because it's all over your reddening face," she observed.

"He obviously didn't want me to know. Or any of us for that matter. What I need to find out is why."

"Doesn't his mum know who she is?"

"Nope."

"How odd."

"Exactly."

"Well, perhaps he doesn't want to build her up too much. He probably would prefer us to meet her without any expectations."

"Hmm."

They carried on eating, but Randal did not taste any of his steak. Under different circumstances he would have sent it flying back to the kitchen. He had ordered medium rare, and it was practically cremated, but his mind was doing gigantic cartwheels. He needed to speak to his favourite cousin. Either that or he would telepathically obtain the identity of his wife-to-be, via the usual, but vital, photographic image.

"I can see it's bothering you, so why don't you call Dean now and congratulate him? He might open up about it all," suggested Alison.

"Good idea. I'm just going for a pee and then I'll call him from the lobby. I won't be long."

Alison nodded as she sipped her glass of Chateau Palmer red wine. She was full of curiosity about Dean's enigmatic future bride.

Randal scrolled down his contact list and called Dean the second he was out of sight. It was on answerphone, so he left him a message.

"Hi, it's me. Give me a bell as soon as you can. It's about the new programme."

Dean rang back as Randal was finishing his lunch.

"Hi, Rand, sorry I didn't call you sooner, only I've been tied up with some stuff."

"With some stuff or someone?"

"Ha, ha, very funny. Now joking apart, what's the problem?"

"You tell me."

"What do you mean? You called me about the new family quiz show, didn't you?" puzzled Dean.

"Did I? So, I did. But that can wait. There's a more important issue to discuss and that can't wait."

"Such as?"

"Such as your impending marriage. Why didn't you tell me? You know I've always had your best interests at heart to say the least. I'm delighted for you, Dean, so why am I the last to know?"

Dean's tongue stuck to the roof of his mouth and he blinked repeatedly as the palms of his hands began to sweat.

Oh, God. This is crazy. He's going to find out. They all are. So maybe it's just as well he's called. I'll tell him now, so he's prepared.

Randal sensed Dean's anxious reticence. He could feel his alarming discomfort transmitting itself from a distance, without the need for speech or proximity.

"You're not going to like it. None of you are," admitted Dean, swallowing hard.

"Why not? Is she the Yorkshire Ripper's firstborn?" asked Randal with deliberate irony.

"She's… she's… oh, what the hell. It's Maddie Flint. As in Carlton's daughter. Don't freak out. Please. I love her. I truly do."

Randal felt a violent surge of fury spearhead into his brain and shoot through every single blood vessel and living part of his whole body. It was so ferocious that he thought he would pass out with the force. He heard himself reply in a spectacularly controlled but vehement fashion. Really, he wanted to explode. Alison looked baffled when Randal got up out of his seat and continued the call in the lobby.

"Maddie Flint! Out of the millions of beautiful women in this whole wide, wayward world, you've picked Maddie Flint to be your future wife? The daughter of a lunatic mother, who slaughtered two friends with her versatile meat cleaver! Who injured her husband but was still after his head on a plate! Who was so deranged that she abseiled out of her prison window without a fucking rope! You're as crazy as her! She should come with a health warning, never mind a marriage certificate!" he raved, forgetting that he had orchestrated the whole tragedy.

"Don't, Randal! Please don't do this to me! That's why I couldn't tell you, or even confide in you. I wanted so desperately to consult you, but I know how you feel about her family," he groaned.

"What family?"

"Her depleted family," Dean sighed.

"Family? You call that a family? Her mother's flown way over the cuckoo's nest and her foiled father hammered on heaven's door with a hole in his back from the aforementioned axe. All that, together with a morphine overdose, administered by the nurse with a curse. The cringe with a syringe. Take your pick! Maddie Flint's got more baggage than Gatwick Airport! She's been sectioned so often that she's got a timeshare in The Priory! What the fuck are you thinking of, Dean? Wake up to yourself and smell the corrosive coffee before you make the biggest mistake of your much-admired life."

"You don't know her like I do. She's been through so much, Randal, but she's still got all this love to give. She just wants to move on and focus on a new life. Yes, she's fragile, but with my help she'll learn to laugh again," he urged.

"Fragile? She's in permanent bits! You told me that often enough after you'd visited the Flint fallout zone. Dean, I'm being cruel to be kind. Your mum will go ape."

"My mum will understand. She knows exactly what it's like to be a victim by association. When my real father was murdered, her life was a mess. She was single, pregnant with me, and before he died, he offered her money to have an illegal abortion, but she braved it all out with the love of our family. You in particular, Randal. Why can't you be more magnanimous towards Maddie? It's not her fault. The blame lies solely with her maternal bloodline," entreated Dean.

"Exactly, Dean! Exactly! Her maternal bloodline! What if she's inherited the flawed chromosome? What if she suffers from the same genetic transmission? Maddie Flint may well be a decent girl, with many attributes, but she's got a damaged disposition, and no amount of love, compassion or understanding will eradicate it all. I want the best for you, Dean. The very best. I know your heart's in the right place. I get that and I feel sorry for her deep down, but the simple truth is that you're far too good for her. Think about the negative publicity that will follow you around. The intrusive media sniffing at your front, back and side door. Believe me, I know what that's like, to go from hero to zero in newspaper print, and it isn't easy to overcome."

"She's worth it."

Randal knew he had lost the argument with those last three words. His advice was like water off a devoted duck's back, and Dean would not budge from his passionate position, so any guidance would go in one ear and cannonball out of the other.

"Look, Dean, I'm dead against your choice and I can't lie about that, but you're obviously smitten so there's point in carrying on with this conversation. You mean far too much to me and I don't wish to hurt you."

"And you mean the world to me, Randal. I'd be lost… I'd be half a person without you in my life. I love you," he croaked.

"Let's just agree to disagree then," relented Randal, but inside he was furious.

The starman's daughter will be part of my family and I can't harm her, otherwise it'll destroy Dean! But if mad Maddie steps out of her loony line just once, I'll remove her so fucking fast that her Flint-toed feet won't touch the gruesome ground beneath her.

There was a long pause before the conversation continued. Randal felt compelled to instruct him further.

"Dean, listen to me. I think you should tell your mum exactly who she'll be meeting and greeting. Prepare her, otherwise her mixed emotions may be very visible and that will be uncomfortable for Maddie, and yourself," he advised, the acidic bile rising in his throat at the mere mention of her name.

"Well, now that you know who she is, it's only right that everybody else should also be aware. I'll speak to my mum, stepdad and Shannon, but do me a massive favour and tell the rest of the family. Please, Randal. Please put in a good word for her. You're naturally persuasive and they'll listen to you. Don't bring Maddie down, no matter how much you want to. It'll just make it so much worse. I'm marrying her and that's that. She's going to be my wife and I want her to have the respect she's been denied, that she deserves," said Dean passionately.

Randal cringed inwardly. His devotion to Dean would make him comply with his wishes, but his deep loathing for Carlton and his kith and kin was still burning away like an out-of-control forest fire that refused to be extinguished.

"I'll do my best for you, but you know where I stand on all this. However, I wouldn't want you to be unhappy over my opinion, so I'll just keep it to myself and ask the family to accept the situation. I'm far from pleased with your choice, but your welfare has always been my number-one priority. I'll accept it for your sake," complied Randal through clenched teeth.

"That's far more than I expected. It means such a lot to me. *You* mean such a lot to me! You always have and you always will," replied Dean emotionally.

"See you both on Sunday then," confirmed Randal.

They said their goodbyes and Randal's whole body was trembling from anger and the pretence of his compliance.

How the fuck am I going to tell Roxanne? She hates the name Flint so much that she's even scrubbed the word out of her dictionary! We both made a massive mistake. We should have removed the whole blighted bloodline! Dean was forever visiting the two sisters after the starman snuffed it. Why didn't I see this coming? I'm absolutely livid with myself!

Randal's mobile rang in the middle of his furious contemplation. It was Roxanne.

"Daddy, can you pick me up from school? I've missed the coach and I'm stuck here. Everyone's gone home. I had a long shower after tennis and misjudged the time. Pretty please?" she cooed.

"No problem. I'm on my way. I need to talk to you anyway."

"What about?"

"I'll tell you soon enough. Wait for me inside."

"OK," she replied as he cut her off, but she had felt his fury through the airwaves.

Randal told Alison. She had mixed emotions as he dropped her off at home. He drove at breakneck speed to Roxanne's school. He parked the car then made his way to the main door only to see Roxanne waiting outside.

"It's not safe to be hanging around on your own! I thought I told you to wait indoors!" he barked.

"I did. I saw you through the window, so I came out. What's wrong? You're late. What have I done now?" she pouted.

"Get in the car and we can talk," he instructed. "There's something you need to know."

Roxanne felt his fury, but her sixth sense told her that it was nothing to do with herself. She tried to raid his head, but he had closed off his thoughts to her. She opened the door and sat down in the car as he lit up his logotype cheroot and joined her in the driver's seat. He inhaled deeply and blew out a stream of rich tobacco. He turned to the side and spoke.

"Now, I've got some very unwelcome news about a very unwanted guest appearance. It's stomach-churning. I'm opening my mind to you so that you can hear the name telepathically, because I'm loath to say it aloud," he almost spat.

It's Maddie Flint.

Maddie Flint? What about Maddie Flint? Daddy, talk to me out loud!

"She's going to marry Dean."

"What! No! It's not true!" she screeched.

"I'm afraid it is. He just told me, and we're all going on a jolly journey to meet her this Sunday, in Chester, at Aunty Dot's. Won't that be nice?"

"Mad Maddie Flint in my family? The starman's deluded daughter! No way! It's so not going to happen!"

"Now listen to me! Dean, for some unfathomable reason of his own, has fallen for her. You know how precious he is to me. You know all about the Sterling removals and the Haynes family fatal displacements. Everything I did was out of my devotion to his well-being. He's more than aware of my feelings about his bacterial bride-to-be. That's why he's kept it a secret and has sprung it on us all. He knew I'd erupt, but I've had to play it down because Dean's happiness means more to me than my venomous desire to liquidate her. I promised him that I'd put my ill will to one side. So that's what you must do, too. For him. For now," he instructed.

"But I hated the starman more than I've ever hated anyone! I helped you kill him, Daddy! I put my own safety on the line because of my love for you. He nearly won! I didn't do all that for nothing and use 'the gift' so that malfunctioning Maddie could worm her way into Dean's bed with a rattle-brained ring on her finger. I won't be able to control my gaze when I look at her floodlighted, flaunty Flint-face!" she raved.

Randal wanted to laugh at her choice of words, but the situation was far too serious for any light-hearted levity.

"Well, you're going to have to behave yourself or else Dean will be heartbroken by our condemnation. Do your protesting with me in private, but I promise you this. If there's the merest, miniscule sign that the starman's off-putting offspring goes off her traumatised trolley and causes Dean any paranoid problems, she'll be explosively expunged. Her wedding vows will be short-circuited like the deviation of an electric current. Cut off indefinitely. Burned out and shut down!" he elaborated cruelly.

"Promise?"

"I already did, and I don't ever go back on my word."

Roxanne sighed dramatically.

"Have I still got to go to Chester? Can't I stay at home alone, instead?" she frowned deeply.

"Best get it over with, pumpkin. Let the actress in you play the part. Just kill the bride-to-be with kindness, instead of 'the gift'."

She nodded with great reluctance, but Randal knew she was burning. They both felt identical rancour: a twin detestation born out of the spiritual rivalry and deep hatred for Carlton Flint and all of his kind.

"I was hungry before you told me about Maddie madhouse, but now I've lost my appetite completely," she moaned, with a gathering molten-glow in her slate-grey eyes.

"Now that's a pity. I've booked a table for all of us at your fave Italian restaurant." He smiled, stroking a loose strand of vibrant, red hair away that had fallen across her beautiful face.

"I'm not in the mood. I just want to stay in my bedroom with my lack of appetite," she moped.

"No, you don't."

"Oh, I so do!"

"Don't."

"Do!"

"Roxanne Dawn Forbes, just stop this right now! You know who you are! You're head and shapely shoulders above them all. Let's get back, get changed, look good and eat out as a family. It's not often we do that with my busy schedule, so less of the drama queen and more of my chosen child in her element and rightful place. Why let a lesser mortal like Maddie malfunction put you off your lasagne?"

Roxanne's full lips twitched into a wry smile at Randal's witty but wise words.

"You're right. As ever. If Dean wants to marry a lamebrain, why should I object? He'll find out for himself the folly of his tasteless choice," she said in a superior tone.

"Do you know the actual meaning of the word flint?" asked Randal.

"Do tell, Daddy dear," she mocked but with adoring eyes.

"A flint is a very hard rock that produces sparks when struck with steel, or an alloy used for producing a spark in lighters."

"And your point is?"

"My point is that if the future Mrs Gibson misbehaves, I might incorporate that theory into her departure zone. It's only wise to have a preliminary plan in place."

"Oh, I do love you, Daddy!" She grinned, throwing her arms around his strong frame.

"Of course you do. So, how's your appetite now, pumpkin?"

"I could eat every single dish on the menu. That's how it is." She smirked.

Randal threw back his head and laughed out loud.

This is what it's all about. Fuck Dean's bad taste. It all pales into matrimonial insignificance compared to having my beautiful, rightful daughter at my sizzling side.

***

By the time the weekend rolled around, the family were well aware of the identity of Dean's intended. Although they had sympathy with her tragic situation, they were judgemental about Dean's choice. His sister, Shannon, who was now twenty-two and still full of it, was positively disgruntled.

"Trust my soft-hearted brother to fall for a walking disaster. Honestly, Mum, she's toxic by proxy," she objected strongly.

"Don't be mean, Shannon. I'm not happy either, but you can't judge a person without meeting them first," admonished Dottie.

"But Dean's so eligible in every single way. She's just taking advantage of his sympathetic nature, not to mention his thriving bank balance," she sniped, flicking her long, blonde hair back in dramatic agitation, as she batted her long eyelashes.

Dottie sighed deeply. She felt exactly the same way, but her precious son had made it very clear that Maddie Flint was his one and only, and he did not want an awkward atmosphere on the day, or any snide comments thrown her way.

"All I want for Dean is to be happy and loved. I'll know instinctively whether Maddie fills that role when I meet her. We can't possibly evaluate or surmise if she will, or won't, until she's sat at my table," added Dottie.

"Well, it's going to be hard for me to bite my tongue. For once, I'm in complete agreement with Roxanne, and that's saying something," admitted Shannon, who was always aware of the constant rivalry between herself and Randal's inheritress.

"Don't be confrontational, Shannon. It's going to be difficult enough for me to cope with one problem at a time. Put a smile on your pretty face. For Dean. For me."

"I will, Mum, but it feels so shoddy. Almost sordid. Maddie Flint's mother was a basket case. I just hope her daughter hasn't inherited her psychosis."

"So do I, sweetheart. So do I," repeated Dottie without malice, and with deep concern for her irreplaceable son.

Not one of the extended family knew that Randal and Roxanne were totally responsible for Maddie Flint's jeopardised sanity. It was so ridiculously surreal that they would never even come close to the truth. Randal especially was now the backbone of the family, the benevolent philanthropist forever helping the disadvantaged bounce back. Or so it seemed. There were no detractors left to suspect him. He had annihilated them all.

For the last eight years he had taken a removal sabbatical, worn out from the spate of telepathic killings that had been necessary to maintain his spotless standing. Clive was privy to all of his homicides, except Spencer's demise. That would be kept a closely guarded secret forever.

Only Roxanne knew the whole truth, but neither of them realised that Randal's up-and-coming tyro was still waiting quietly in the wings. Patient but fiercely telepathic!

***

Tyrone Pendle was twenty-one. He opened his many presents and faked a dashing smile on his handsome face. His party was in full swing, but he was not enjoying being the young man of the moment. It was all so tedious and meaningless.

His seventeen-year-old sister, Tiffany, was dancing her dainty feet off to the beat of some tuneless, bass-thumping distortion of a song, while his parents looked absurd trying to keep up with her relentless foot-hopping. They had spent a fortune on the lavish celebration. Money was not an issue for his wealthy parentage. But his contempt was.

They've got as much rhythm as a starched shirt with stage fright! Clueless! But I won't feel like this for much longer. I've waited eight years for this fated introduction, and nothing, absolutely nothing, is going to spoil it. Not even the christening of my tiresome nephew next weekend, although that will be a monumental task for my hidden, dark disposition.

Tyrone felt that he was on the verge of something magnificent. His heart kept skipping essential beats, but it was only due to his mounting, unbearable excitement. He looked across at his new influential friend who appeared to be assimilated, but he knew that they were both putting on an act for their own very different reasons.

Tyrone's disconnection was all too familiar. He had always felt superior and unappreciated in equal measure. As for his companion – well, he was detached and permanently analytical. But their newly formed, amicable connection was going to be Tyrone's passport to salvation. The answer to all of his frustrated, unattainable ideals and aims. What a prize amigo! Fate, and a lot of groundwork, had delivered him right to Tyrone's tyrannical door!

Ryan Forbes! The eldest son of his saviour-to-be, Randal Forbes!

Tyrone had worshipped Randal for eight solid years, from

the second he had clapped eyes on his sinful aura that had catapulted through the television screen and into his living room. It had affected all of his six senses with a devastating disturbance of the most awe-inspiring kind.

As a result, he had researched Randal's profile with obsessive zeal. He now knew every single aspect of his life on earth. Tyrone's own telepathic ability showed him the startling long list of lesser mortals who had succumbed to Randal's wrath. The Full 'Murderous' Monty.

But he had felt an unbearable exultation, instead of overpowering repulsion.

Both Tyrone and Ryan had followed in Randal's academic footsteps, winning unconditional places at Beaumont College in Oxford, where they had first crossed each other's dysfunctional walkways. It was more design than chance because Tyrone had purposely set out to imitate Randal's life path.

Ryan was also out to impress his father, and, just like Randal, he genuinely felt at home within Oxford's dreaming spires and historical splendour. He had chosen the history of art because it appealed to his own creative appreciation.

Tyrone was highly gifted and excelled at most subjects. He was studying English literature, yet again an acknowledgement of the Randal Forbes factor. Tyrone worshipped Randal, albeit from a distance.

We'll be the modern-day, straight version of Randal and Clive. I feel closer to Ryan than any of my own family, even though he's younger than me. I know that his father is the main attraction, but I'm still impressed by Ryan's capacity for learning.

He holds all his cards close to his chest, but that's because he feels second best. His sister, Amber, identifies with the same inferior standing. His little brother, Oscar, is too young to analyse the pecking order but he has potential powers. However, they're watered down by his maternal line but could be revived.

Ryan's present-day unhappiness is mostly to do with his so-called stepsister, Roxanne, but she's far from unrelated. I know that she's his blood half-sibling, but she can't tell him. He told me that he loves her and it's very complicated. She only wants a platonic relationship. But it's for the best.

She's the most fascinating, beautiful creature I've ever seen, albeit in a photographic image. I'm deeply in love with her myself. We are exactly the same. She'll know that the minute we meet. But firstly, I have to show her father that I'm worthy, that I'm a kindred dark spirit in need of his guidance and respect.

Tyrone was more than ready for an immediate apprenticeship. He was ferociously telepathic but could not reveal his unrighteousness to another soul, not even to Ryan, because he knew he had not inherited 'the gift'. The fact Tyrone had become very close to his idol's firstborn was joyous in itself and helped him cope with all of the dark leanings that were officially stunted.

I have to throw myself at Randal's feet and show him that I'm more than ready to begin and I've been learning in frustrated secrecy, without his acceptance or government.

I need to prove that I'm a worthy candidate and I can add my own brand of sorcery to the magical mix, so that when I achieve premium, paranormal status, I can offer his daughter my love and devotion, regardless of her youth.

Just like he knew that Alison was the chosen one, regardless of the age gap, I'll make sure that the pattern will continue and 'the gift' will live on, through my glorious graduation. In the company of my cosmic cap and gown. With Roxanne.

Randal was totally unaware of any other dark alter egos. He was basking in the ownership of his ever-blossoming benefaction and had attained his ideal status with his chosen daughter. As far as he was concerned, they had complete control over their own dominion.

Tyrone was wading into choppy waters, but his dark edge had a stunning advantage compared to Carlton Flint, who had fought tooth and nail for purity and virtue but had lost the war. There was a glaring reason why Randal could welcome his besotted admirer. One major, singular advantage.

Tyrone's powers were also pitch black and kicked saintliness into permanent touch.

***

Early Sunday morning, before Randal's entire maternal family drove down to his Aunty Dottie's, in separate cars, he woke up with a gigantic erection. He reached over to Alison, who was lying on her back, and stroked her full breasts. Her nipples stood to attention even though she was fast asleep.

He pushed back the duvet so that he could see the erotic result of his fondling. He put his hand up her nightie and played with her vagina, fingering her labia until she automatically became moist to his touch.

Randal released his throbbing phallus through the front of his boxer shorts, all the while groaning with passion. He began to masturbate so that he would be extra stiff before he woke her up. He played with himself for quite a while.

He spoke aloud even though she was still gently snoring and not aware of his arousal.

"I want to fuck you, my gorgeous wife. I'm so hard. Wait until you see the size of it and witness what you've done to me. Ooh! Ooh!"

He carried on moaning as he massaged his humungous member with one hand, while the other one played with her breasts.

"Oh, I'm bursting and heavy with love juice. I think I better let you know how close I am to coming all over the place."

Alison stirred and felt Randal's touch. He reached inside his shorts and pulled out his swollen testicles so that his whole manhood was exposed.

"Ah, you're awake my precious. I want you so badly. It's like the first time all over again," he whispered into her ear.

Alison came to and Randal stopped jerking off. He pulled her hand towards his humungous erection.

"You take over now. I want you so badly," he groaned.

"Oh, Rand," she responded, now totally aware of the passionate clinch.

"Yes, my love. Make me come. I've got myself so worked up; I can't hold it in. You know that happens a lot. My prick's on fire. It needs your touch. Oh, I'm so hard!"

"Why didn't you wake me up?" she said softly, feeling very aroused.

"You looked so beautiful, I just wanted to feel you first. Then I ended up touching myself because you're so sexy and now I've reached the point of no return."

"Oh, Rand. I'm on my period. Oh, heck."

She turned round so they were lying face to face. Her hand glided up and down his manhood which was red from all the massaging. It twitched, throbbed and seeped at the top. A small stream of semen shot out and Randal moaned even louder.

"It's just a rehearsal. It's going to explode."

"I want to come too," she groaned, and placed his monumental member in between her legs, so that the tip just rubbed against her clitoris but did not penetrate as such. She could feel it sliding backward and forward, and the friction felt exquisite.

"Mmm. That's right. Can you feel me?" he said thickly.

"I can feel you. It's so good."

"Sexy lady. My sexy lady," he whispered.

"Ooh, Rand."

"It's close."

"Tell me when it comcs."

"Won't have to."

"Still tell me."

"It's on the way."

Randal started to rub faster and pant louder, as Alison prepared herself for their synchronised climax.

"It's here! I'm coming! Now! Now! Now! Now!"

They both yelled out loud as a cascade of thick sperm spurted multiple times in between her legs. Randal though it would never stop and Alison squealed with the intensity of her multiple orgasms. She was soaked but relished every drop of his love stream. She adored him. She could never get enough. They lay there, kissing and stroking each other until they were ready to face the outside world. They both climaxed again. Alison wished she could spend the rest of her life in bed with him. Her love for him was timeless.

***

Ryan felt very hung-over from Tyrone's celebration, but Alison insisted that he should still show up for Dean's sake.

"It's so important that we're all there to support him because it's crucial to Dean's future," she told Ryan, when they were on their way to Chester.

"I've got such a headache. In fact, I've got a whisky-and-Coke ache," he groaned, still half asleep and looking worse for wear.

Randal swore to himself behind the wheel as he looked at his son's pained expression reflected in the front mirror of his six-seater Mercedes Benz.

"You shouldn't have drunk so much last night! You knew we were coming here today!" he admonished, taking out his discontented mood on his eldest son.

"Dad, please. My head hurts. It was a party and that's what happens at these crazy celebrations. You should know."

"What's that supposed to mean?" barked Randal, and Ryan just shook his head.

"Was the birthday boy drunk as well?" pumped Roxanne.

"He kept off the whisky and just drank the Coke. I wish I had."

"Very wise, but very dull," she quipped. "Anyway, who is he? This twenty-one-year-old reveller. Anyone interesting?"

"Tyrone Pendle," mumbled Ryan.

"Tyrone Pendle? Isn't his father the property magnate? Pendle Enterprises and the rest of the world?" intercepted Randal sardonically.

"The very same," confirmed Ryan.

"Well, at least you got plastered in notable company. Where did you meet the son and heir?"

"At Beaumont College. I would have told you about him, but you're always too busy to listen. He's older, but we hit it off right away. He's studying English literature, so you'd probably have a lot in common. Now, all of you, just leave me alone. I need to close my eyes and switch off. Please!" he requested in a raised voice that made him wince.

Ryan was thankful that Oscar was fast asleep on Amber's lap. At least he was spared the constant chattering and hyperactivity. Roxanne contemplated as she stared out of the window.

Tyrone Pendle? Why do I know that name?

She entered Ryan's fuzzy head on a very flimsy, subliminal level and searched his recent recollections. An image flashed before her of a tall, dark, good-looking student with deep-set, bewitching brown eyes. He was riding his bike, looking down from his lofty station. His handsome face looked imposing with an imperious expression.

Roxanne's heart skipped a beat at the vision and Randal felt her puzzlement and arousal. It was very strong and stopped him dwelling on Maddie Flint. He had also received a mental image of Tyrone and it abruptly halted any other rumination.

Hell's bells! This guy's powerful and he's on my case. I have to know more about him.

"Ryan? Ryan! I'm interested in the birthday boy's background. Tell me more."

"He's sleeping, Dad. He must be shattered from his late-night partying," observed Amber.

"Leave him then. I'll interrogate him later," Randal reluctantly complied.

He looked at Roxanne on the back seat through the mirror. She was deeply engrossed in her telepathic infatuation. He frowned deeply.

There are two major issues here. Dean's undying love for Maddie flipped out Flint, and now Roxanne's teenage passion for the mysterious Tyrone Pendle. There's always someone or something spoiling the perfection!

By the time they arrived at Dottie and Neil's house, Randal was brimming over with unmitigated unrest. He rang the bell and his aunt opened the door, smiling widely as she ushered all of them into the large living room. Randal felt her insecurity about their reaction to her future daughter-in-law. Dean had a protective arm around Maddie's shoulder as they greeted them.

"We're both so glad you could come today. It's much appreciated," he enthused, but his fingers were trembling as he shook hands with Randal.

"Hello, Randal, it's nice to meet you again," Maddie almost whispered.

Randal and Roxanne were simultaneously struck dumb by her uncanny resemblance to Carlton. It was quite unnerving, as if his female form had fallen to earth in order to perpetuate his rivalry and disgust. Randal forced himself to greet her politely, but his eyes spoke a different language. He could not control the luminous glint in his fixed stare. Roxanne followed suit as she congratulated them, but her body language was not cordial.

Randal's parents were both present, along with his Aunty June and family. The sight of Maddie Flint kissing them all on their cheeks made him want to throw up.

My mum's side are all infected by this inferior interloper. My treasured Aunty Dottie went through hell and back, carrying and raising Dean, giving him undying love and protection. So, how does he repay her devotion? He chooses to champion this simpering, whimpering spawn of the starman! This so-called, credit-worthy cretin in crisis. This Flint-flop, flimflammer! And try saying that after a bottle of wine!

"Randal, how lovely to see you again! I swear that you look more handsome as the years go by," fawned his Aunty June, her attractive features lighting up at the sight of her favourite nephew.

"You flatter me, kind lady, but I like your style," he responded, smiling disarmingly, glad of the diversion away from his foul mood.

June's husband, Christopher, shook Randal's hand firmly, and their daughter, his cousin Heather, waved to him across the room with her husband Larry.

Dean's sister, Shannon, scowled as she caught sight of Roxanne in deep conversation with Amber. She had never come to terms with her permanent presence in the family, and the way she seemed to manipulate everyone around her.

"Hi, Shannon," croaked Ryan, still bleary-eyed.

"What happened to you? You look positively done in."

"Oh, I didn't get much sleep last night. Out on the razzle-dazzle."

"So, you won't be wanting any pink champagne then?" she teased, pointing towards the drinks table.

"Er, best not. Dad will go ape."

"Since when did he become tea-total?" mocked Shannon.

"Since his long drive here and back," chided Randal into her ear, and Shannon jumped.

"Randal! I didn't see you!"

"It's your loss," he said lovingly to his youngest cousin. She hugged him a little too possessively and caught sight of Roxanne's jealous stare in her direction.

Alison came over with Oscar, who was wide awake with a mouth full of crisps.

"Daddy, when can we have something proper to eat? I'm hungry." He sulked, tugging at Randal's sleeve.

"Very soon. Now go and speak to your grandma. She wants to tell you about the trampoline in her garden. She bought it especially for you."

"Trampoline! Wow! Can we go there now?" he exclaimed excitedly, forgetting all about the food.

"Another time," said Randal gently.

He looks like me. Red hair and red-faced, with the thought of something exciting in the offing. But a trampoline would be the last thing to stimulate my seven-year-old self. In my case, it was the well-planned elimination of John Sterling!

Randal felt a hand on his shoulder.

"I want to speak to you. Come with me, while I keep an eye on my rhubarb crumble," requested his Aunty Dottie.

He sensed a strong uneasiness in her request as they slipped away into the kitchen.

Dottie wanted complete privacy, so she shut the door behind them. She cleared her throat before she spoke.

"Now, Randal. I need your honest opinion on Dean's immovable fixation. You knew Carlton's wife. Did you ever suspect any psychosis? I'm terrified that Maddie may have inherited her mother's illness. I'm so worried for Dean's welfare. I can't sleep," she grimaced.

Randal felt sincere sympathy for his aunt's plight. He was fractionally guilty over his part in Francine's deranged downfall, but then his offence was quickly forgotten when he thought of Carlton's devout, dedicated deliverance of the desperate. Pure hatred instantly replaced any misgivings.

"I only met Francine Flint three times," he lied, omitting their hypnotic, pornographic 'Scarlet Pimpernel' episode in the hotel bedroom. "Once at Christmas, then at her house with

Alison, when she invited us both for dinner, and again, at the last disastrous show of *Celestial Bodies* when Carlton was injured by the falling monitor. She seemed quite grounded."

"So, what possessed her to do it? What made her kill two friends and then attempt to do the same to her husband?"

"I can't answer that. I don't honestly know. She must have had a hidden psychotic streak. Her smiling, wholesome nature was a sham. Her manner was cordial and charming, but it was concealing a powerhouse of insanity," he fabricated, not acknowledging that he ironically fitted the same description as his falsified explanation.

"That's just it, Randal. That's my biggest concern."

"You mean you've sensed it? Has she shown any irrational behaviour?"

"No. Maddie's very sweet and eager to please, but what if she becomes violent for no apparent reason? If Carlton Flint couldn't control his wife after all those years of marriage, then what chance would my beautiful, big-hearted son have, if Maddie snapped? I'm so scared, Randal. I've not discussed this with Neil or Shannon. They don't know how frightened I really am," she choked.

"Shh. Come here, Aunty Dot. Don't get upset. I hate to see you so distressed."

His concern was genuine as he held her in the circle of his strong arms, his eternal hatred for the Flints fermenting in his boiling blood.

This is all wrong. Maddie Flint's all wrong. For eight solid years I'd put 'the gift' to bed. I thought long and hard on its re-emergence and I still let it remain dormant. Clive's been elated by my cosmic complacency. Roxanne's fundamentally frustrated by our redundant removals. But I don't want to damage Dean with new reprisals. I must placate my beloved Aunty Dottie, though. I simply must.

"Aunty Dot, listen to me. I'm going to persuade Dean to put the wedding on ice. I'll suggest that he should get to know her even better. I'll do it in such a way that he'll see the sense in my proposal," soothed Randal, stroking the side of her face.

"Would you? Oh, Randal." She sniffed, blowing her nose on some kitchen roll.

"Now there's something you all don't know that might show her true colours," he added.

"What? Tell me."

"A fellow author of mine has written a book on the Flints' downfall. When it hits the shops, it will affect Maddie's state of mind for sure. Dean will be able to use it as a template to judge her reaction. He'll see if she goes over the top and becomes totally uncontrollable. Then he'll realise just exactly what he's letting himself in for, and that only professional help will be effective."

"But what if she harms him, Randal? What if she becomes violent?"

"Then I'll make him doubly aware of that possibility so he can protect himself. Let him come to his own conclusion about their future together. It might be her undoing but his salvation. When push comes to shove, it's only Dean who matters. It's only Dean who's so precious to us all," he concluded with dramatic passion, like an actor in a staged play.

"What would this family do without you? You're everything to everyone," she praised with an adoring expression, her eyes brimming with unshed tears.

"You'd all carry on arguing," joked Randal, and Dottie laughed and cried at the same time.

Don't you worry now, my sweet. I'll find a way to change Dean's mind. I'd never hurt him because that would wound me too. I just need to protect him as I always have done.

So, I won't remove his flappable fiancée. That would destroy him. But what you don't know is that I'm the author of the aforementioned book. It's written under an alias.

When it's published, I'll perform a dual hypnosis, so that Maddie

Flint will react totally over the top to its contents. Dean will see exactly what he's up against and decide for himself, with a little hypnotic help, that she's far too dangerous. This will leave him free to look elsewhere and find a more suitable candidate for a place in his heart.

He hugged his favourite aunty and she spoke to him earnestly.

"Don't tell anyone what we've discussed, not even your mum. She'll only worry that I'm worrying. She still thinks I'm her baby sister in need of her mother-hen protection. I'm confiding in you, so let's keep it between ourselves. Please?" she entreated.

"Of course! I'll fight tooth and nail for Dean's welfare. You know that. You can trust me with anything."

"Yes, darling. Thank you for comforting me today. I needed it."

"I'm glad I've helped." He smiled, kissing her tenderly on her cheek.

For you, and for Dean, I'll use 'the gift' in a hypnotic, rather than a cut-throat fashion. Roxanne won't agree. She's itching for a Maddie murder, but that's not the answer. I want Dean unscathed and eligible.

So, it's a simple solution and it leaves me free to concentrate on the next powerful, puzzling project. Tyrone Pendle. Tyro or tyrant? It all remains to be seen.

4

Roxanne put the finishing touches to her striking eye make-up and applied another layer of volume-lash mascara. She pouted so that her shapely mouth complimented the glossy, scarlet lipstick, that had a provocative look and left the observer bewitched.

She wore a tight-fitting, sleeveless, deep purple shift dress, with spaghetti shoulder straps. The outfit clung to her curves and her luxurious, long, red hair framed her beautiful face in a natural explosion of shiny curls.

She inspected herself thoroughly in the mirrored wardrobe door and smiled at her own reflection.

I've got Maxine's vampish-stance and glorious hair, but my features are identical to Daddy's. The shape of my face is Randalesque, as is my height and sexy aura. I'm positively outstanding and I crave no part of modesty or chastity. I know who I am and I know what I want.

Randal was downstairs in his study when she sashayed into his space with a grand entrance. She needed his constant approval and admiration. It was so important to her that he sanctioned her every move.

"Daddy, how do I look? Will I pass?"

He looked up and dropped his pen, as well as his jaw.

"Stunning! You're just stunning, but where are you going dressed like that?" he asked, frowning, his curiosity instantly aroused along with parental concern.

"I've got a blind date. Well, it's part of a double date, actually." She smiled cheekily, batting her eyelashes.

"A double blind date? Who with?"

"Ryan's got a new girlfriend, and he's bringing his student buddy with him, for my own entertainment." She smirked.

"Is he indeed? Are we talking Tyrone Pendle?" asked Randal with sparking eyes.

"We are. He wants to see me. He's seen my photo and now he wishes to meet me in the flesh," she bragged.

"Hmm. Let's rephrase that, shall we? He wants to meet me primarily, so he's using you as an intermediary," he replied sardonically.

"No, Daddy. He told Ryan that he thinks I'm really hot and he would love to take me out," she stressed.

"Would he now? Does he know you're only sixteen and still at school?" He glowered, his gaze becoming more intense by the second.

"I suppose. Ryan must have mentioned it." She glared back at him.

"Well then, here's a bit of advice. As amazing as you look, I want you to get changed out of that fabulous unsuitable dress! You're beautiful and you'd look just as good in an outfit where you're covered up. So, do that. Now!" he ordered.

"No way! We're going to a trendy, posh restaurant and then on to a show. I want to look the part and I do! I've not spent the last hour making myself irresistible for nothing. Get used to it. Why shouldn't I look this way? I'm not your baby anymore!" she rebelled.

Randal stood up and looked every bit of his intimidating and domineering six feet two inches.

"I won't ask you again. I was twenty-one once, like your

devious date, and I know what he'll be thinking when he claps eyes on what you're half-wearing! So, get up those stairs. Right now!" He bristled.

"*No! I won't! So there!*" she yelled, stamping her foot down hard on the floor in the old familiar childish tantrum.

Ryan heard their raised voices and entered the room to investigate.

"What's going on here? Why are you shouting?" he queried.

Randal's eyes were on fire and about to ignite. He quelled the action with enormous willpower.

"What the hell are you thinking of, Ryan?" he snapped.

"Thinking of?"

"Yes! Just that! How old is your new girlfriend?" he barked.

"Tamara? She's my age. Why?"

"And Tyrone Pendle? Let me guess. He's three years older?"

"So what?"

"So what! I'll tell you so what! Roxanne's still in school uniform and I'm not happy with the age difference. I've not even met your Beaumont buccaneer yet, and from what I know, neither has Roxanne," he argued.

"Dad, you sound like a dinosaur. It's the year 2000, not 1900. We're only going for a meal and to the theatre, for God's sake. Roxanne will be with me all the time!"

"While she's in that dress, Mr Pendle will be after his dessert before his starter! She needs to get changed. That's the compromise," he insisted.

"I've worn this outfit before to a party and you never complained. In fact, you said you preferred it to my green silk dress with the plunging neckline. The one on New Year's Eve!" she protested.

"I lied! It isn't a case that I prefer it. I just hate it less," he growled.

Amber walked into the room at this point, also curious about the discord.

"What's the matter? Why are you all arguing? I can hear you in the hall."

"Ask your sister!" carped Randal.

"What's the problem, Roxanne? Can I help in any way?" she queried.

"Our father thinks I look like a trollop and I'm far too young to be seen with a twenty-one-year-old, Oxford college student," she growled, glaring at Randal.

"Oh, Dad! That's tosh. In case you've forgotten, my boyfriend's almost twenty and you're not overly bothered about him. So why is it different for Roxanne?" objected Amber, more annoyed over his obvious favouritism.

"Because it just is!"

"Why? Why is it? I'm the same age as Roxanne. Could it be that you're more protective of her? More caring? More interested? More paternal? In fact, I'd go so far as to say that I seem like the adopted sibling, instead of your real daughter. That's how you make me feel, and how you've always made me feel. Like an interloper. A lodger," she said bitterly.

Randal shook himself out of his disgruntled state when he saw Amber's face crumble.

Who'd be a father of teenage girls? Won't somebody save me from their hormonal harassment! But Amber's right. I do favour Roxanne for obvious reasons known only to us. I must learn to be more generous with my affection, or at least appear to be. I don't want my other children suspicious or upset. It genuinely pains me to see them distressed, because after all, they are my own flesh and blood.

"Look, Amber, I'm sorry you feel so neglected but I truly have no favourites. Perhaps it's the very fact that Roxanne's adopted that I worry more about her," he lied. "Please don't ever feel unloved. All of my children are special to me in different ways."

"You wouldn't think so, Dad. We feel pushed out and ignored. I'm glad that Amber's brought this up because I feel the same way. I have done for years," braved Ryan, seizing the moment to express his own pain.

"I'm so sorry. It was never my intention. I get too caught up with my work and sometimes my priorities are all wrong. I'll try to make it right," assured Randal.

"Then start now, with Roxanne, and let her have a memorable night in the dress she prefers. You have to trust her, Dad. You can't control us all every second of the day," urged Ryan.

"I do trust her. It's Tyrone Pendle who worries me. And that's why I need to check him out," he preached.

"Well, you'll get that chance because he'll be here any minute. He's a great guy, Dad, and you'll like him. All your concerns will be put to bed."

"As long as it's only my concerns," he intimated suggestively, through a narrow-eyed sideways glance at Roxanne.

She opened her mouth to object and the doorbell rang at the same time to interrupt her disapproval.

"Talk of the devil," said Ryan, not realising how close to the mark he was with the phrase. "Tyrone's here now."

"Well then, let him in," drawled Randal as he lit up a cheroot.

Roxanne looked at Randal with appealing eyes and spoke to him telepathically.

Don't you dare show me up, Daddy. I'm a good girl, really.

Then don't give me cause. Let me assess the situation and you'll know instinctively if I approve. I know something that you don't. Your Mr Pendle has already hypnotised Ryan out of his fixation for you. That's why he's not bothered about you dating his new best friend.

How do you know that?

Because I know everything.

But why didn't I know?

Because you aren't looking for defects. I've been on his case just like he's studied mine. Nothing escapes me, so don't ever underestimate my powers of deduction. Now, just let me greet this Beaumont buccaneer and assess his suitability for my most precious daughter.

I'm sorry I shouted at you, Daddy. I didn't mean it. I know you want to protect me.

They smiled their special smiles at each other and all prior discord was forgotten.

I still don't like your dress, but I guess I have to accept the fact that my baby girl is all grown up.

I'll always be your baby girl no matter what.

Just be safe, pumpkin. Just be safe.

Randal heard the sound of laughter in the hallway as Ryan welcomed his fellow student and new best friend.

"This is Tyrone," announced Ryan, unnecessarily.

"Hi, everyone!" he enthused as he looked directly at Randal. "It's been my long-term wish to meet you, Mr Forbes, and I can't believe it's actually happening."

Their eyes met and in that one split second, Randal knew that he had a genuine, kindred, dark spirit standing before him in human form.

He felt their mutual loathing for lesser mortals reaching out across time and space. Their absolute contempt for the 'flock mock'. Their thirst for knowledge and their love of literature. Their need to rule the unrighteous roost and rid themselves of any suspicious encumbrance or impediment. Randal's heart sang unexpectedly.

"Welcome, Tyrone, to my kingdom. I'm glad your lifelong wish has happened. Very glad indeed," he almost crooned, as both their eyes sparked in primeval recognition of 'the gift'.

***

Clive Hargreaves did not know whether to feel bemused, confused or abused. He lit up his cigarette, dragged far too hard on its filter tip, coughed because he inhaled it badly, took a gulp of cold coffee and then slammed down the cup in a gesture of exasperation. Its contents splashed all over his desktop, but he ignored the splodges on his handwritten paperwork because he was trying to breathe normally while he was deep in thought and full of agitation.

Why, oh why, has this had to happen now? I've had eight wonderful years of peace, love and joy. No bad vibes, no dark deeds, no worries, no stress and, most of all, no Randal removals! And now I've got double the malevolence. Two for the bloody price of one!

How long has Tyrone Pendle been lurking in the shifty shadows, besotted with the love of my life? According to Randal he's the real death-defying deal. A student of sacrificial slaughter, twiddling his thumbs and just waiting for a chance to prove his satanic status, or words to that effect.

And on top of all that, he's stepping out with my mesmerised Roxanne, whose own gruesome gift has just been sleeping. And now, it's wide and flash-eyed awake! Perilously alert.

God give me the strength to cope. I thought I was safe and gloriously immune, but this latest development has got me sitting on the edge of my supervisor's seat. I'm now a protector of three: a tyrannical trio of trick-or-treats, just waiting to create a heretical hurricane of havoc. How's that for alliteration?

He tried to continue proof-reading Randal's current manuscript. He strongly disapproved of the subject matter because he knew it would only cause more pain and heartache for Carlton's devastated daughters. Even the title was naff.

The Flawed Flints, written under another alias, namely Lloyd Byron, was outrageous – a twist of the famous name, and a nod to one of Randal's favourite poets.

As if to add fuel to the flammable situation, Tyrone had already been very vocal in trying to impress Randal. In his ultimate quest to win Roxanne's heart, he was relentless in his pursuit of acceptance, as he spoke earnestly to his new mentor.

"You know I'm fully aware that Roxanne's underage, but I'm prepared to wait for her, just like Alison waited for you to grow up. I say that with the greatest of respect because I know what she means to you, and regardless of the five material years between you both, you knew right from the start that she was the one. Just as I know that Roxanne's my soulmate," enthused Tyrone.

Randal blew a stream of cheroot smoke across the room before he replied through glinting eyes.

"I'm championing you, but you still have a long way to go. Roxanne is my true inheritress and my most precious child. I want the very best for her, and I mean the cream of the double cream, and nobody less will serve at her side. I've never been actively seeking a tyro, or a suitor, for my outstanding daughter. You've been thrust upon me and I don't know exactly what to do with you just yet. 'The gift' is very powerful and you have undoubtedly been touched by its majesty. So, we'll just take it day by day, but make no mistake, I'm still pleased that you've applied for the vacancy."

Tyrone looked at Randal with an expression of pure reverence.

"You and Roxanne totally get me. My parents and siblings think I'm out of step with everyone and everything. In a sense they're correct, forever lecturing me on the rights and wrongs of the artificial, social merry-go-round. How to win friends and influence people is my father's mantra. He wants me to take over the reins of his business empire with my older brother, Tobias, so he's training us both up for the future. He's forever banging on about tenacity, tenacity, tenacity. He's purposefully chosen our names to begin with the letter 'T', as in Tobias, Tyrone and Tiffany. It's pathetic," he complained.

"I don't blame your parents for wanting you to get ahead. There's nothing wrong with that. In their mortal eyes they want the best for you. My mother, father and sister have always supported me, as have certain members of my extended family. That's fine as long as you hide your true benefaction. You can still be loyal to the ones who are loyal to you," preached Randal.

"But they're such a king-size drag! What they want for me is so far removed from my inner self. Dad can't understand why

I'm at Beaumont College, studying what he calls 'lightweight literature'. If it doesn't have a money-ring to it, then in his eyes it's all pointless. He's as spiritual as an agnostic android and his only goal in life is to outdo the outdoers."

"You can't afford to rub their noses in your superior knowledge. You have to take a step back and go with the flow. You're drawing attention to yourself with your non-compliance. The trick is to let them think you are all they want you to be. I realised that from a very early age. Deception is better than derision," advised Randal.

"But I feel stifled. I need your guidance. I now know for sure that I have 'the gift', but I don't know what to do with it. I've spent so many years hiding it, fighting it and feeling scared of it. I've always felt special but isolated. I couldn't reveal my true standing or use my powers openly. Help me to function. Show me how to shine," he almost begged.

Randal looked into Tyrone's bright brown eyes that were alight with frustration and passion. He blocked off his thoughts to his student, whose pulse points were throbbing with expectation.

He hero-worships me. I don't blame him. However, it's all about his adaptability but most of all his suitability. He's a very willing pupil and I'll take him under my wing. There's so much for him to learn.

He should not feel scared by his benefaction. He should embrace it without doubt or culpability. We need to have a trial run. We'll start from scratch and build up slowly.

"What are you doing at the weekend?" asked Randal, lighting up another cheroot.

"Not a lot."

"Then come for dinner. I need you to meet someone special. My lifelong protector, Clive. He can be trusted one hundred per cent. He's also my lover, but you know that already. Never, ever reveal that to anyone. Our relationship is sacrosanct, and if anyone should ever hurt him, they will feel the full power of my homicidal wrath. You understand me?"

"I get it. Clive's your paranormal patron. You're very lucky to have him as a friend, don't you think?" Tyrone chuckled, feeling smug and close to the source of it all.

Randal's slate-grey eyes flashed with ominous yellow, sparking glints.

"Now watch my mouth and let me answer that last sentence point by point. Number one, Clive's so much more than my guarantor. Number two, he's just as lucky to have me as an ally. Number three, the word 'friend' doesn't even come close. He's like family, my precious loyal partner and companion. He's touched my heart, and that's not an easy thing to do. Very few can. He's my same-sex soulmate, my creative soundboard and the designated, appointed, pledged protector of 'the gift'. My life would be half-empty without him, so don't you dare try to analyse our relationship in one casual, glib, throwaway statement," he reprimanded, with a menacing stare.

Tyrone's heart stalled and he took a number of deep breaths before he replied.

"I'm s-so sorry. I didn't mean to insult you both. I would never d-do that so early in my apprenticeship," he stuttered.

"Let's rephrase that apology. I don't want to hear such an asinine comment at any time in your probationary period, early or late, otherwise it will be terminated before it's even begun. I'm very particular about descriptions of the people who matter to me the most. So, engage your brain before your tongue."

"I understand. I only want to learn, so please be patient. This is all new to me. I'm going to make mistakes, even small ones," he beseeched.

"You're digging a bigger hole for yourself, Tyrone. Your mistake was not a small one. It was demeaning and misguided. Take note and don't slip up again," he instructed.

"Message understood. I promise to do just that."

"Good. Now, I'm going to call Clive and invite him to dinner. You're the newcomer, so treat him with the respect he so rightly deserves. He might not have 'the gift', but he's still very special and irreplaceable. You're unlikely to meet anyone else of his kind in your lifetime."

"I'm honoured. Truly," responded Tyrone with a half-smile.

"And so you should be."

Tyrone exhaled, not realising he had been holding his breath in anticipation of Randal's hostile response. He could feel his bubbling wrath transmit itself through their dual telepathic frequency, but he did not have to be psychic to realise that he had committed an unintentional, disrespectful offence.

Randal's presence was overpowering and imperious, and kicked his own dark disposition into touch. The last thing he wished to do was get off on the wrong foot, but through his lack of thought, he had touched a raw nerve.

"I'm in awe of you, Randal. Please remember that," beseeched Tyrone.

"Don't instruct me. You've a long way to go, so let's start off as we mean to go on. I'm the master and you're the tyro. The word's in your name. Live up to it."

"I will. With your help," fawned Tyrone.

"Indeed."

Randal called Clive on his mobile, while Tyrone sat opposite him with his eyes downwards. He felt like a schoolboy who had just been given a detention for bad behaviour. He stayed silent while Randal made contact.

"Hello, you," said Randal warmly when Clive replied.

"Hi, what's up now?" asked Clive, his heart thudding at the sound of Randal's sexy voice but still feeling the after-effects of his latest contemplation about the re-emergence of 'the gift'.

"Why should there be anything up? I'm inviting you to dinner tomorrow evening if that's OK?"

"Oh, I see."

"Well? Are you coming?" asked Randal suggestively, and Clive felt hot at his double-edged insinuation.

"I'll always come for you," he replied just as improperly, and felt aroused at the mere thought of Randal's nearness.

"We've got another guest," added Randal.

"Anyone I know?"

"Tyrone Pendle. I've told him all about you, well, all about us, and what you mean to me. As he's from the same source, it's important for the future of 'the gift' that you encounter another kindred spirit. Roxanne especially wants you to meet him. She's insistent."

Clive hesitated and Randal felt his reluctance. He knew that he had misgivings about the whole scenario.

"I'm… I'm not sure that I'm ready for this, Randal. I've thought about it a lot and I need more time to adjust to the situation." He frowned.

"I understand. That's why I think it's best that you come tomorrow because all of your doubts and uncertainties will be laid to rest. Please, Clive. For me," he urged.

"Is he with you now?"

"Yes."

"Have I lost you to him?" asked Clive, with a slight break in his voice.

"Never. You should know that," assured Randal.

"Then I'll come. For you, and with you. Be gentle with me. I'm feeling fragile with the resurrection of 'the gift'. I've had eight years of peace and I don't know what to expect."

Randal's heartless heart melted and his only concern was Clive's welfare. He was his number-one priority.

"Why don't you shut up shop and drive over to me now? We can grab a bite to eat together," suggested Randal softly.

"Where are you?"

"I'm at Astral TV. I'll wait for you in Studio One."

"What's Tyrone doing there anyway? I thought he was back at Beaumont with Ryan," uttered Clive in a flat voice, as vivid recollections of their own youthful time in Oxford served as a poignant reminder.

"By rights he should be, but he just needed some extra advice, some guidance."

"And did you give it to him? Did you take time out of your relentless, intrusive, hectic schedule to pamper his every need?" Clive scowled, hating himself for his uncontrollable jealousy.

"Get yourself down here pronto. We need to talk. You need to talk. That's evident. Please?"

"Not if he's there."

"He won't be."

Clive felt very low, as an ugly resurgence of his former depression was beginning to snake its way into his present vision. His head hurt and felt heavy with unwanted thoughts.

How can I compete with a twenty-one-year-old genius who has 'the gift'? Tyrone's got it all. Youth, brains, good looks, all fused with telepathy.

Roxanne's hooked on him and the love of my life is rejuvenated with the exultation of his tyro's apprenticeship. I'm pushed out before it begins.

I don't want a notorious novice on the scene, a newcomer who's straight but still besotted with Randal.

That doesn't mean a thing. Randal could seduce Casanova if he wished to. He could have anyone with a pulse at the snap of his shapely fingers. Oh, God. He's probably picking up on every negative, possessive, insecure thought in my head right now. Well, let him!

Randal heard all of Clive's unnecessary but painful ramblings, and it only increased his desire to appease him.

"I'll tell you what. I'll drive over to you. Stay put, Clive, and I'll be with you in about, say, half an hour. I'm on my way. OK?"

Tyrone felt the urgency in Randal's movements as he put down the receiver. He had a mental flash of Clive in intensive care and of Randal reviving him with 'the gift'. Then he realised it was in the past and not a future portent. He also knew that Randal did not want a repeat performance, and that was why he needed to get to Clive and talk him out of this latest depressive episode.

"Let's wrap it up for today. In fact, I think you should go back to Oxford and stop neglecting your studies," advised Randal, grabbing his jacket and car keys.

"What about dinner? With Clive?"

"It's on ice. For now, at least."

"Is there a problem? I'd hate to come between you both." Tyrone frowned.

"It's nothing insurmountable, and don't flatter yourself."

"Am I still your pupil? I need to know because I picked up on a lot of envy and animosity towards me from Clive. Will this put a halt to our relationship?" he asked anxiously.

"I'll sort it out. Clive feels threatened and there's no need. Now stop asking me questions or else I'll terminate our alliance. Just get back to Beaumont and I'll be in touch. Our liaison is far from over. OK?"

Tyrone half-smiled and looked appealingly handsome as he felt relief and concern simultaneously.

"I can speak to Clive if you wish and put his mind at rest. He needs to know he's an integral part of 'the gift'," he enthused.

"Have your train ticket to hand and take your misplaced enthusiasm and irritating suggestions back to Oxford. I'll call you. When I'm ready. Come with me and I'll drop you off at the station," advised Randal in a superior, no-nonsense tone.

Tyrone nodded and knew when to stop. He tried to stem his thoughts but failed.

I need Clive on my side, not on my case. He's an invaluable asset and advocate of 'the gift'. I know he's jealous of me. He should realise that I love everything that Randal is, but I'm not 'in love' with him. It's Roxanne who's captured my heart and soul. She's the main attraction and my ultimate goal. I have to do everything possible to prove that I'm worthy of her. In Randal's eyes. Clive's too.

They drove to the railway line in silence but could hear snatches of each other's thoughts. Randal was too concerned about Clive to talk.

The last thing I want is for him to be depressed again. I'll nip it in the bud before it takes hold. He's so sensitive, always has been. He should know by now that my love for him is genuine and eternal. But there again, his human emotions get the better of him every time.

He's far more delicate than I thought. Eight years of respite is a long time, and I just took it for granted that he'd be able to pick up from where I left off. He seemed to cope well with my last killing spree, but there again he's had quite a few years to come to terms with it all. Time is a great healer.

There will be more removals. I have to teach Tyrone the right way to use his powers. I think Clive's more concerned about my feelings for my absolute beginner. Well, he needn't be. If there's to be any closeness it will come down to the way my apprentice performs. It's about pride not passion. Clive has my full desire. Not my tyro.

By the time Randal reached the office, Clive was halfway through a bottle of wine. The need to blot out his self-doubt was all-consuming and the alcohol would numb his vulnerability. He looked up through bloodshot eyes as Randal walked through the door.

"Welcome, your lordship. I've taken a break from proof-reading your latest, hurtful piece of non-fiction. *The Flawed Flints* is another masterpiece of destruction. Well done!" slurred Clive, swivelling round to face his lifetime's obsession.

Randal pulled up another chair so they were practically touching knees. He stared deeply into Clive's eyes and stroked his cheek in a gesture of tender caring.

"Now listen to me, you clown, because you've got this all so wrong. Put down that glass of wine and watch my lips," demanded Randal.

Clive began to tremble at his tender expression of concern. Even after all the years he was not immune to the Randal-effect.

"You have absolutely no need to feel threatened by Tyrone Pendle. He means nothing to me emotionally. He represents an unexpected challenge, not as a rival but as a pupil. I've never come across anyone like him before. He needs me more than I need him. All of his life he's had 'the gift', but he didn't know what it was. He thought it was more of a curse."

"He's right."

"No! It's only a curse if it's redundant, if it's allowed to fester with fear and misuse. He needs our support, Clive. I have to see what he's truly capable of because he loves Roxanne. If they are meant to be together in the future then I have to evaluate his worth, to judge for myself if he's the right pillar of our paranormal society so that he can support and worship her in the right way. I won't be here forever, so I need to leave her in the hands of a successor: a true recipient of the same gift we share. It's imperative that she has that protection and reassurance. At the moment I don't know if he's the one, but I need to test his powers and suitability."

"Where do I fit in, Randal? Where the fuck do I fit in with your grand plans? Am I going to be relegated to the sidelines again or just hanging around while the three of you play happy gift-hood? I'm powerless. Literally." He grimaced.

"You're anything but! You have the power to feed the power. Do you see anyone else in your role, Clive? Is there another person on this earth, apart from Roxanne, who is privy to everything I am? Who else nurtures me after 'the gift' has drained me? Is there another protector who holds my head and rocks me to sleep when I'm exhausted after a removal? Do you see another guy who I touch physically? Who I'm passionate with? There's no-one. Just you. Tyrone could never, ever come a fraction close to what we have. To what we've built. He's a tyro, not a toy boy. Your fears are unfounded. Do you understand that? Do you?" declared Randal, his eyes on fire with passion and fervour.

"Oh God, Randal. I got it wrong again! I'm just so… so scared of losing you, of failing. I don't want to go down that gut-wrenching road again. Ever."

"The only road you'll be going down is on the motorway when we travel together with another project, when we work as we've always done on more creative themes. I want you with me, Clive. As long as my flashing eyes are open, I want you by my side and in my bed. You've always been free to choose another partner. I told you that a long time ago in Oxford. If that were to happen, I would be partly bereft but delighted for you at the same time. As long as you need me in your life, just as I need you in mine, nothing, or nobody, will ever get in the way of our relationship. It will always flourish and survive."

Clive began to cry softly. It was a mixture of relief and deep emotion.

I love you so much it hurts. Why does it hurt so much? Will I ever get used to the pain, passion and power?

"Stop torturing yourself," said Randal, upon hearing Clive's thoughts.

"Where you're concerned that's how it's always been. A myriad of emotions. I find it hard to think logically around you. It's torture. You're torturous."

"Isn't it about time you realised that you could save yourself from all the doom-ridden scenarios that you conjure up in that frizzy-haired head of yours? Just look at me, Clive. Look closely into my eyes. What do you see?"

"Right now?"

"Yes."

"It looks like love, but it could be an act. I never really know. Do any of your worshippers truly have a piece of your heart? Do you blame me for my cynicism? When you have that misty expression in your gaze, I could almost believe that you truly care, but then the illusion is shattered by that ominous, molten glare when you're in full monstrous throttle." Clive shuddered.

"What do you want from me? You know who I am. What I do. What I've done. How many times can we go over this?" sighed Randal.

"It's not you, it's me. I guess I didn't expect 'the gift' to show itself again. I got used to being distanced from it all. But this is so different, Randal. Now there's another *exactly* like you. It was deadly enough with Carlton Flint. This time, I truly don't know what to expect. It's taken me years to accept my role, and more recently with Roxanne. But this new interloper? This stranger who's studied your life and copies everything you do? Even down to the student wire? He purposefully chose to go to Beaumont. It could have been any of the colleges, but he wanted to mimic your footsteps. Don't you find that creepy? Isn't that a trifle alarming?"

"It's for me to find out and for you to accept. I don't feel anything adverse; I just feel his frustration and fervour. He hero-worships my level of ability and wants me to show him the sovereignty and authority of our twin benefaction. That's it."

"And then what? What will he have to do to prove his ascendancy? How many removals before he's passed the tainted test? Are you both going to sit down and work out some kind of dramatic script together? Have I got to wipe his brow as well as yours? Hold him in the circle of my arms and help him breathe?"

"It depends. If he's worthy of his endowment then he'll need your support. I truly don't know at this stage if he's creditable. I have to think of the future preservation of 'the gift'. Of my daughter's inheritance. You know that. One day I'll be gone. You must see that, surely?"

"Stop! Stop it! I can't bear to think of that! Don't ever go there!" bellowed Clive, with agitation and distress.

"Shh. Calm down. I'm talking practicalities not immediate circumstances. Now come here," he soothed, opening his arms.

"I need another drink, not a pitying hug," moaned Clive.

"No, you don't."

"Watch me!" he argued, reaching for the bottle of wine, still somewhat inebriated from his previous alcoholic state.

Randal grabbed it out of his hands before he could pour it into his glass.

"Now you're acting like a child! This is what Roxanne does when she can't get her own way! Let's get this whole thing straight otherwise I'll just walk out of here and I won't come back!" threatened Randal.

His words struck a chord in Clive's troubled soul.

That's the last thing I want to happen. Why can't I just accept his explanation and advice? He's made it perfectly clear. Why am I still arguing? Why?

"Your thoughts are more mature than your actions, Clive. Listen to your conscience. It's telling you to agree with me. There's absolutely no reason why you should carry on with this pantomime. Just believe me when I tell you that apart from my wife and family, you're the most important person in my life. I would never hurt you intentionally. If I've done so in the past, it was the selfishness of youth. We've grown up together emotionally. I've also learned many lessons along the way. Forgive me for my former mistakes. You mean so much to me, Clive. So very much."

Clive looked at his stunning face, still unlined and youthful.

He looks in his mid-twenties, nothing like a man in his forties. He's just so perfect. That's why I hate it when things spoil that perfection. But he's right. I need to accept this new situation and do my best as his protector. It's not going to be easy, but I simply have no choice. No choice at all. Because without his love I'm nothing.

"I'm sorry. I think I'm ready now. Ready to move on to the next phase. And if that includes Tyrone Pendle, then I have to prepare myself for that extra responsibility," said Clive out loud.

"Thank fuck for that," he expounded, his words totally at odds with his passionate expression.

"Love me," pleaded Clive, as he fell into his arms.

So Randal held him close, and made him whole again.

5

Oscar Wilde Forbes was feeling disenchanted and thoroughly discontented at school. He was super-intelligent, so the syllabus for the average seven-year-old did little to stimulate his interest or advancement.

His hyperactivity was a consequence of frustration because he had no outlet for his boredom. Just as Randal had been, he was light years ahead academically. He was also bubbling on a low light with the stirrings of 'the gift', which so far had been sleeping and struggling to emerge.

"Miss! Miss Turner! I'm so fed up with this story now! Can't we learn about real magic?" he protested, right in the middle of her reading an excerpt from *Alice in Wonderland* to fire up her pupils' imagination.

"Don't interrupt me, Oscar! It's very rude," she berated.

"But real magic's much more exciting than made-up stories," he argued.

"There's no such thing. Magic is either in fairy tales or performed as an act on the stage," she insisted.

"That's not true! I can do magic and I'm not in a stupid story or on the stage," he pouted.

"Oscar Forbes! This is too much! If you don't settle down,

I'm going to ring your parents! How many times do I have to tell you to keep quiet? It's happening far too often recently," she reprimanded.

Oscar scowled as he stood up.

"If you don't listen to me then I'll *make* you listen!" He glared, his eyes glinting and threatening to glow.

There were a few stifled giggles around the classroom, as the children were amused by his seemingly silly behaviour.

"Right! That's enough! Go and stand in the corner, Oscar! You can stay there for the whole of the lesson! Go!"

"I won't. But you will." He smirked.

Then for the first time ever 'the gift' took hold. He focused his burning gaze on her face and she felt an unbearable surge of static energy filter through her head at a frightening speed, as though she had been struck by lightning. She stood ramrod-still like a frozen statue.

Now, Miss Bossy Boots! You can stand in the corner instead of me and stay there!

She shifted across the room in a robotic fashion. Her eyes were glazed as she obeyed his telepathic command.

Oscar smirked again. The Randal-smirk.

Now say these words over and over and over. 'I love Oscar and magic is real.' Do that! Oh, and stand on one leg while you're saying it. Oh, and don't dare stop until I say so!

"I love Oscar and magic is real. I love Oscar and magic is real," she reiterated like an insane parrot, nearly falling over as she tried to balance on one foot.

A merciless smile spread across Oscar's face as the whole class burst into hysterical laughter at their teacher's repetitive ritual. Oscar's stare was still alight, but all eyes were on his hypnotised teacher and her bizarre behaviour.

Then suddenly he felt his concentration wane and his eyes became normal again, far too soon for his liking. He was still rather pleased with himself, if only for a short while, because it was an entertaining diversion away from the tedious lesson.

"What's the matter, Miss Turner?" he asked loudly, along with the riotous reactions of his fellow pupils.

She failed to understand why she was facing the wall, and stood on one leg! She pulled herself together but inwardly felt very confused.

How the hell did I get here?

"Now do you believe in magic?" whooped Oscar.

She turned round to look at him and frowned as he smiled wryly.

That'll teach her! She won't start with me again. When I get home, I'm going to tell Daddy and Roxanne. They believe in magic. But I can't do it properly. I want to, but then something always stops me. I wish it would last longer. But I know they'll be pleased with me.

Miss Turner felt strange. Her head was still fuzzy and her co-ordination slightly off-centre.

There's something really odd about that boy. I don't like his precocity or his behaviour. What just happened to me?

"Settle down now, class. Please be quiet," she heard herself say with more control than she actually felt. "Now tell me, what did I just do to make you all laugh?"

"I can tell you that, Miss Turner," scoffed Oscar with a supercilious expression.

"If you must."

"You stood in the corner on one leg and told everyone that you loved me and magic is real." He sniggered.

"Now this time you've really gone too far! You're a very rude little boy, Oscar!" she chided.

"It's true, Miss Turner," verified another pupil. "Oscar's not lying. You did what he said."

"You must be mistaken. Now stop playing games and let's get back to our lesson," she instructed, but inside she was quaking.

That little boy is very weird! There's something not quite right. He made me a laughing-stock. How can that be? I'm not happy teaching him. Not happy at all.

★★★

Back at home, Oscar knocked on Randal's study door. He knew that if it was closed that his father was working hard on a new creative project, and he did not want to barge in unwanted.

"Come in," said Randal, irritated at being interrupted.

Oscar peeped round the door, his cheeky face full of enthusiasm.

"Daddy, something happened today at school and I have to tell you what I did! It was really ace."

"Was it now? Well, quickly, because I'm in the middle of an important scene in my new book," he answered distractedly, looking up with mild interest.

"Guess what I did? You're good at that."

"I'm not in the mood for guessing games, Oscar. So just tell me what happened."

Oscar walked up to him and climbed on his knee, just like Roxanne had done as a child. He whispered in his ear with his hand cupped around his mouth.

"I did some magic. Proper magic, to my teacher, because I was bored."

"Oh?"

"She doesn't believe in magic, so I made her do a very funny thing."

"Made her?"

"She told me off and I got cross with her, so I made her stand on one leg and say, 'I love Oscar and magic is real.' She said it over and over and over." He giggled.

Randal looked intently at him.

"How did you make her do that?"

"My eyes went twinkle-twinkle, and I got inside her head with my voice, so she did what I asked. I've tried to do it before, but it never worked. But this time it did! It so did! Now I can do proper magic!"

"Can you now? So, what happened to your teacher?"

"Well, the magic didn't last so she stopped. But she didn't know why she did it. She didn't believe me when I told her what she'd done, but another boy said I was telling the truth. She had to believe me then. She looked at me really funny. I think she was scared." He grinned.

Randal looked into Oscar's nearly identical eyes.

He's got a diluted variety of 'the gift', but it's far from top form. He's not taking it seriously. It's just a daft game to him. Roxanne knew that we were the same. Oscar doesn't realise the significance. I don't think it's safe in his hands.

"Daddy, don't you think it's good that I used the magic? You look upset. I thought you'd be happy for me."

"I am. You're a clever boy, but I don't think you should tell anyone else about this, apart from me and Roxanne," warned Randal.

"Not even Mummy?"

"Especially not your mummy."

"Why?"

"It's a secret. And the magic won't work if they know about it. So, let's just keep it to ourselves, huh? For now."

He's only a fraction of the way there. If he was a true inheritor, he would feel very differently about it all. Even at his tender age I always knew, as did Roxanne, and now Tyrone. As much as I love my son, I don't think he's equipped to deal with the seriousness of it all. I would have to sit him down and explain everything, and I know that would overwhelm him rather than inspire. No! He's got to be de-gifted. I'll have to work something out. A gentle hypnosis possibly. I'll talk to Roxanne first. See what she thinks.

"Don't you think I did a good spell?"

"You did a very, very good spell. But you must keep quiet about it. Promise me?" requested Randal, stroking his son's flushed cheek.

"If you think so. But what about my class? They all saw what I did to that horrible teacher. And what about her?" he insisted.

"They'll all put it down to a joke. The teacher will say she was playing a game."

"But she wasn't, Daddy. I made her do it."

"I know that. But I'll magic what you did away; otherwise, everyone will want to know how you did it. It all has to be kept very, very quiet."

"How can you magic it away?"

"Easy-peasy. I know what to do, so you just leave all that to me."

"OK then," he sulked, "but I want to do it again to somebody else. I want to do it to this stupid boy in my class."

"Of course, you do, you little tinker. But in the meantime, just listen to your daddy and do what he says."

"I will, but I get so bored at school. All the others are really dopey compared to me."

Randal smiled widely. There was no doubt that Oscar was academically advanced.

But that's his only true gift. Pity! I could have had two offspring to tutor, as well as my tyro. But Oscar will still achieve great things to make me proud in a mortal sense. Now where's that photograph of his classmates and teacher? I'll do a mass hypnosis so they'll just forget about today and Oscar's daft game.

***

Leighton Pendle was feeling furious with his son. He had arranged a very important business meeting and Tyrone had failed to show up.

"I just don't get that boy! Why can't he be more like you, Tobias? I've worked my fingers to the bone to give our family the best things in life that money can buy and what does he do? He throws it all back in my face, just so he can read up on those debauched poets and writers who flounced about in some forgotten century or other. Just what has that got to do with modern life? How's he going to forge a living with his head in the clouds, studying the irrelevant ramblings of those immaterial rhymesters!" he snorted, his handsome features twisted up in protest.

"He's not like us, Dad. He's… well, he's different."

"Oh, he's different all right! Do you know what he did the other day? Or should I say what he preferred to do?" objected Leighton.

"I don't know, but I'm sure you're going to tell me regardless."

"He actually had the barefaced cheek to walk out on one of my most influential friends, with the flimsy excuse that he had a tutorial in the afternoon. I told him to leave that day completely free. But, oh no! Beaumont College is more important than a peer of the realm! Lord Arkin Benton of all people! Lord Benton, would you credit it! He was really put out and I don't blame him. How could Tyrone do that to me? It's positively ludicrous!"

"We're not all cut out to be like you, Dad. I'm more business-minded, but Tyrone's always favoured the arts. You can't make him into something he's not. He'll just rebel. He's finding his way."

"Well, if he doesn't pull his monogrammed socks up, he'll be finding his bloody way out of the house and into the street. Let's see who'll fund his college fees if I cut all ties, if he's got nobody to back his dramatic daydreams!"

"Well, surprisingly you're wrong there. He's very friendly with Ryan Forbes, who's also studying at Beaumont. They're pretty damn close from what I've heard," argued Tobias.

"Ryan Forbes?"

"The eldest son of the one and only Randal Forbes. You know, the famous author and entrepreneur. You've admired him for a while yourself, and all the business ventures he's cultivated along the way. Now he's a poet, but you don't deride him."

Leighton stopped ranting and rubbed his chin.

"Randal Forbes, eh? That's the best thing I've heard yet! He's not let his airy-fairy poetry get in the way of his business acumen. He's a great success. Now he's a gold-edged contact to have. I'm very pleased with that one. Why didn't Tyrone tell me about the connection?"

"He didn't think you'd be remotely interested."

"Oh, but I am! Randal Forbes is a tour de force. He's built an empire of his own. I'm impressed. Maybe Tyrone's got far more ambition than I credit him with," he mused.

"Aha! So, suddenly Tyrone's got the go-getter, green light?" replied Tobias sardonically.

"Well, it's a bloody start and makes a change from his head being in a backsliding book all the time."

"I doubt if Randal Forbes would agree. He's primarily one of the most successful authors and playwrights worldwide, not to mention his poetry or his blockbuster film *Fiesta* which started life as – how did you put it – 'a backsliding book'? He wouldn't take too kindly to his self-penned, much-acclaimed novel being described in that way," scorned Tobias.

"There's a huge difference here. He's had the drive to marry his creativity with enterprise," enthused Leighton.

"Well then, Beaumont College did him the power of good, as did his degree in English literature, the same subject that Tyrone's studying. In fact, he told me that Randal's his absolute role model, and befriending Ryan is the icing on his creative cake. So, you see, Dad, you should be encouraging him, not ridiculing his ambitions," pointed out Tobias.

"Tell me more about Randal," queried Leighton, lighting up a cigarette, totally disregarding his eldest son's advice. "Does he have other children, apart from Ryan?"

"According to Tyrone, he has two daughters, Amber and Roxanne, who are both the same age as our Tiffany, sixteen or thereabouts. Apparently, Roxanne's adopted. Also, he has a younger son, Oscar, who's about seven. I have to tell you that Tyrone's besotted with Roxanne. He never stops talking about her."

"So, then Randal's got two daughters the same age?"

"It appears that way. Amber's beautiful, but Roxanne's stunning. In fact, the whole of their clan is amazing. And that includes the extended family."

"And Randal's wife?"

"Alison Whitaker, the famous classical pianist and composer."

"I'd like to meet them. I think we should, especially now that Tyrone's so close to Ryan and sweet on Roxanne."

Tobias frowned as his father prattled on.

"I could put in a good word for Tyrone, because if he's as creative as you say, then Randal Forbes is the ideal contact to further his aims and turn his dilly-dallying into a vocation. He needs someone with drive and ambition behind him, but most of all, power! The power to influence him so that he can capitalise on his studies and not just walk around with a head full of fanciful notions, but mostly the power to propel him into a prosperous future. Randal's the ideal mentor for him. I'm very excited with the connection. In fact, I'm going to speak to your mother about it all," he gushed.

"Whatever you think, but let Tyrone know what you have in mind. He's not a kid, and if you treat him as an adult, then he'll comply with your wishes. Just show him some interest in his choice. He had to be fiercely academic to be offered an unconditional place at Oxford. It's a hell of an achievement in itself. Praise him, Dad."

"Praise him? When he shows me that he's not wasting his time and finally comes to his senses about his future prospects, then he'll be applauded. So far, the only thing he's displayed is his rebellion. He looks at me with those strange, dark eyes, as if he's going to explode or something. I tell you, sometimes it's really daunting. Have you ever noticed the expression in them when he's annoyed or confronted?"

"Not really. I very rarely annoy or confront him," replied Tobias with more than a hint of contradiction.

"Well, trust me! I've witnessed it, and I don't like it one little bit. It's unsettling and quite formidable."

"I just think he's frustrated because you're always looking for the negatives and don't see the potential in the positives. Tyrone could go on to be a famous author like Randal. His gift for the written word is just wonderful. You've never took the time to read his stuff, have you?" argued Tobias.

"Not really, and even if I did, I'd still want him to have that ambitious work ethic, to be driven, not ferried. You won't get anywhere if you don't capitalise on it all. He needs influential contacts. That's partly why your mother and I arranged a huge party for his twenty-first birthday. Did he thank us? No! Did he look remotely grateful? No! Did he throw himself into the celebratory spirit? No! He appeared thoroughly bored and disconnected. That's not normal. He's not normal. I don't understand him one little bit," insisted Leighton.

"He's just not comfortable in a crowd. It wasn't ingratitude that you saw, it was uneasiness. At least that's the way it appeared to me."

"You're too soft, Tobias. Believe me, the expression on your brother's face was one of contempt. He looked down on the whole thing. Sometimes nothing pleases him, and that was a prime example," scorned Leighton.

"I still think it would help the situation if you gave him more support," chided Tobias.

"You're right in one aspect. I'm going to ask your mother to organise another of her magnificent functions. We'll invite Randal and his family. It'll be the perfect setting for us all to meet," he enthused, with an expectant light in his eyes.

"Don't you think you should ask Tyrone first? I mean, he might find it all a bit too overwhelming. He's struck up a close friendship with Ryan, but I don't know exactly how friendly he is with the rest of his relations," advised Tobias.

"You've just told me to encourage him. What's more praiseworthy than issuing an invitation to his new circle of friends? Look, there are tons of students at the various colleges in Oxford. The place is teeming with them, but it doesn't mean they'll all be successful, does it? Randal is the key, not some insignificant graduation day with a dubious diploma to nowhere. Tyrone needs a wake-up call and he's stumbled across it, albeit randomly."

"OK, Dad. I can see you're determined to forge a relationship with Forbes & Co."

"Tyrone doesn't realise what an amazing opportunity this is for him. By the time I've finished with Randal Forbes, he'll be putty in my hands. Just stand back and watch."

***

Leighton's wife, Corrine, had been ridiculously busy at her husband's request in preparing invitations for the world and its wealthy wife, to what promised to be, so far, *the* social extravaganza of the year, with a glittering guestlist of who's who, and what's new.

Things were falling into place and an air of exciting anticipation was stirring at the Pendle estate. But then a shocking bombshell occurred on the morning of the actual jamboree, and it was all over before it had even begun.

Tiffany Pendle went missing and it was totally out of character.

The last they saw of her was when she'd gone for her Saturday-morning jog, wearing a blue and white tracksuit, with matching headband and trainers. She did not return for lunch as promised, and her mobile was permanently unavailable. She had no cash on her and had every intention of coming back home in good time to get her hair done for the evening's big event.

Twenty-four hours later she was still absent, and the police, press and TV cameras were crawling all over her family and associates.

Her parents and Tobias were out of their minds with worry. Tyrone was more puzzled as to her disappearance rather than anxious, and he had consulted Randal over the phone to compare telepathic findings.

"I stared at her photo, just like you instructed me to do. I know she's still alive. What I can't understand is why I only see darkness around her, and yet I feel she's still breathing," he stipulated, with confusion rather than emotion.

"She's been abducted for money. Her kidnappers will get in touch with your father any time now. She's locked in an unlit, rundown shack, somewhere very isolated. They've blindfolded and gagged her. The hijackers are wearing masks, so I can't see who they are, but I've listened in to their conversations," explained Randal, his eyes glowing in his study, as he traced Tiffany's image with his fingers.

"Why couldn't I get all that information from her picture as well?" Tyrone sulked, more concerned about his level of power than his sister's welfare.

"You will, with more practice. You really don't care much for your family, do you? I can feel total detachment."

"I feel nothing for them. I told you that when we first talked. I don't like them and they don't get me," he replied callously.

"That's irrelevant. Your sister's the same age as Roxanne and these scumbags have snatched her off the street. They have every intention of blackmailing your father in exchange for her life. They mean business, dirty business, and it's up to us to get her out of there. I won't tolerate teenage abusers. They all need to die. Do you understand me?"

"You mean they'd actually go that far? They want to kill her? Are you quite sure of that?"

"What planet are you on, Tyrone? We need to use 'the gift' to save her. The police are too slow. Now pull your stupid, selfish, designer socks up pronto, and follow my instructions. Is that clear? You're testing my patience and I expect instant co-operation from my tyro. Your sister's badly traumatised. Now that might not bother you, but it infuriates me!"

"You've not even met Tiffany, and yet you're so concerned. It seems contradictory because I know you didn't really want to bring your family to that huge party my parents should have thrown yesterday. I knew instinctively that you were coming out of curiosity, rather than desire," stated Tyrone, feeling mystified.

"What the fuck's that got to do with this top-priority situation?"

"It's just bewildering. That's all."

"This isn't the time for absurd analysis!"

"I'm sorry. No disrespect intended. I was just thinking out loud."

"Just engage your brain and listen closely to what I'm going to do. Are you receiving me?" asked Randal, his query saturated with sarcastic disdain.

"I am."

"I'm now locking my study door because I don't want to be disturbed and then I'm going to shanghai one abductor's head. That's the best way to go. He'll do exactly what I want, and what *you* should really want!" scorned Randal.

"How many of them are there?"

"It's a motley crew of three, but it only takes one telepathic hypnosis to affect a result. I don't trust any of them with your sister. They're all turned on by her young flesh. I need to get full control of the situation because it's urgent."

"Won't the other two be suspicious? Can I help you in some way? I really need a trial run," suggested Tyrone.

"Not this time. Roxanne's helping me and she'll incapacitate their reactions."

"Roxanne? She's doing that for me?" he fawned.

"No! She's doing it for Tiffany! In case it's not sunk in, your sister's been dragged by her architect hair extensions into a den of mercenary iniquity and is in mortal danger. Because of your obvious indifference, I don't trust you with this assignment. I need a passionate intervention. We'll talk again about your lack of concern. Any vital undertaking of 'the gift' should be executed without contemplation. The fact you're not close to your sibling is immaterial. What matters is the annihilation of her detainers," stipulated Randal.

"I understand that now. There's no room for analysis. All my life I've wrestled with my thoughts. It's a hard habit to break."

"Break it, Tyrone. Otherwise, I'm wasting my time."

Randal beckoned Roxanne over to him. She was in the room and had listened in to the conversation, both audibly and telepathically, and she was more than ready for her first designation in eight years.

Tyrone had to see how powerful she was and learn from her, because she was in love with him and desperately needed Randal's approval of her choice. Otherwise, her future would be marred with dissent.

"I'm ending this call now, Tyrone, but I'll contact you later to tell you what's transpired. We'll also discuss your unacceptable attitude towards your benefaction and family."

"Please let me help you both," beseeched Tyrone.

"Just do as I say! This conversation is over," affirmed Randal.

Roxanne sighed deeply. She could feel Randal's displeasure wafting over her in waves of disappointment and disdain, and felt obliged to come to Tyrone's defence.

"Daddy, he doesn't mean to let us down. He's still learning, and if you don't guide him, he'll never be able to grasp the essence of it all. Let me teach him too. Please?"

"So far, he's bottom of the leaderboard. Tiffany is in grave danger. That should be his only objective!" he admonished.

"I'm only pointing out—"

"Don't bother! Are you going to assist me or not?" chastised Randal. "Time is of the essence."

She nodded and bit her lip, deeply upset by his wrath. As much as she felt a blossoming love for Tyrone, her father remained in pole position. She hated displeasing him and only felt whole when he smiled at her with complete adoration.

He had no equal. He was omnipotent in her eyes. She looked for his qualities in every other man, but they did not come close. Tyrone might in time. But even he would never eclipse the all-consuming obsession she had for Randal. How could anyone else overshadow him in her life?

Who could possibly match the genius of his literary inventions? His irrepressible physical presence. The absolute power he held over all lesser mortals with his unconquerable application of 'the gift'. His very existence on the same earthly plane.

"I'm ready, Daddy. Always."

"Good. Now come nearer and concentrate on Tiffany's image. You'll be able to see and hear everything that's transpiring. I'm going to raid the head of the degenerate who goes by the nickname of Jet, due to the repulsive black hair dye he uses. I had a psychic flash of him applying it to his greasy, long mane. I'll use him to restrict or destroy the others, but I'll need you to add your highly individual brand of extermination."

"Yes, Daddy," she complied, but underneath she was still sulking about Tyrone's absence.

"Now, stop brooding and be my special girl. We work well together, so remind me how good you still are, eight years after our Flint obliteration."

He smiled disarmingly and the sun shone again in the room. Her low mood lifted instantly and she felt the adrenaline pumping through her veins at the re-emergence of another joint vengeful venture.

"Just watch me!" she enthused, as he kissed the tip of her nose.

The kidnappers were talking, while Tiffany made fearful noises as she lay on an old flea-ridden mattress in the middle of the floor. She was terrified by her ordeal as she heard every one of her captors' words.

"Hey, Jet! Just look at her wriggling around. Her tracksuit's all crumpled. Maybe we should take it off. What d'ya say?" asked the gang member nicknamed 'Big' due to the size of his ding-a-ling.

"Bags I get first go." Jet laughed cruelly behind his disguise.

"Hey, dude, it's my idea! You'll have to wait in line for little Miss Moneybags and her charms!" answered Big threateningly.

Jet ignored him and was just about to pounce on his captive when an electric shock rushed through his entire framework. He began to choke and fell to the ground heavily, clutching his throat as he gagged inside his face mask, his skin turning blue and his bloodshot eyes bursting out of their sockets.

"What the fuck's up with Jet?" asked the detainer nicknamed Flick, due to his love of knives.

"I can't breathe! Help me!" screamed Jet in response.

They had no choice but to remove his visor. The two of them tried to pin Jet down but he lashed out, punching the air with both tattooed fists, smashing Big's jaw and fracturing it with the force. The injured party retaliated and kicked him in the face, breaking his nose in the process.

"What the hell's going on? Why are you knocking the shit out of each other? Is it over that stuck-up teenage bitch?

Arguing who gets there first? Forget it! We're after the money, not the fucking honey!" yelled Flick.

Jet suddenly stopped squirming. He stood up with the blood pouring down his face from both mangled nostrils. He looked totally robotic under Randal's control as he walked over to Tiffany.

"She can't breathe. We need to remove her gag and blindfold," he advised.

"Are you crazy, man? She'll scream the place down and know who you are, even with your bloody mess of a face!" argued Flick.

"She won't care. She needs to use the toilet or she'll mess up. It's only right," he said mechanically.

"Ooh, do you want to pull her tracksuit bottoms down then? Was it worth breaking Big's jaw?"

"She needs the toilet," repeated Jet.

He bent down to undo all the restrictions and then helped Tiffany to sit up. She was panting heavily and her eyes were glued open with shock.

"Don't hurt me, please don't hurt me," she reiterated through trembling dry lips.

"I won't harm you. Tiffany, isn't it? Come with me," instructed Jet in a gentle caring manner, totally in tune with Randal's commands.

"Yeh, come with him!" sneered Flicker crudely.

Jet turned his head round in hypnotic disgust as Randal vanquished his brain.

"You total apology for a human being. You deficient, debauched, contaminated, faulty and inadequate prick. This world would be a far cleaner place without your defective ugliness," Jet expounded, in unmistakable Randal derision.

"Yer what? What fucking language is that?"

"The language of observation, loathing, repugnance and poetic justice."

"Listen up, man. I'm gonna punch you in the gut so hard, you'll throw up that dictionary you've just swallowed."

Flick rolled up his sleeves in readiness only to be stopped in his tracks by Big, whose lower jaw was so broken that his line of teeth was completely uneven. He was bleeding from his mouth through torn gums. Big pointed a hand-held gun at Jet's head and pulled back the trigger.

"Please, let me go, let me go," cried Tiffany as she shivered uncontrollably at the whole perilous situation.

Roxanne felt her terror and her telepathic gaze laser-beamed into the room at the speed of light.

Under her control, Big turned his firearm on Flick instead and shot him at close range through the head. Then she made him point the gun at his own temple. He fired and his brains blew out, all over the wall.

Tiffany was so traumatised that she had gone into apoplectic shock and was temporarily deprived of all voluntary motion.

"Don't be afraid, little lady. Jet will look after you now. We'll take the gun with us for protection. You need to go back home."

He picked her up and carried her outside to the rust heap he called a car. He carefully laid her on the back seat and covered her with Big's coat, which smelled of stale tobacco and sweat.

"That'll keep you warm," he purred.

Jet drove along the dirt track until he reached the road that led to the motorway. His shattered nose was still streaming with blood, both eyes black and bruised, but he did not feel any pain as Randal guided him ahead.

I want you to follow my directions and when you reach your designated destination, take Tiffany out of the car and transport her up her driveway. There will be a police presence.

As soon as you hand her over safely, take the gun out of your pocket and shoot yourself through the mouth. That will stop you using foul language and preying on other teenage targets.

I know you've done this before: assaulting underage girls! But never again! Your sort needs to die in the womb. I'll abort you instead and all of your kind to come. Annihilation instead of castration. That's the motto. Evermore.

Randal hugged Roxanne with pride and she clung to him willingly.

"That's that, then. Tiffany's safe thanks to your help. You never fail to impress me," he praised.

"I'd do anything for you, Daddy. 'The gift' is mighty and we have to use it when and where it's wanted. Tyrone has to learn that, and not let any doubts or human weakness get in the way of a crucial removal. That's where he's going wrong. It's not about his ability. It's all about his application."

"I couldn't agree more, pumpkin. However, he's disappointed me so far. I've yet to see commitment and enactment from him, rather than hesitation or inspection. I'm not too sure about his allegiance to the cause. The power is powerless without backbone or drive," he said with a furrowed brow.

"He'll learn. I'll teach him too. It would be sacrilege to let his benefaction remain hidden or misused. We can't let that happen. We just can't," she implored.

"Can't we now? He'll need to show me far more dedication."

"While we're on the topic, what about Oscar?" she enquired.

"Oscar?"

"Yes. He's got the stirrings of 'the gift'. He told me what he did to his teacher. I know it was only a fun thing but he's brimming over with enthusiasm."

"It's not enough. He should know instinctively the full extent, but he's playing games instead. Removals would only disturb and damage him. I don't feel he's in the same class as yourself or your wavering boyfriend. Now, if Tyrone had Oscar's keenness, and Oscar had Tyrone's capability, I'd have two more ideal students to coach. Neither of them is up to scratch."

"You're not abandoning Tyrone, though, are you? I'd hate that. Your opinion matters to me the most," she implored.

"I'm not too sure if he's worth the bother. Your Uncle Clive's very disturbed by his emergence in our lives, although he's convinced himself he can cope. If push came to shove, I don't have to tell you who matters more."

"But he's only at the beginning of his apprenticeship. Every tyro needs guidance. Please try to help him. For me?" she pleaded with matching eyes.

Randal looked deeply into her corresponding gaze and relented.

"I'll give him one more chance, but if he lets me down or questions my tuition, then his initiation period will be ancient history. He simply must learn to separate his lesser mortal reactions from his superhuman gift."

"He will, Daddy. I know he will."

"Maybe. Fate will decide. Not us. He's either your soulmate or your subordinate. I hope it's the former. For you and for the future conservation of 'the gift'."

6

Amber was spending the weekend with her paternal grandparents back in Cheshire for two reasons. Firstly, she was very close to them, especially her grandfather, Edward Forbes, who shared the same birthday as herself. Secondly, she was constantly hurt and annoyed by Randal's preferential treatment of her 'stepsister' Roxanne.

Even if she knew that her adopted sibling was really a blood relation, it would have made no difference to her rancour. Randal had taken great pains to conceal Roxanne's true identity, otherwise it would be the end of his marriage and family life.

"Honestly, Granny, I'm so sick of that smug look on her face. She sucks up to Dad constantly and he melts. I've never been able to get that reaction from him. Ryan feels much the same. We're both out in the cold even though Dad tries his best to make us feel wanted. It's never enough, though. As long as that red-haired minx is hanging on to his coat tails, we all feel second best. I'm sick of it! So sick of it!" cried Amber with a crestfallen expression on her pretty face.

Margaret Forbes was feeling very saddened over Amber's distress and furious with Randal for displaying obvious favouritism.

"Oh, darling, don't get upset. It makes me very unhappy when you do. Your father's so full of his work that I'm amazed he's got time for any of you," she justified, softening the blow, but inside she was blazing and totally agreed with Amber.

"Oh, he's got time for his work all right! Mum caters to his every whim and puts her own talent on ice to prop up his ego. Clive buzzes round him like some besotted honeybee, and Oscar, well, he's also got the Randal-bug. Dad's closer to him than Ryan. I don't know why I'm upset, really. I should be used to it by now." She sniffed, as Edward passed her his handkerchief.

"I'm going to have a word with that son of ours, Margaret. He needs to know how his behaviour is affecting both of our grandchildren. He's bang out of order here and he has to be brought down a peg or two! I've never quite understood why he displays such blatant affection to the adopted one, and not his own flesh and blood!" he barked.

"Oh God, no, Granddad! It'll only make things ten times worse! He'll think I've been gossiping behind his back and then he'll be even more distant, or he'll have that unnerving glint in his eyes when he's annoyed."

"I'll give him unnerving glint! He might be in his forties, but he's still my son, and I won't tolerate all this best-loved behaviour towards the adopted daughter at your expense, Amber. He needs to be told! The sooner the better!" he thundered.

"If anyone's going to tell him it will be me," insisted Margaret. "Edward, you won't get anywhere with him in that mood. I know Randal inside out. We need the iron-fist-in-the-velvet-glove approach."

"I know he's a wonderful son to us, but he needs to be a doting father as well. I'll not have Amber, nor Ryan, feeling inadequate to Maxine and Saul's orphaned daughter. You're way too soft, Margaret! You've always spoiled him! He got away with murder as a child!" maintained Edward, far nearer the twisted truth than he realised.

"Let's not talk about this anymore. It's making Amber worse. I'll raise the subject with him in a very calm and diplomatic way so that he'll think it's my own observation," reasoned Margaret.

"If you must," agreed Edward reluctantly.

"Now, Amber, darling, tell us about your school trip to Bruges," urged Margaret, putting a protective arm around her.

They listened closely to Amber's newly found confidence and enthusiasm for her last break. She shook off her low mood as she expounded excitedly on her historical knowledge of West Flanders capital, and her interest in the canals, cobbled streets and medieval buildings.

Her appreciation of aesthetics was very evident in her description of the Museum of classical Flemish art. In this way she was more like Randal than she actually realised. She had inherited his love of history and craftsmanship.

Margaret listened eagerly but her mind was doing cartwheels. Her intense dislike of Roxanne surfaced intermittently and spoiled Amber's vivid descriptions of her travels.

I really can't come to terms with that girl's residency in my son's household. I don't like her at all. She's arrogant, self-indulgent, presumptuous and quite unsettling.

Why Randal goes along with her temper and tantrums is beyond me, especially at the price of his true daughter's self-worth. Doesn't he realise what he's doing to both Ryan and Amber? Surely, he must see that they feel pushed out and neglected?

His obsession with Roxanne is unnatural. I've never seen him behave like that with any of his children except her. Why? He told me eight years ago that both he and Alison felt desperately sorry for her as an orphan, so they showered her with love and attention. I even asked him if Roxanne was his own secret child. He convinced me that she was just needy and disturbed, and he would never step out of line or be disloyal to Alison. He looked quite shocked when I suspected him.

But that was then, and they adopted her when she was a little girl. She's a teenager now and Randal's over-indulgence is still going on. Roxanne's a vibrant young woman and been part of our family long enough to feel settled and secure. She still persists on hogging the limelight and Randal's complete attention. And he lets her. In front of us all. Constantly.

Alison's never complained. She's a wonderful wife and mother, and has welcomed Roxanne into the fold. But I'm really worried. I care deeply about my grandchildren and it pains me to see this resentment and unrest in our family. Randal must stop this unjust favouritism. He should know better than to openly display such hurtful and unfeeling conduct.

"Granny, do you want a cup of tea and some of my sponge cake?" asked Amber, interrupting her unsavoury thoughts. "I baked it yesterday for you."

"Of course, I do. I thought you'd never ask," she joked, disguising her unease, her thoughts still swirling around.

I'm going to tell Randal what I think of his cruel nepotism. It's about time he knew!

***

Randal was in a very black mood and was taking it out on everyone within hearing range.

"Yes? What now!" he exclaimed, when Alison interrupted his creative writing, although his inspiration had already deserted him as he stared at the blank page.

"Pardon me for breathing! What's got up your nasty nose then?" she shot back.

"All I want is peace and quiet to concentrate on my next novel. Is that too much to ask? You, Ryan and Amber laughing in the other room like a trio of hysterical hyenas. Roxanne's fantasising vocally over Tyrone for a change. Oscar's hyper-activating, but most of all, my bloody mother's giving me earache over the phone! Why don't you all disappear for a while? Give me some space!"

Alison could not understand his sudden vitriolic rant. He had been in a state of arousal only one hour before and had pulled her to him, kissing her fervently and running his hands up and down her shapely body in the familiar, spine-tingling fashion.

"I could take you right here and now, up against the wall," he had said thickly, as his hot tongue flicked around her ear.

She felt his hard erection against the top of her legs as they threatened to give way while she succumbed to his lust. He was just about to unzip his jeans when Oscar intruded on their passionate clinch, crying that he had trapped his finger in the door.

"It hurts, Mummy!" he'd yelled, as he ran to Alison, who had to pull herself out of her hot-blooded moment.

"Oh, Oscar! How did you manage that?"

"It's bleeding and it won't stop!"

"Go and see to him. Then afterwards I'll see to you," Randal had said suggestively, with an intimate gaze that caused her legs to buckle once more.

Back in the present she was very puzzled by his abrupt change of behaviour.

"You were all over me like a rash before. What's happened since then to make you so stroppy?" she queried.

"My mother apparently thinks I'm a bad father! She's just lectured me on the rights and wrongs of parenthood!" he bleated, his eyes kindling with menacing light.

"What on earth does she mean?"

"Oh, just some stupid points about getting my priorities right. She's rubbed me up the wrong way. I'll get over it." He half-smiled but inside he was burning.

"Well, don't take it out on all of us. We're just innocent bystanders. I only knocked to see if you want a coffee. I've got the percolator on and it's your favourite blend."

"OK, that'd be good. It might wake me up. I didn't sleep too well and I've got a lot on my mind," he replied, yawning widely.

Alison nodded with innate understanding as she vacated the room, leaving Randal alone with his racing thoughts.

I won't be dictated to by my mother! I'm forty-fucking-two, not a kid! I've tried my best to include everyone in my shows of affection. Ryan and Amber have been objecting behind my back about my preference for Roxanne. Yes, she's my most treasured child, but I've cut down considerably on displays of priority in public.

It seems there's still a massive bone to pick with me over all this. Roxanne's an extension of my true self and that's hard to ignore. In human terms it does look suspicious and she seems to be habitually preferred. She's toned down her superior standing at my request. She's gone out of her way to include her siblings in conversation and outings. So, what the fuck do they want?

They don't complain when I'm giving them a lifestyle that most families would only dream about. I don't see Ryan refunding me for his Oxford education or new car.

Amber's pretty eager to give the chain stores a miss and frequent the designer shops without price tags. They're quite content to reap those rewards on a daily basis!

My mother came out of the caring closet and castigated me over putting all my paternal eggs in Roxanne's blameworthy basket. She's never liked her much and Roxanne reciprocates the feeling. If only I could reveal that Roxanne's her blood granddaughter and not some adopted waif. She'd change her mind so quickly that Oscar's tortoise would look like the road runner.

I wish I could come clean about everything. It's such a drag: a drain on my true purpose. I'll have to apply myself more diligently on a human level and pump up the gregarious gas. Add another layer of saccharin to the sickly sweet charade of falsified fatherhood. Play the game of legitimate life and rise to each overwrought occasion.

I do love my family, inasmuch as I can ever care about lesser mortals. But I must protect Roxanne more than any of them. She's the only one who matters in terms of the true inheritance. I love all of my children but she's the real deal. So I have to protect her legacy more.

In future I'll do that very discreetly. In terms of human emotion, I suspect that Ryan feels left out and Amber's jealous. It's up to me to turn on the magnetism and show them my affectionate side. Perhaps they're right in some ways. I've been too frugal with my love.

I can't spend my life hypnotising my family. It's far better to win them over naturally, then I'll know if I've reached the correct level of deceit. Anyway, it's much more satisfying. Hypnosis is the easy way out and does not test my true strength or charm offensive. I'm capable of winning anyone over without autosuggestion.

It's unfortunate that I recently eradicated Oscar's weak standard of 'the gift'. I know my son, and he's not capable of handling such responsibility. Any homicidal activity would only harm him emotionally.

And now there's the tyro! He's maddeningly inept, but his benefaction is intact. I need to see what he can achieve on his own without my tuition. He's got to show me a lot more compliance and fervour.

Roxanne's got faith in his aptitude, but I'm concerned. He has a propensity towards analysis instead of application. That's got to be scrapped. All this nonsense needs to be sorted out, and quickly. I'm the best thing that ever happened to my family and friends.

In fact, I'm the best thing that ever happened. Full stop!

***

Tyrone was sat in silence with Ryan in the Beaumont College refectory. He felt instinctively that Randal and Clive had sat at the very same table, back in their day.

"What's the matter? Are you still upset about Tiffany?" asked Ryan caringly.

"What? Oh no, I'm glad she's home. There are just a few things on my mind."

"Well, you know I'm here for you. Anyway, got to go now

for my next lecture. See you this evening for a drink at the students' bar?"

"Yeah, catch you later."

Ryan stopped on his way out to acknowledge a few students as Tyrone sat in silent contemplation. He was having very unwholesome thoughts about his family and recalled his last visit home when his parents had fussed around his sister as if she were a piece of cracked porcelain about to break in half. The commotion had got on his nerves, as did his brother Tobias, together with his sister-in-law Harriet and their baby, Rupert.

If my father asks Tiff one more time if she's OK, I swear I'll incinerate him. Get over it! All of you! She was kidnapped then returned unscathed. Anyone would think that she died. A motley crew wanted to screw her. Well, they didn't! Thanks to Randal, Roxanne and 'the gift'. Tiff's a bloody airhead anyway. I'm surprised she had the brains to object. Cretin!

Randal wants me to be more gracious towards my family. How can I be? I've never been. He's just got to understand that I've no allegiance to any of them. He's far more intertwined with his clan. I know he protected them in the past and has this amazing loyalty to certain members. But me? All I feel is scorn. I want to harm them all and I've held back for so long. But now I'm going to use my powers to rid myself of their unwanted interference.

Even Randal had failed to measure the actual true depth of Tyrone's detached psychosis. When they had first met, Randal felt their twin desire to cleanse themselves of all 'the detractors'. That had sat well with him, but he failed to grasp the fact that where Tyrone was concerned, this theory would apply to the whole of the Pendle dynasty.

Tyrone recalled one of their conversations.

"You show promise, but your antipathy towards your kith and kin is unpalatable," Randal had scolded.

"I'm not like you in that respect. I've no reason to feel loyal or concerned. I've absolutely nothing in common with my close or extended family. Quite frankly, if I never saw them again, I wouldn't miss them or have any regrets. Your parents put you on a pedestal. My lot pull me down. Constantly!"

"Tobias doesn't. He defends you!"

"How do you know that?"

"I've tuned in to his conversations with your father. I've listened to them sporadically because I need to know everything about you and your family from a mortal standpoint."

"Tobias is a 'yes' man. He knows which side his inherited bread and butter is on. Don't be fooled."

Randal's eyes had glowed and the recipient of his wrath had felt the heat.

"Fooled? You're walking on thin ice, Tyrone. Nobody fools me! I'm the true master of trickery. The demoraliser of the duped!"

Tyrone came back into the present in the washroom, as the hustle and bustle of student life interrupted his reflections. He made sure the toilet cubicle was completely locked.

Randal wants me to prove I can use 'the gift' to its full frenzy in the way it should be implemented. He has committed multiple murders without regret. They were necessary. Well, mine are too. Randal will simply have to understand that.

He stared at his father's photograph. His gaze became so illuminated that it penetrated the image and threw two spotlights against the inside of the door.

Leighton had met up with his wife, Corrine, and they had brought Tiffany with for lunch at their favourite Italian restaurant. Suddenly he began to choke and turned blue as he clutched one hand around his throat.

"Oh, Leighton! What's wrong?" cried Corrine.

"Daddy! God, what's happening now?" screeched Tiffany, her nerves stretched to their fullest from her recent traumatic experience.

Tyrone stepped up on his telepathic hold, exalting in the

power he held over his father. A dominant manipulation of the most formidable kind. It felt euphoric. It was Herculean. A commanding role reversal.

Now, 'Daddy Cool'. In your jacket pocket you'll find a plastic bag. Take it out and put it over Mum's vacuous head. Hold it there. No matter what! Do it! Do it right now!

Leighton stopped retching and rose up in a robotic fashion. He pulled out the bag and shoved it over Corrine's head, yanking it tightly around her whole face so that she could not breathe. Now it was her stint at turning blue.

"Daddy, what are you doing?" shrieked Tiffany. "Help! Somebody, help!"

Leighton was relentless in his hypnotic quest. The manager of the establishment came running over to assist but the strangulation carried on. Tyrone had imbued his father with superhuman strength so that his hands could not be prised off his deadly target.

Oh my! I never saw such devotion to a cause. Keep it up, Dad! What's the Pendle motto? Your particular dictum? Tenacity, tenacity, tenacity. Well, this is my diligent version of that maxim. Proud of me now? Better than my head in a backsliding book? Now start to laugh and let go. The bag has a life of its own.

Corrine Pendle slumped to the floor with the bag glued indelibly to her asphyxiated face as Leighton chortled and everyone looked on with horror and disbelief.

And that was the end of Mrs Leighton Pendle. In full view of a packed restaurant.

"Call the police! And an ambulance!" shouted a well-dressed diner, but it was far too late.

***

Leighton Pendle had gone from economist to round the twist. He had been arrested and thrown into a prison cell, and was a rampaging version of his previous form, rattling the bars like a frenzied caged animal.

"Let me out of here now! Do you know who I am? I need to speak to my solicitor!" he raved.

"Calm down, Mr Pendle, or else we'll bang you up in solitary! After what you've done it won't be a lawyer you'll need. It'll be a head-shrinker!" jibed the warden.

"What the hell are you going on about? I don't even know what I'm supposed to have done! I can't remember a damn thing!" he ranted.

"Well then, it's a bloody good job there were witnesses!"

"Witnesses! What witnesses? Where? To what? I'll sue the sodding backsides off the lot of you!" he roared.

"Stop pretending, Mr Pendle. At least ten people saw you kill your wife!"

Leighton's blood ran cold as if a mountain of ice was shifting through each vein and artery. His tongue froze and felt suctioned to the roof of his mouth.

Tyrone was watching the action through his telepathic link and the smile on his face eclipsed any other thoughts of revenge he had ever harboured.

Oh, Daddy dear. You so need to be full-stopped. But I have to admit to plagiarism. I stole Randal's plot, notably the Flints' homicidal theme. But the other way round. I hypnotised you to kill Mum, then wiped your memory clean.

You think it's wrongful arrest and want your heavyweight legal team of super crooks to exonerate you. Some hopes! You're going deeper and down.

It's kind of sad that Mum had to die, but she never got me either.

All my life you both demoralised me. I never received one single word of encouragement or support. I hid behind a mask of aloofness. A cloak of indifference. A reticent ruse. Not anymore.

Randal's my only inspiration now. Because of him, I know how and when to use 'the gift'. I can remove any encumbrance and my parents were a lifelong menace to my true standing. It's as simple as that. As easy as pie.

Tyrone nodded to himself with smug satisfaction. He got ready to meet Ryan, feeling somewhat frustrated that he could not confide in his new friend about his first successful annihilation.

He wished that Ryan had 'the gift' so they could work together. He felt close to him, partly due to the Randal connection, but strangely more so as a platonic kinship. They seemed to click together through their emotional isolation.

Ryan will be a brilliant brother-in-law when I marry Roxanne. I can't even tell him that she's his blood sister. I wish I could. Maybe Randal will relent one day and admit it. After all, it's been years since the Maxine episode. Times change.

Alison's been with him forever and perhaps she'd forgive him the one little dalliance. Well, that particular one anyway. What a charismatic Casanova!

He's such a cool dude. Just wait until he hears what I've achieved today with my first rewarding assignment of 'the gift'.

***

Randal and Alison were having an early night and were all over each other in bed when the late-night news of Leighton Pendle's arrest was reported on their bedside radio, which was still switched on. In between the heavy breathing, the announcement resonated, and Randal jumped off Alison, his passionate embrace totally culled.

"Oh, Rand, where've you gone? I want you," she moaned in protest at his withdrawal.

"Shush! I just remembered something that needs sorting out. Sorry, sweetheart, but I'll be back very shortly," he promised, blowing a kiss in the doorway as he pulled up his jeans that covered his obvious arousal.

"Well, don't be long!" she shouted, but he was already halfway down the stairs.

He switched on the TV in his study and stared at the screen with glowing eyes as images of the Pendle clan flashed on and off in between the account. It took him all of five seconds to know that Tyrone had caused the whole homicidal mess.

He's stolen my Flint script with a role reversal! He's used his father to kill his mother instead! His hatred of them was far stronger than he allowed me to believe or perceive. He blanked out his deepest, abhorrent thoughts.

I've given him the green light to annihilate them!

He's used 'the gift' to rid himself of their interfering presence. They weren't that bad! I've tuned into both of them and they just needed to be steered in the right direction.

He could have easily influenced them. They weren't a threat to his benefaction! He's a million times more detached than I realised. He thinks this removal will impress me. He needs to think again!

The phone rang in the middle of his scrutiny. It was Ryan.

"Dad, it's me! Have you seen the bloody news?"

"Yes. I know. I'm watching it now," replied Randal in a controlled voice.

Ryan's cheeks were high in colour as he voiced his concern.

"I can't believe it! I just don't get it! Leighton loved Corrine to distraction. They were ideally suited. Why the hell did he do it? In front of Tiffany! As if she's not been through enough recently. It's... it's monstrous," protested Ryan.

"I agree. Have you spoken to Tyrone?" asked Randal in a deceptively gentle voice.

"I'm supposed to meet him for a drink, but I can't get hold of him. His mobile's permanently on answerphone, and he's not in his room, or anywhere to be seen."

"Well, when you do catch up with him, ask him to ring me right away, please."

"Why?"

"Because Roxanne will be worried about him and I need to

know his state of mind before he talks to her. I don't want him leaning on her too much. Apart from you, I'm the best person to console him. Do you understand that?"

"Totally. He looks up to you, more than his own father, and now he's got more cause than ever to detest him. I always thought he went over the top about his dislike of him. He called him a contemptible control freak. That's an understatement. His dad's psychotic!"

"It certainly looks that way," answered Randal through gritted teeth. "Let me know if you hear from him first."

"Will do. Speak soon."

"Ryan."

"Yes, Dad?"

"Be careful and look after yourself. I don't want you bogged down with Tyrone's emotional upheaval. Don't get too involved. Let me take the brunt of it all."

"That's good of you. Really good of you, but I need to be there for him too. He's my closest friend."

"I understand that, but remember that I'm also here for you. Always."

Ryan felt his heart sing. For once he did not feel sidelined, and it was a wonderful feeling to know that Randal cared for his safety and welfare.

"I'll be in touch soon. Love you, Dad," he whispered.

"Love you too, son."

Randal put down the phone. His eyes were still alight as he dipped into the desk drawer for his packet of cheroots. He lit one up and his blood began to boil with anger at Tyrone's unnecessary escapade.

He's got this all wrong. All wrong! His parents were not enemies of 'the gift'. They were just out of tune with his disposition. How many times have I told him that he possesses the power to move on from his former frustration? To resolve all the issues surrounding his childhood. To charm his way into their good books.

So, what does he do for his first removal? He kills his mother! Because technically it wasn't 'Daddy Pendle' who did it. It was my half-assed, bone-headed tyro.

He just won't listen! He looks up to me but turns a deaf ear to my advice. If the pupil disregards the teacher, then he'll fail. So, what's the point? At first, I was over the dark side of the moon that I'd found a true kindred spirit in waiting. It was a joyous discovery and totally unexpected. But he disappoints me on every level. He defies all guidance and instruction.

He's ferociously intelligent and telepathic. Even I could not get to the true root of his disaffection. He's deceived me. Me! So how can I trust him with Roxanne? She's begging me to give him another chance. How many opportunities does she want me to afford him?

I'm not happy. Not happy at all. I need one more face-to-face discussion with him and it will all hinge on that outcome. Further failure to comply leaves a monumental stumbling block. I have to weigh up whether he's suitable. Whether he's a threat to me or the application of 'the gift'. Or both.

Because ultimately, he absorbs too little. But regrettably, he knows far too much!

***

Dean was feeling very anxious because Maddie had reacted extremely badly to the published book about her family. *The Flawed Flints* had become a bestseller for all the wrong reasons, and neither of them knew that Randal had written it under an alias in order to cause her present mania, so that Dean would call off their engagement for good.

"Maddie, calm down! I can't reassure you if you're behaving like this! Please! Let me hold you and take away your pain," he almost begged.

"You can't and you never will!"

"That's because you won't even let me try! At least talk to me. It's a badly written book and designed to hurt you, but it's just another nasty, avaricious, unfeeling scumbag, making money out of the whole tragedy. I'm going to find out who this Lloyd Byron is and I'm going to sue him on your behalf."

"It's too late! It's far too late! I'm so sick of it all. It never stops!"

"Let me have a word with Randal. He's got major contacts in the literary field and he'll know this Byron guy. Let him deal with it. Believe me, Maddie, the toerag won't know what's hit him if Randal takes him to task. I know the book's already out there, but if anyone can get fair play for you it's my beloved cousin. He hates injustice with a passion."

Maddie sobbed, but Dean's words rang a promising bell and she felt less manic as a result.

"But Randal's so very busy with all his business and family commitments. When would he find the time to help me? He might refuse so I don't want to build my hopes up. He probably thinks the same as the book anyway. They all do," she blubbed.

Dean agreed with her inwardly, but he hid his concurrence of opinion well.

Randal's just got to realise how much I love this girl and how badly I want the author brought to task. I don't know what else to do because Maddie has reacted violently to the whole issue. I daren't tell him that she threatened me with a knife the other night.

I truly don't know if it's a reaction to all the negative publicity or whether she has a propensity towards insanity like her mother. I felt very panicky when she was brandishing the blade. I've got to do my best, and I need Randal's help. If he can just be made aware of the situation, he'll be able to suggest some form of action.

Unbeknown to them both, Randal was now behind Maddie's total downfall in every sense.

Step one, his book was the literary aperitif.

Step two, he would cause hypnotic hysteria towards Dean and everyone in sight.

Step three, would be her downfall.

Step four, he would effectuate the ultimate conclusion whereby Dean would decide, of his own accord, to pull away for his sanity and welfare.

His sadness would be fleeting because Randal would heal his heartbreak and hypnotise him to believe that his fiancée was not equipped to be his future wife. Another special woman would fulfil that role perfectly.

And her name was not Maddie Flint.

Dean rang Randal while Maddie was sleeping.

"Hi, Rand. I need your help badly."

"What's wrong?"

"It's about the book *The Flawed Flints*. It's really set Maddie off. I know you don't want me to marry her, but she's still my fiancée and I love her to bits. I can't control her moods, though. She's really going over the top about it all," sighed Dean.

"So how can I help?" he asked cunningly.

"I want you to find out who Lloyd Byron is."

"Lloyd who?"

"Lloyd Byron, the author. I want to take him to court, on Maddie's behalf. The book's scandalous and scrapes the bottom of the barrel. He shouldn't be allowed to release such muckraking libel. It's unethical and immoral. Have you read any of it yet?"

"No." *I've not read it, but I wrote it.*

"Well, you should. You're a man of principal, the perpetual voice of the underdog. Help me sue this lowlife!" stressed Dean.

"I know how you feel, but I really don't see what I can do to help. I've no control over publications or their content, however poisonous they may be."

"Find out who the author is and where he lives. That's all I want. I know you can do that, Rand, even though you don't care for Maddie. Please! Do it for me," beseeched Dean.

Randal felt for Dean but could not help smirking behind his compassion.

Oh, the irony of it all. He wants me to reveal my identity and address so he can prosecute me. Dean, Dean, Dean. I'm doing all of this for you and your beautiful mother. My dear Aunty Dottie, who's out of her mind with worry over your choice of bride.

I'll go along with your request on the surface, but behind the scenes I've already put the wheels of Maddie's ruination into motion. You know I could have left her alone, but you had to go and stir it all up by bringing her back into our lives.

But I'm afraid that she's got to go, so be prepared for her wrath and subsequent arrest. I won't remove her; I'll just get her sectioned. She may as well live up to the Flint family history.

"Look, Dean, I'll do my best and make a few enquiries. I just want you to be safe. I don't trust Maddie's temperament and this is obviously exacerbating it all. Please be careful. Your welfare's far more important to me than hers," he elaborated.

"I just want Lloyd Byron's head on a plate. It's only poetic justice."

And it's only poetic justice, Dean, that Carlton Flint's family are consigned to historic hysteria, remembered with revulsion and read about with disgust. I rest my case.

***

Roxanne was beside herself with angst, as she argued with Randal in his study.

"But, Daddy, you of all people must know how it feels to be superior and slighted at the same time. Tyrone had nothing but insults from his father all his life, and his mother followed suit. It's irrelevant who they are!"

"Oh, but it's very relevant. Each removal has to be an enemy of 'the gift', full stop."

Roxanne's cheeks were flushed with annoyance as she continued her tirade.

"I hated Maxine and Saul with a passion! I wanted them both dead! So did you, and that's what we worked towards, even though I was only a little girl. We did it together! You killed my real mother on stage and I helped you murder Saul, my so-called father, in the cemetery along with two other lesser mortals! It's so hypocritical of you to condemn Tyrone!" she raved.

Randal's eyes looked like two points of glowing lava about to erupt and destroy everything in his line of vision. Roxanne flinched at his expression as he lambasted her with his own brand of home truth.

"Let's take your infantile, offensive and insolent outburst apart, shall we? Now listen very, very, very carefully to what I have to say or else I won't be accountable for my actions! Are you listening?"

She backed down, her heartbeat thumping in her chest wall, her thrusting confidence momentarily dented.

"I repeat. Are you listening? Answer me!" he exploded.

"I'm all ears," she whispered.

"Right! Don't you dare compare your hatred for Maxine to Tyrone's abhorrence of his father! Your dearest mummy was dangerous. She was a suspicious loose cannon who deduced too much. A veritable stumbling block in the way of our joint legacy! I had to claim you back and the only way forward was her demise, followed by Saul's. Tyrone's father is just uninformed, a trifle ignorant and bombastic, but he was never, ever a threat to 'the gift'! Neither was Tyrone's mother, Corrine! Now, regardless of Leighton Pendle's lack of sensitivity and appreciation, Tyrone possessed the ability to turn it all around. A simple charm offensive would have sufficed!"

"But—"

"But nothing. Rest your mouth and let me finish!"

Roxanne felt the blood drawing out of her face as Randal drained her with his ultra-violet gaze, as he continued to flare up with disgust.

"Tyrone's public, plastic-bag removal, was amateurish, crass and absurd! But I'll tell you what's even worse than all that, dear daughter of mine. Are you still listening?" he thundered.

She nodded, her fear mounting with his uncontrollable wrath.

"What's even worse is your boyfriend's astounding selective hearing! All my tuition has been disregarded! Every conversation we've had has been dismissed! The bulk of my valuable time, which I willingly afforded him, in the hope of nurturing another successor, in anticipation of a befitting suitor for you and future generations, who may inherit 'the gift' – all of that has spectacularly backfired and made me very dubious and sceptical about his suitability for the role!" he fumed.

Roxanne licked her lips before she summoned up the nerve to reply.

"Please, Daddy! Please! Don't abandon him now. He adores you, as we all do. He's still learning after a lifetime of running away from his true self. He's trying so hard to please you but somehow failing in the process. I still think he'll eventually succeed, though," she implored.

Randal's gaze narrowed so that his eyes looked like two dazzling slits as he responded.

"And I know that he never will. He's deceived us both! He's used our connection as a passport to demonstrate his insanity. He's functioning under the pretext of being my tyro. He's unpredictable. I've handed him a homicidal handbook with the right script, but the wrong cast!"

"But… but *you've* committed multiple removals! Some of those could have been avoided too, but you chose to destroy them! Sometimes the deceased were disconnected from the real culprit, like the Haynes children! Yes, you got rid of the main wrongdoer, namely Nick Haynes, because his loose mouth caused Dean such heartache and pain, but his two little sisters were just bystanders! They weren't guilty at all!" she braved.

"Oh, weren't they now? Not guilty? Not guilty! They came out of the same wanton womb as Nick Haynes's fishwife mother, who kick-started the whole fucking malicious episode. They had to die!"

"Don't swear at me. Don't you fucking swear at me! I'm just trying to show you that mistakes can be made in the heat of the moment. Nobody's infallible. Not even you!" she shrieked, hating herself for insulting him.

Randal got up off his chair and threw it across the room.

"Get out! Get out now!" he stormed.

"No! I need to get things right with you!" she screeched.

"Do you now! I'll tell you what's right! I was going to give Romeo one last face-to-face talking-to, but your ungrateful, disrespectful attitude towards me has severed that possibility in the amputated bud! I'm done with him! His apprenticeship is terminated forthwith!"

"But, Daddy—"

"But, Daddy nothing! When my chosen child questions me over my methods, and puts the welfare of some crackbrained, asinine newcomer above the advice of her omnipotent father, then it's time to call it a day!"

"Does that include me? Are you calling time on me?" she sobbed.

"I'll pretend I didn't hear that nonsensical question."

"I want to be with him, Daddy. Don't stop me seeing him. Please have that last meeting with him. I'm so, so sorry I said what I did," she begged.

"Stop petitioning me! It's so demeaning and totally beneath you," he chided.

"But I didn't mean to question or belittle you. You're my whole world. I can't bear it when you shout at me. I love you so much!" she cried.

"Is this apology solely for the benefit of our relationship, or are you trying to bribe me with affection in order to keep Tyrone on the paranormal payroll?"

"If it came to a choice between you and him it's a no-brainer. I just want you to go ahead with your original plan of one last meeting with him. I made you very angry and I'm really sorry. I know Tyrone's messed up, but it's too early in his trial period to pull the plug on him," she entreated.

"You've got rose-coloured glasses over your inherited flashing eyes. Your infatuation is overriding your intuition. Believe me, Roxanne, he's never going to be a credit to 'the gift' or to you. His certifiable detachment will always be present. He'll block off his deepest thoughts and carry on in his own merry unstable way, not sharing his true intentions with either of us. I can't trust him. He's using 'the gift' as payback for twenty-one years of forbearance, for falsifying all toleration of his kith and kin. I think he's going to annihilate his whole immediate family," he prophesised.

"No way! He's never given the slightest indication of that!" she contradicted.

"He never gave you the slightest indication that he was going to kill his mother! Did he? Hmm?"

"Well... no... but..."

"There's no buts, Roxanne. And now he's going to remove them all."

"You can stop him; I know you can. You can talk to him and show him that it's inadvisable and unnecessary. That it's wrong."

"I'm his mentor. Not his conscience."

"I don't know what to say or do now," she croaked.

"You say and do nothing. You leave it to me."

"Are you going to remove him? I don't think I could cope with that!"

"I'm not sure. I need to keep him sweet. He knows every single, solitary thing about me. About us. I'll play him at his own game. I'll block out my thoughts until I decide which way to go. I don't want a non-communicative, tight-lipped, taciturn assassin in my daughter's life. You should both be able to share ideas for any removals openly. With mutual trust. He's too self-contained. He has lofty ambitions and will eventually turn on me. Even he doesn't realise it yet. He'll bite the hand that feeds his authority. Each experimental removal will exacerbate his need for yet more needless and unmerited ones," he preached, as he mentally meditated.

I've made my own breakneck bed, but that doesn't mean I have to lie in it. The sheets can be easily stripped and destroyed. The bed can be comfortably dismantled. And 'the gift' will be in safe hands once more.

7

Randal and Clive were deep in conversation, in between answering office calls. They switched the answerphone on to avoid multiple interruptions.

"So, as you can see, I'm not jumping through hoops over my absolute beginner," concluded Randal, about Tyrone's lack of teamwork and unity.

Clive sighed deeply because all of his innermost worries had come to the fore.

"I told you that I had grave doubts about this whole association. You were on such a high that you'd found your 'successor' and I couldn't burst your expectant bubble, but truthfully it all had an ominous ring to it. When you're in that other-worldly zone, I'm always afraid of disagreeing with your opinion. You either shoot me down in flames or try to butter me up. Either way, you end up doing exactly what you want and to hell with the consequences."

"I know, I know. This is another first for me. I didn't see it coming, would you believe? I thought he was my spiritual doppelganger, and that was so exciting, Clive, not just for me, but for Roxanne too. I didn't approve of his sexual desire for her, but eventually that could have sprouted wings when she was older. And I might have sanctioned it. But now? No way is he coming near her: not emotionally, physically or telepathically. He's yesterday's greenhorn news! The biggest problem is that he knows everything there is to know about all of us, and if I don't handle this carefully it could end very badly. Very badly indeed," he pondered with a sinister expression.

"So, what have you got in mind? Anything I should know about? Another removal on the horrendous horizon? I need to prepare myself before it's a further shock to my struggling system. You're not dealing with a powerless new kid on the block here. He's got 'the gift' and now he intends to use it after years of inertia. He's esoterically let loose. I'm scared for you, and Roxanne," agonised Clive.

"No need to be. Whatever happens I always win. Anyway, he's coming down to see me tomorrow. I told him we need to talk. He's got a good idea that I'm not impressed with his first assignment, but I've blocked out the bulk of my anger and frustration. There's no need to panic at this stage."

"At what stage do we prepare ourselves for alarm?"

"Early days, Clive. There'll be ways round this. Trust me. You know I won't let you down."

"I'm not so sure this time. It was a nightmare with Carlton Flint but at least he was virtuously gifted."

"In the end that made no difference to his telepathic wrath. It was lethal."

"So, what's the tyro going to be like if he turns? You told me his power is jet black. He's going to be a formidable foe!"

"Possibly. But at this moment in time, I'm still his idol, so let's not run away with a hypothetical conclusion. My main unease is the data he has mentally absorbed of my life's work. That's the worry. Not the extent of his capability."

Clive scratched his head in agitation.

"I know we've discussed most of this before, but I've got

to tell you how resentful I am of all the attention you pay that dumbass tyro." He scowled.

"He's no dumbass. It wouldn't be so maddening if he was. That's what really bugs me. He's pretty clued up on most things, but his legacy is wasted on him. He needs to throw out the disorganised dishwater and effect a resourceful removal, but his entrenched psychosis is now active and he's targeting his family tree. He was full of repressed lunacy, but now he knows exactly what to do with the madness."

"And you're still full of him! Whether he does right or wrong! I never hear you talk about anything else these days! Hello? I'm still here! Permanently pasted to your hip. When was the last time we spoke about us? What happened to the creative projects you said we'd work on together? I feel unwanted, unnecessary and dispensable," he bellyached, his jealousy very evident.

"That's crazy and you know it. I'm not even going to justify that ridiculous claim."

"It's not ridiculous! It's how I feel and if I can't admit that after all our years together, then something's missing in our relationship. We still have one, don't we?"

Randal had too much on his mind and Clive's constant insecurity over Tyrone's presence in their lives was another issue within the predicament.

How many times can I tell him that he's special to me? I can't do with this headache right now. But look at his face. His eyes are full of love and hate. Oh boy. Let's put his mind at rest once more. His fragility is surfacing and that's not a good thing. Clive, Clive, Clive. Why oh why can't you be more confident? Your place in my life is sacred. You are the other same-sex half of me.

"Stop looking at me like that. It's so frustrating," preached Randal.

"Like what? How am I supposed to look at you? I never know which expression to pull out of my emotional bag. You've made me how I am. You've shaped my whole life. My different personas. My brittle acts of happiness. My simulated smiles. We can go over all this a million times, but it will always end in the same way. You're mine and then you're not. Someone, or something, else, always comes along, and spoils the symmetry."

"That's life, Clive. Even if I didn't have 'the gift', different people and situations would still crop up. Other than handcuffing myself to your bed post, I don't know what else to do to prove I'm all yours. Do I? Well? Do I?"

Clive's heart skipped its usual beat at the seductive expression in Randal's unusual eyes.

I can't stop myself envying those who grab his attention. Oh God, why can't I stop this crippling jealousy? I've had thirty-five years' practice and I'm still struggling.

"I'm scared, Randal. The years have flown and I'm more vulnerable with the passing of time. All I've ever wanted is you. And now I find myself in yet more jeopardy in the name of 'the gift'. I'm petrified of the outcome. For you. For me. For Roxanne."

"Don't be. Look at me, Clive."

"There's nothing you can say to make me chill out."

"There is. I've thought about this on and off over the years, and I should have suggested it a long time ago."

Randal's serious expression filled Clive with nervous tension.

"What is it? You're not giving up on me as well, are you? Am I to be relegated with your disposable tyro? Well? Am I?" He panicked.

"Your response makes my suggestion even more applicable. You're so paranoid, always over-suspicious!"

"I'm always negative when you're on the verge of another lethal performance, when you're obsessed with someone else."

"Now listen to me. I can help you with all of your insecurities. Let me... just let me hypnotise you into loving me less. It will take away all your pain and even leave the way open for you to find another partner," proposed Randal.

Clive shrank back into the emblematic shadows. He looked shocked and horrified.

"Hypnotise me into loving you less? Leave the way open for another partner? You want me to back off after all we've been through together, after what we mean to each other? Fuck you, Randal… fuck you!"

Randal shook his head in despair.

"What do you prefer, Clive? To carry on suffering or to free your soul? I'm trying to help you! I'm doing this out of love and compassion. Out of concern!"

"For me or for you?" croaked Clive, his eyes full of pain.

"For you! I can handle us, but you can't! Do you think I get a buzz from seeing you distressed? The days of me lording it over you are long gone. I was young, full of it and totally insufferable," he admitted.

"And now you're older, still full of it and as fucking insufferable as ever! You want to eradicate the whole reason I exist! My love for you has always been painful, but I wouldn't change one single, agonising second of its unbearable ecstasy. I've had plenty of other relationships over the years, behind the scenes, with umpteen closeted gay men. I've even stepped out with beautiful women who leave me stone-cold. I never told you that I dated Maxine's cousin, Guy Hale, the hairdresser you met at her wedding. We were together for almost twelve months. But you know what? Every touch, every caress, every tender expression from him was second-rate. I shut my eyes and all I saw was you. *You!* Do you think I've spent a lifetime adoring you to be dismissed with one click of your fucking fingers? I'll cope with this new shit! I always do in the end!" he hollered.

Randal knew about Clive's secret dalliances. They had helped him to manage and overcome extra stress, but now he was unstable again because of Tyrone.

Randal drew a deep breath before he spoke. It had to be said in such a way that Clive would accept hypnotic intervention.

"But you haven't coped, Clive. You tried to top yourself because of me. Eight years ago, I needed to kill Carlton Flint, and you took a handful of pills with a bottle of whisky. You call that managing? You nearly died!"

"But I didn't! Because you saved me! Because you knew I wanted to be saved! To carry on, to love you, to be with you, to protect you! I'd rather be long-suffering than Randal-free. Love is always painful no matter what, or with who. So, you can stick your hypnotic assistance where the sun doesn't shine!" he snapped.

Randal smiled regardless of the heated debate.

"Now that's a bit paradoxical because you always tell me that the sun shines out of – how do you so quaintly put it – out of my mystical backside?" he jested, but with a loving expression.

"You know what I mean. You so know what I mean. There's nothing more to say or suggest now! Is there? Well?"

"I guess not. You've said it all."

"Good! That's all sorted then!"

"Do you fancy coming with me to Scotland next week?" asked Randal, changing the subject completely.

"Scotland?"

"I've rented a cottage in Perthshire for a fortnight. I need some peace and quiet to finish my book. I also have to work out what I'm going to do about the tyro. I can't think straight at home, too many distractions."

"Won't my company be a distraction?" asked Clive indelicately.

"Probably."

"So, what do you want me there for?"

"Oh, you know. I might need help taking off my sporran. Not to mention the kilt," Randal quipped suggestively.

"So, we're back to the same old sarcastic, bawdy repartee now, are we, Mr Forbes?"

"Would you want it any other way, Mr Hargreaves? Especially now I know you're a glutton for punishment."

"No. No, I wouldn't want it any other way. Ever! Now you do understand that, don't you?"

"Totally," replied Randal as they fell into each other's embrace.

***

Before he left for Scotland, Randal decided to drive to Oxford and get together with Tyrone there. His mind was working overtime as he pulled into a parking space near Beaumont College. The familiar surroundings brought back a host of vivid images, together with poignant memories of his early years and adventurous youth.

Oh, but it was such a good time! I was adored by many. They would flock round me in worshipping herds and I had them all under my theosophical thumb. I've brought that power with me into the present. And now my darling daughter, Roxanne, is a shining star, following in my fabled footsteps.

He was meeting Tyrone at the Randolph Hotel for lunch, but it was much more than a social confab. It was an underhand motion. In fact, it was a crafty ruse on his behalf because it was imperative to keep on top of his novice's unpredictable behaviour. He sat behind the wheel for a while and lit up a fresh cheroot. He inhaled, then blew out its rich tobacco. His car embraced the aroma as he meditated.

I never thought I'd return here as a mentor to a student tyro, a reticent rebel without a just cause. I walked along these streets, full of so many dreams and plans, with unwavering ambition. Fame was my only goal, and nothing, absolutely nothing, was going to get in the way of my advancement. Such exciting, exhilarating moments in time, and spectacular removals!

What a script I devised for Robbie Sterling and Marcus Pennington. Gone but not forgotten in terms of my telepathic effectuation. Oh my, I was so creative. How old was I when they succumbed to my control? Let me think. It was 1977, so I'd be all of nineteen. One year older than Ryan. And look what I achieved! Remarkable!

That reminds me, I must pay the Penningtons a visit, specifically the lady of the manor. She's a pensioner now in human terms but still ravishing and nowhere near her age in looks or ways. She still rolls out the red-hot carpet for me. Some things don't ever change, do they, my sweet Fiona?

And then there's her eldest son, Marcus the meddler, remaining hypnotised in his twilight zone. Wishing I was his lover, not remembering I was his hated enemy. Oh, these insane fantasies of the afflicted with enforced memory loss. He's still in the dark. He thinks I walk on water. I probably could.

Randal laughed to himself as he got out of the car. He strode quickly towards the hotel, his long legs still agile and athletic. His thick, red hair glistened in the sunlight and complemented the tan leather jacket, coffee-coloured shirt and brown chinos that flattered his six foot two-inch frame like a fashionable second skin.

The yellow glints in his slate-grey eyes added another devastating dimension to his handsome facial features. Heads turned, but he was oblivious to the stares and gasps, as he glided through the doors, like a male model on a photo shoot.

"Oh, just look! It's Randal Forbes!" squealed one star-struck woman.

"He's so sexy!" replied her equally affected, middle-aged friend. "He's even more handsome in the flesh. Oof!"

"What's his wife's name again? She's famous, isn't she?"

"Alison thingy. You know, the classical pianist. Talk about looking forward to bedtime!" she drooled, and they both giggled like teenagers.

Tyrone was waiting impatiently for Randal in the lounge. He spotted him as he waltzed through reception, standing head and shoulders above the other guests.

Wow! Isn't he the real deal?! I don't have to be his kindred spirit to see he's a class act. No wonder Roxanne's so special. She couldn't be anything less with Randal as her father.

Randal smiled widely and falsely as he shook Tyrone's hand. He had jammed all undesirable thoughts so that only his constructive ones were audible.

"So happy to see you." Tyrone beamed. "I've not had a proper chance to discuss things with you since the parental debacle. Dad's in the slammer and Mum's pushing up daisies, but it's no great loss. I know that you told me to try and get them onside, but 'the gift' spoke to me and it was so strong that I really didn't have any other choice."

"Let's get a table before we launch into a full-blown discussion," suggested Randal, dismissing Tyrone's annoying confession.

"Of course. You must be hungry after your drive."

"I am."

Randal was attended to immediately by the restaurant manager, who instantly recognised him.

"Good afternoon, Mr Forbes! May I say it's a pleasure and privilege to have you here as a guest," he fawned.

"You may. In fact, you should," he quipped satirically, with the Randal-smile.

"Indeed. Please come this way. I've got just the right table for you and... I'm sorry, I didn't catch the young man's name," he hinted, looking at Tyrone.

"His name's irrelevant. We have a lot to debate, so I'd appreciate a very quiet corner," requested Randal in a no-nonsense tone.

"Of course. I've just the ideal spot. Please follow me," he cajoled as he led them to their seats.

"Can I get you anything to drink?" asked the waiter, who appeared out of thin air the minute they sat down, lighting a scented candle on the pristine table-cloth.

"Just some spring water for me, I'm driving," instructed Randal.

"A glass of your house wine would be nice." Tyrone smiled.

"Certainly, sir," he replied, as he handed them the à la carte menus. "Anything else?"

"You can give us some space. My time's limited," answered Randal tersely.

"Of course, sir," he responded subserviently.

Tyrone grinned at Randal and looked like a mischievous schoolboy.

"Do you find me amusing, Mr Pendle?" asked Randal as he perused the bill of fare.

"I just love the way that people dance to your tune. It's so entertaining. I'm aiming to get that level of respect."

"Are you now?"

"I sure am."

"Well then, just take a leaf out of my birthright book. If you're going to marry my daughter, she's used to immediate, first-class attention."

"I'm learning, day by day. You've taught me to embrace my benefaction instead of being afraid of it. I've got so many ideas. Who to save, who to remove, etc. It's so exciting. I can do anything or be anyone I want."

"You mean you can do anyone or be anything you want," wisecracked Randal.

"There you go! You've always got the right banter."

"So, it's banter now as well, is it? Well, stick with me, Tyrone and you'll be able to plagiarise that too. You've already stolen my plot. Shame on you," he drawled.

"Plot?" he queried with a frown.

"Yes. My Flint script. You tailored it to fit your first removal."

"Oh, I see. I didn't intentionally steal it. Now that Mummy dearest is no more, and Daddy defective is looking at life behind bars, well, it was the ideal solution. I feel as free as a bird. Almost," he admitted.

"Almost?"

"There's still the matter of the rest of my family. Tobias and his nauseating wife and screaming baby, not to mention Tiffany and her irritating, airheaded, spoilt, dingbat ways. They are an encumbrance, Randal. I've thought about them a lot, you know, when you told me to be more altruistic towards them. Well, I have grave doubts over that advice. They represent years of misery by association. Surely you understand that feeling? You felt much the same way about your cousin Spencer. He was family. You put up with his supercilious nonsense all your life. You simply had to eradicate him. I get that. I so get that."

"What do you fancy for lunch? My treat," he replied, completely dismissing Tyrone's opinion and blocking out his spiralling fury.

He's completely lost the plot. Literally. Spencer was my extended but not immediate family.

I could never remove my parents and sister, even if they suspected my powers and deeds. At one time Patricia did to a degree, but I used my charm and a little hypnosis to get her back on side.

Tyrone's built up this ridiculous vendetta in his paranoid head and is now ready to annihilate his own flesh and blood. All because his father preferred making money to writing poetry. So what? Tyrone could do both.

"I took the liberty of perusing the menu beforehand, so I know what I want, if that's OK with you?" presumed Tyrone.

Randal signalled to the waiter to take their order and he came hurrying over to attend to him.

"Yes, sir. Are you ready to order now?"

"I would have thought that was obvious," drawled Randal, still frustrated with Tyrone's take on 'the gift' accompanied by an 'above his station' attitude.

"Of course."

"I'll have the pan-fried sea bream with seasonal vegetables, followed by the pistachio mousse."

"Certainly. And you, sir?" he asked, addressing Tyrone.

"I want the loin of venison and the milk chocolate truffle, please," he said in a self-important tone.

"Thank you. Anything else?"

Randal shook his head and Tyrone followed suit.

The stately dining room was very elegant and reflected the university history of Oxford. Randal felt totally at home but had grave doubts about his tyro. His closed-off thoughts were still operative, as he poured himself a glass of water.

"So, tell me, Tyrone, what exactly have you got in mind for your remaining family? Is it another homage to my past movements, or have you thought of something a bit more original?"

"Are you annoyed with me for tweaking your idea and passing it off as my own? It only goes to show how much I revere you. I didn't mean to infringe your copyright. I thought you'd be pleased with the similarity. It was my first assignment and I didn't want to mess up, so I felt it only right to utilise a removal that had been tried and tested, so to speak. You are my peer after all." He frowned deeply, his brown eyes darkening with instability.

"I'm not annoyed. I'm just disappointed that you couldn't conjure up something more innovative, more imaginative," lied Randal, but he hid his displeasure well.

"I understand that to a degree, but what I have in mind for the rest of my clan will rectify that. I'm working on it."

"Are you now? Brief me."

"Aha, it's a secret. I don't want to dilute the shock value by telling you. I want it to be mind-blowing. I'm only halfway through the script. I'm following your guidelines by writing everything down and going through it with a toothcomb to make sure it's one hundred per cent workable. I'm approaching it as if I'm creating a story, just like you've always done. That's the way forward. It all makes perfect sense now."

"It makes perfect sense to use 'the gift' appropriately. What you're planning is a waste of psychic energy because there are numerous enemies out there who mean you far more harm than your family. Your brother and sister are not adversaries. They are lesser mortals who happen to be related. They should be left alone to carry on with their insular but harmless lives," instructed Randal.

"So, you still don't think I should have used my father to remove my mother? How else was I going to get him off my back for good?" he objected.

"By proving your true worth, which you could have done so easily and turned the whole thing round. It would have been far more satisfying to see your father's face full of respect and admiration," lectured Randal.

"You just don't get it, do you? When did your father last tell you that you were a failure? That you were a waste of space? That you would never amount to anything? You're used to adulation. I grew up with condemnation. If you're told often enough that you're an oddity, a minnow, that you're inferior and lightweight, well, you end up believing it. I was screwed up because deep down I knew I was superior to them. I could read their minds. They thought I was crazy because I used to break things around the house in a temper. I didn't even touch the ornaments. I just stared at them and they'd shatter in response. But I was scared of my powers because I didn't know what they were or why I had them. Now I do. Thanks to you. So, it's payback time. They all need to die. It's as simple as that. Plain sailing," he deliberated with glowing eyes and a viciously cruel smile, prompting Randal to cringe.

He's completely unbalanced and disturbed. No amount of tuition is going to put him on the right road. He won't ever let go of this grievance, so the rest of his family have to be annihilated in order to balance the books. He's only at the beginning of his apprenticeship and he's parked the bus.

Randal could not see that his own perception of poetic justice was just as twisted as his tyro's. In his mind, Tyrone's methods did not fit in with his particular reasoning so therefore it would all have to be blackballed, overruled and quashed. His pupil was turning a deaf ear to his tuition which was the ultimate error and offence, so it had to be invalidated. But this would be very tricky because they both possessed equal intensity and strength.

"Do you really need me as your mentor now? I mean, you're obviously single-minded. Maybe it's meant for you to find your own way. Perhaps it's how 'the gift' tells us both that you need to be free. I think you're totally aware of your powers and should have free reign to use them. Practice makes perfect. Who am I to hold you back? What do you say, Tyrone?" he advised cunningly, disguising his disgust.

"Your opinion matters to me regardless of our variance. Do you really think I'm ready to go solo?"

"I do."

"Then I will. I'll always be grateful to you for showing me the way, and when I marry Roxanne, I'll be the finished product and you'll see how far I've come!" he bragged.

You won't live long enough. Your days are numbered, Tyrone. If you think I'm letting you within one inch of my daughter, think again, screwball. What was your father's motto? Tenacity, tenacity, tenacity. He was right. It's the final countdown.

***

Randal summoned Roxanne to his study when he arrived back home. She was working on a number of short stories with a dark edge, and knew she was the absolute, genuine author to create the characters, all of them so vivid they were leaping off the page. In this sense she took after Randal. Her writing was imaginative and authentic, at the same time.

So, when her father interrupted her, she felt the same as he always did if he was disturbed in the throes of his creative flow.

"Oh, Daddy, I need to get back quickly to my writing. I'm just in the middle of this amazing plot and I don't want to lose the thread. So, can you be quick?"

"I don't do 'quick' when there's a bleak, fatalistic crisis to discuss," he reprimanded.

Roxanne received a mental flash of Tyrone and instinctively knew it was all about him. She took a deep breath and prepared herself for her father's unavoidable sermon.

"What's he done now?"

"What's he done now? Everything and nothing! That's what! He's unemployable and strictly out of bounds! I met him in Oxford and the penny finally dropped. He doesn't need a mentor. He needs a fucking shrink."

"A fucking shrink?"

"You heard me, and don't swear."

"I'm only repeating what you said. They're your words, not mine." She pouted, on the verge of a tantrum.

"Never mind getting on your high horse again. Just calm down and listen to what I have to tell you. I don't want you to interrupt. There'll be plenty of opportunity to discuss it all when I've finished."

"This doesn't sound good."

"Oh, believe me, it isn't! Behind those dark eyes of his lies a powerhouse of unadulterated insanity. He's drunk with it all. 'The gift', which he once called a curse, has gone to his head. He's unbending, inflexible, uncompromising and entrenched in bitter hatred for people who mean him no harm. His family are not the enemy yet he's still hell-bent on removing them. He disagrees with my advice to steer clear of all unnecessary homicide. So, because he's rejected my instructions, so early in the game, I've decided to abandon his training. In fact, I've decided to relinquish the association altogether. He's not worth the trouble."

"But, Daddy, I—"

"I've not finished."

"I need to say something. I really do." She sulked.

"You can have your say when I've reached the end of mine. This is crucial to the future of 'the gift', so listen very carefully to the rest of my judgment," he advised.

Roxanne's eyes began to smoulder with the stirrings of her wrath.

"Don't you dare look at me in that way!" warned Randal with a similar expression, his own gaze speaking the same language as his chosen daughter.

"Don't you dare look at me with that glare!" she cautioned.

"Are you questioning my ability to judge a dangerous situation? Why are you so defensive of Mr Pendle? You're love-struck but it's pure infatuation. He's swept you off your first-crush feet. That's all it is, Roxanne." He glowered.

"Don't tell me how I feel. I love him! I really do! I'll never find another like him. He's unique. And he makes me feel so special. In every way," she burned.

"You love him? Well, here's the thing! He's fooled you! He'll stop at nothing now to achieve domination! Nobody's safe! Not even me!"

"But this is so crazy! Only recently you were praising his eagerness to learn. You were so excited that you'd found someone with the same benefaction. He's the opposite of Carlton Flint. Right up our street. The same contempt for lesser mortals, the same desire to eliminate all enemies of 'the gift'," she argued.

"He's delusional. He wants to eliminate solely for the sake of revenge and spite. His primary targets are innocent of suspicion. They have never been a threat. What have I always told you? Huh? We have to guard against danger. Against any risk which threatens our standing and we have to eliminate the root cause if it persists. In Tyrone's case he's determined to kill his immediate family, and he's obsessed with the deed. Any tyro who can put up such resistance to my superior counselling will never adhere to the chosen path. He will make up his own rules. He's out of order, non-functional and in disrepair!"

"I still want to see him! You can't stop me seeing him!"

"Oh yes I can! I'm warning you now that his days are numbered! Trust your father's sixth, seventh and eighth senses! He sees you as the ultimate trophy. He rates me highly but deep down he intends to outstrip my status. I feel it so strongly and I'm only sorry that I couldn't predict this situation. I let my excitement and enthusiasm override the possibility, because, like you, I was elated to find such a rare kindred spirit. Well, not now!"

"I don't get it! He's never given me any cause to doubt him. I can feel the love he has for me. When he holds me close and kisses me, I feel so aroused but secure and safe as well."

"What!"

"Don't yell at me!" she screamed.

"What else has he done, Roxanne? He swore openly to me that he'd never touch you until he had passed his apprenticeship and proved his worth to me as a suitor! He lied!"

"He's... he's... touched me everywhere. But I wanted him to, Daddy," she insisted.

Randal turned away as his eyes floodlighted the whole room. His fury was uncontrollable and scorched everything around him.

"He's a dead man!"

Randal took time out to breathe. He wiped the back of his hand across his mouth and turned to look at her. His eyes were alight and he was burning as he tried to control his monumental wrath before he spoke.

"Who do you trust more? Me, or him? It all boils down to that one thing. Have I ever misguided you? Have I ever given you cause to doubt me? You're my most treasured child. He's crossed a fine, perverted line, and defiled you against my wishes! He's broken all his promises! The hatred I have for him at this very moment in time is on par with Carlton Flint! In fact, it's three steps up! I'm so boiling mad! So furious and incensed it's beyond belief!"

"I can't turn off my feelings for him like a tap! I still care! I do!" she cried, her bottom lip wobbling with emotion.

"No, you don't! If I've got to hypnotise you into a state of indifference towards him then I bloody well will. It's either that or I'll incinerate him right now! Today! Don't fight me on this one, Roxanne! I know what I'm talking about! He might have the same powers as us, but he's going to use them unsuitably, ill-advisedly and dangerously! Why are you arguing with me about it? Why are you defying me?"

"Because.... because I'll never find anyone else like *you*! You're everything in one! I could spend my whole life searching! I'll be alone one day with 'the gift' surrounded by lesser mortals! What happens, Daddy, when you're no longer with me? What then? Nobody else will fit the bill. I'll be totally on my own with our benefaction. That's why I want Tyrone because... because... he's like *you*!"

Randal felt his anger rapidly drain away and it was replaced by an all-consuming tenderness and caring for his special child.

Oh my word. She's looking for me! She's so feisty and yet so fragile. So loved but so lost. I should have realised. I should have known!

She heard his thoughts as he opened his arms to her and she ran into them, sheltering from the insecure storm.

"Now listen to me, my precious pumpkin. I truly believe that there's another 'me' out there. By that, I mean a further kindred spirit who totally fits the bill. This world is a vast place. As I've got older, I realise that we're not the only ones to have been chosen. I know you'll find your soulmate. I swear. Believe me," he stressed, stroking back her hair and looking deeply into her eyes.

"Promise?" she wept.

"I promise," he whispered as they stood in emotional solidarity.

And now I'm going to remove my disobedient tyro so you can find your true heart's desire. The promised one. 'The gift' will deliver him to your dynamic door. Trust in your benefaction. Trust in your daddy. He'll never let you down.

"What are you going to do to Tyrone? Will it be violent?"

"I want you to knock all thoughts of Tyrone Pendle out of your head. By that I mean everything. The good, the bad and the oh-so-ugly. He doesn't exist. He's totally inconsequential. It's just you, me and 'the gift'," he soothed, stroking her wet cheeks with his thumbs.

"But you said he wants to outstrip you. So did Carlton Flint, and without my help, he would have killed you! I'm so scared of a repeat performance."

"So, what are you saying? Are you offering me your unique brand of combat? An inherited helping hand in the destructive mix? Hmm?"

"I want to assist. You're my number-one priority, Daddy. Nobody else comes close," she said adoringly, all previous dissent forgotten and dismissed.

"I can't lie to you, pumpkin. It will be nasty and a true test of my station. Just because he's younger and less experienced is not a benchmark for failure. He's stored up twenty-one years of frustrated power and now he's about to unleash its damnable force. My hatred of his treacherous and disgusting behaviour towards you is raging inside me! I'm literally trying hard not to explode!"

"He's not entirely to blame on that score. He responded to my flirting," she admitted.

"Hogwash! He knew the score! We agreed on it. He was to keep any touchy-feely business out of the equation at this stage!" expounded Randal with a resurgence of sparking eyes.

"So, what will you do now?"

"What will I do now? I'm going to kill him stone dead! How? I'm not sure yet, but he's a marked man walking on wafer-thin ice, and he's going to fatally slip up."

"I don't really love him. It's just that he's the same as us. I thought I'd have a boyfriend who was as magical as my spellbinding father. I wasn't defending him. I was just safeguarding the notion. I'm so sorry," she confessed, biting her lip.

"Nothing to forgive. You're safe in my arms now. There's no need for any imposters or apologies."

As Roxanne nestled in his embrace he pondered on his next assignment, cutting off his thoughts so as not to alarm her.

Tyrone Pendle, I'm coming to get you! It's the dramatic showdown of the new Millennium.

The demise of the tyro and the rise of the maestro. That's a good title for a book if ever I concocted one. Even though it's a trifle too long!

It will be 'the gift' versus 'the gift'. I'll take you apart. You're dead meat. I'll chop off those hands that sullied my child. Prepare yourself for pain.

So now, let the music play and the revue begin.

Act One – Damnation. Act Two – Demolition.

8

Tyrone was admiring Randal's photograph on the rear side of his last novel, when he felt a creeping premonition of something quite formidable.

At first, he thought it was just the telepathic link he had with his icon, and that he was picking up on Randal's awesome power. But then a flash of acrimonious, contemptuous disapproval issued out of Randal's eyes, and grabbed him by the throat, until he thought he was going to choke. He flung the book across the room as he struggled to breathe and think straight.

What the hell was that? A definite warning, but why? Ryan told me that Randal's in Scotland with Clive, working on another creative project, but I've just had a psychic caution.

'The gift' wants me to look behind the scenes. I've inadvertently tuned into Randal's rage. He's full to the brim with indignation and resentment! Over what? I'm going to enter his subconscious, like he taught me to do, and find out.

Wait a minute! It's best I go through Clive. He won't suspect anything unusual. I can use him as a host body to analyse Randal's pitch-black mood. Now where's that photo of him? Here goes.

Clive was making some percolated coffee in the cottage

kitchen as Tyrone slid effortlessly into his subconscious. Clive popped his head round the door.

"Do you want a drink?" he asked Randal.

"Sure. No sugar, though, I'm sweet enough." Randal smiled.

"That's highly debatable," replied his protector but with obvious affection.

Tyrone weighed up the scene behind Clive's eyes.

This is really odd. Randal's in a good mood, so why did I feel such rancour? Something's telling me that it's nothing to do with his present disposition. Whoa! It's all to do with his hatred of me!

I felt his hostility emanating out of the psychic airwaves through his photographic image. But that doesn't make any sense! We parted amicably even though he gave me solo licence to practice and use our legacy. I'll just hang around a little longer for a possible clue.

"How do you feel now?" asked Clive, as he gave Randal his coffee, lovingly stroking a loose section of red hair off his forehead that had flopped into his slate-grey eyes.

"A bit better. The sound of silence is very cathartic. I've written another chapter, you've knocked it into grammatical shape for me and, on top of that, I've also worked out a long-term plan of how I'm going to eradicate the tyro."

"Don't overdo it. You need to relax. Just writing a new novel is enough without planning a psychic showdown. Anyway, it's not that urgent. Pace yourself. Tyrone's still in awe of you and doesn't suspect a thing."

"Just the mention of his name is enough to set me off. The thought of his dirty hands all over my daughter stirs me into immediate lethal action! It's taking me all of my time to control the urge to snuff him out right now! It has to be a slow but painful exit. He's dead meat. He's earned all of his brainsick brownie points!"

Tyrone's hair stood on end. Every single cell and pulse throughout his whole body rebelled against Randal's words. His face flushed with rage and shock.

What? What! He wants me dead? All because I pawed Roxanne! He thinks that's a monumental betrayal? She was so up for it! And now she's snitched to her daddy! She's not what I thought her to be! She swore she'd keep it just between us! She's ruined everything! Everything! I must calm down and listen to this conversation. I must hear where it's heading. Clive's talking.

"You know I feel exactly the same as you about Roxanne. She's still underage and Tyrone should have known better, but it doesn't merit another telepathic removal. Can't you just tell him to leave her alone now, and let him go on his merry, wandering-hands way?" advised Clive.

"It's not just about Roxanne. He's a total waste of spiritual space. A reluctant pupil full of idiotic ideas. A fantasist who believes he has to kill his closest family to attain psychical status. A complete pain in the defiant derriere who needs to be taught a fatal lesson for lack of dedication and consolidation. His father was right. He's worthless and inept."

Clive sighed and nodded his head in resignation. Randal was in his unmovable mindset and would not be swayed away from his murderous objective.

"Just one more question. Will Roxanne be helping you, like she did with Carlton?" asked Clive anxiously.

"I'm not sure. We'll just have to see how it all pans out, but one thing's certain, my former tyro will be history. A brittle blip on a promising horizon who could have shone but faded away instead. Disloyal, dismissed and destroyed!"

"I get the picture and I'm terrified. I can't lie," groaned Clive.

"There's no need for fear. I'll beat him hands down, from out of the air and into the ground. He's finished, Clive. Over! Now let's get back to some work. I don't want my latest book to be overshadowed by that no-mark novice."

Tyrone had to remind himself to breathe. He pulled out of Clive's head and slumped back into his chair. His heart was thumping so hard he thought it would burst through his chest wall.

I worshipped a fake! A deceiver with a winning smile! He was my ultimate icon. My unequalled hero of heresy! I'm speechless with shock.

He's the same as my father, but with 'the gift'. Demoralising detractors. Roxanne too! If they suppose I'm going to roll over and die, they need to think again. I'll kill them both! Randal's made a massive mistake! I'm more than ready for his wrath! He taught me well, regardless of what he believes.

And now I'll employ all his own tactics to destroy him. My power will outstrip his fortification and dismantle his reign. I'm the new holder of 'the gift' and I don't have to walk in his fake footsteps, because I'm more than capable of engaging my own spiritual warfare.

His worshipful, deluded circle need a little telepathic word in their ears to know what a two-faced, deceitful, despotic demon they have in their midst. I'm going to activate his complete downfall beginning as of this minute. Right now!

***

Marcus Pennington was reading one of Randal's poetry books for the umpteenth time when Tyrone took possession of his thoughts through his photograph.

Hello, Marcus. Don't be alarmed. I'm a friend and not part of your illness. I mean you no harm, but I need to de-hypnotise you, so that all your recollection of your time at Beaumont College, Oxford, will be restored, and you'll remember everything single thing.

Randal Forbes caused your severe memory loss. I won't go into it too deeply because you must prepare yourself for a big shock. The truth will be hard to bear, but it's only right that you should know.

Marcus leaped out of his chair and took a sharp intake of breath.

Who was that? Don't tell me I'm hearing voices now as well! Oh, God!

Tyrone put his hands around Marcus's photograph. His eyes glowed as he pumped radiant, remedial rays of light that travelled through his splayed fingers, right to the root cause of his recipient's amnesia.

Now, Marcus, I'll fill in the gaps to help you along. Randal Forbes took over your brain and made you tie your grandfather to a chair, soak his rectory in kerosene and set it alight, so that he died in the fire on Halloween, twenty-three years ago.

He forced you to hang yourself but relented with the stranglehold, so you didn't die. Instead, he erased your memory out of respect for your mother, Lady Pennington. He's been her lover since 1977 and it's still going on. It's a lot to take in but now I'm going to withdraw and let you chew it all over. So long and good luck.

Marcus blinked rapidly to dispel his blurred vision. He windscreen-wiped the hazy impression away, breathing heavily from the monstrous words in his head. Then suddenly, a host of lost memories and images came rushing in like strobe lightning, each recollection a punch in the stomach and a stab in the heart.

He looked at Randal's book, still in his hands, and observed his photograph on its back cover. He was so stunned that he spoke out loud.

"Oh my good God! I remember! I remember! He's a fucking monster! Gramps thought he was possessed and wanted to perform an exorcism! I begged him to let it drop! Clive told me that Randal was his own demon! Clive! He was the one I loved, not… not… not that satanic piece of unadulterated shit! Who was in my head just now? He said he was a friend. What else did he say?

"Hell and high water! My mother! He said Randal's her lover! *Her lover!* Is that why he still visits us after all these years? It must be! All the time he's been gloating, egging us all on with a perfect charade of compassion! Who just gave me my memory back? Maybe it's just returned on its own, in a weird way. The brain is a complex centre of thought and sensation!"

Marcus threw Randal's book across the room then stamped on it hard. He spat at his face and wept tears of relief and remorse as he remembered the whole tragic saga.

You let me fall in love with you! You led me to believe you were helping me recover, when all the time it was you who had caused my grief!

You killed my grandfather! You hanged me from a tree! You let me suffer with mental anguish and pain in my throat for years! I was a whisker away from death. I was insane with anguish and torment, not understanding how I could do that to a beloved priest! You don't deserve to live! My wayward mother needs to know who you really are and what you did! Pronto!

***

Tyrone was riveted to his vengeful spot. He needed to inform the people who mattered most to Randal, to reveal the true, treacherous despot behind the benevolent mask.

He knew that the police would dismiss any paranormal, homicidal accusations. It would all sound totally ludicrous, so his aim was not for criminal justice. Tyrone had to hit Randal hard, right in the centre of his private solar plexus.

Subsequently, his next target was Dean. He was devising another programme for Randal's company, Astral TV, when Tyrone rang him on his private line.

"Dean Gibson here. Can I help you?"

"No, but I can certainly help you."

"Who is this, please?"

"I can help you to know what your beloved cousin Randal is all about," sneered Tyrone, dismissing Dean's enquiry.

"Who the hell are you? How did you get my private number?"

"It's irrelevant. Now, do you want to hear the truth? I feel it's very, very crucial that you should. So, don't hang up on me," insisted Tyrone.

"Well, just be quick, otherwise I'll cut you off!"

"Are you ready for this? It's not pretty. But here we go. Randal's really a psychotic psychic. He reads and controls people's minds, issuing commands through their photographic images. He telepathically killed your real father, John Sterling, by creating a shower of shattered, mirrored glass, so he bled to death in a hotel washroom, way back in 1965. Randal hated him for trying to force your mother, his Aunty Dottie, into having an illegal abortion when she was pregnant with you," he expounded, licking his lips with sadistic relish.

"Now if you don't get off the line, I'm going to call the police! I don't know how you've got this information, but you're obviously deranged," snapped Dean.

"Oh, I've not finished yet. Years later, Randal hypnotised Raymond Haynes to stab and kill his wife, Delia, because they had been gossiping about your birth father and your mother's love affair with him. Their son, namely nasty Nick, your childhood enemy, had overheard them and blabbed, alerting you, in front of all your junior-school pals, to the ugly hidden truth.

"Not long after that, you went walking through a winter wonderland in the park with Randal. He caused Nick and his two little sisters to wade into the lake and drown. You fell into a Randal-induced sleep on his shoulder while he murdered them with his mind. Remember?

"A few years later, he willed your half-brother, Robbie Sterling, to jump off a cliff in the Lakeland Fells. He had asked him purposely to join him and Clive so that he could annihilate him.

"Randal told the police that Robbie had slipped, but he lied. He killed him. He killed them all to protect you from the truth. He feels you're his creation, saved from being aborted.

"Now *that's* the real Randal Forbes! Your hero! Your benevolent, altruistic cousin. A psychic, serial killer on the loose, removing others as well, whenever and wherever he can.

To coin one of Randal's barbs after sticking in the verbal knife, do have a nice day!"

Tyrone put down the phone, sat back, grinned and then could not stop laughing.

That'll put the cosmic cat amongst the poisonous pigeons.

Dean did not realise that he was still holding the phone in his tightly clenched fist. He was shocked and confused, disbelieving and open-mouthed, with racing thoughts.

Who the hell was that screwball? But more so, how did he have all that information about my life? How can he accuse Randal of such lunacy? And yet, he sounded so sure, so positive in his accusations.

Oh, God! What am I even thinking of here? My beloved Randal a murderer? Never! I need to see him so badly. He doesn't get back from Scotland until next week. I can't possibly phone him with this shit now! He's gone away for peace and quiet and is probably in the middle of a creative chapter. He'll freak out!

But that caller's a menace! What if he means Randal harm? Oh God! What should I do?

He put down the phone, but it rang again while he was contemplating and Dean nearly jumped out of his chair. He answered it with trembling hands, but before he could even ask who it was, Tyrone carried on from where he left off.

"It's me again. I forgot. Randal's also doing his best to split you and Maddie Flint up. Together with Roxanne, who is his female counterpart and blood child, they killed Carlton, who had the same powers as them, except he used his for benevolent purposes.

"Randal hypnotised Francine Flint to poison Carlton, in order to weaken him. Then, under his control, she sliced Dr Winston Ramsey's head open with a meat cleaver. Roxanne did the same act to Stella Reid and then unsuccessfully tried it on Carlton, who survived the blow.

"When Carlton was hospitalised, his nurse was also under Randal's hypnotic trance and he instructed her to pump a lethal dose of morphine into Carlton's system. The injection that finally saw him off.

"Oh, and by the way, Randal's the author of *The Flawed Flints.* He wrote it under the alias Lloyd Byron to drive Maddie even further into psychosis. Nice guy, isn't he, Dean?"

"You're insane! I'm calling the police! You're a certifiable crackpot!" Dean bellowed, but Tyrone carried on.

"Before he died, Carlton told the police about Randal and Roxanne, and that his wife, Francine, was not responsible for her actions. They thought he was mad. When Francine Flint was arrested and then Nurse Archer, they gave their statements, but they were practically word for word the same: that they couldn't remember anything.

"Detective Inspector Wayne Bredbury researched Randal's background and found that he had been hauled in over several other homicides. It was too much of a coincidence that Randal was connected with every one of them.

"So Inspector Bredbury visited Francine in prison, because he suspected some paranormal skulduggery and was even thinking about reopening the case. Randal found out and hypnotised him to jump under a train. Then Francine followed suit and abseiled out of her prison window, minus the rope."

Dean felt sick. He had wanted to slam down the phone but somehow felt compelled to listen. His stomach was churning and he had a pounding headache.

"Oh, I nearly forgot. Just one more thing, Dean. When you see Randal about my accusations, look into his eyes as you confront him. They will glow! Those eyes are the windows of his dark soul, and when they're on fire, nobody's safe in their flashing path. Not even you. Or me. So be aware. He's evil. Lucifer's right-hand man, and homicide is his best friend. I rest my case. Good afternoon."

Dean nearly threw up. *I want Randal back home, right now! I need to speak to him! Desperately!*

***

Alison was trying to pacify Oscar, who was having a tantrum because she had stopped him eating cake before his evening meal.

"Oscar! It will only spoil your dinner. You can have a slice of it later. Now stop being silly and sit down at the table!"

"No!" he rebelled.

The phone rang in the middle of her frustration.

"Roxanne, make sure he eats his main course, please. That'll be your father ringing from Scotland. He said he'd phone tonight," she explained.

"Will do. Give Daddy my love," said Roxanne, smiling widely.

Ryan and Amber looked at each other in silent protest.

She's always got to be the first in line, they thought simultaneously.

Alison took the call in the hall because she wanted some privacy in case the conversation got steamy.

"Hello? Is that you, Randal?" she asked huskily.

"Sorry to disappoint you, Mrs Forbes, but it's me," replied Tyrone tersely.

"Tyrone?"

"The very same."

"What do you want? We're upset over the way you behaved with Roxanne. I think it's best you don't call her anymore. Just keep well away," she stated firmly.

"The way *I've* behaved? What about the way your *husband* has behaved all these years?" he protested gleefully.

"What's that supposed to mean?"

"I think you better sit down. Your legs may give way with the shock."

Alison frowned deeply and prepared herself for what she thought was his confrontational response to the ban.

"Look, Tyrone, quite honestly, I'm not in the mood for your adolescent grudges!" she scolded.

"Adolescent grudges? Oh, you couldn't be more wrong! Your dear husband has been having a passionate affair with Lady Pennington from the first day they met in 1977. He was nineteen at the time, and I believe she was forty-something when he defiled and corrupted her. You were also invited to that fateful weekend with Clive at Clarendon Hall, Banbury. After you fell asleep, Randal thoroughly screwed the lady of the manor in her boudoir and they've been at it ever since. He can't get enough of her." Tyrone smirked.

Alison took a sharp intake of breath.

"You're a despicable liar! You can't see our daughter, so you're making scandalous mischief. You're pathetic!" she snapped.

"*Our* daughter? Are you sure about that? I think you mean *Randal's* daughter. Roxanne's his blood child, conceived in a frenzied, debauched, one-night stand with the late, great Maxine Hale. Why do you think he's so close to her? Over-protective, often to the exclusion of your other children?

"Number one, she's inherited 'the gift'. Number two, she's contaminated with the same murderous disposition. Number three, she wanted to marry me because I'm like him. Telepathic. Psychic. Dark. Unique. Invincible. And *that*, Mrs Forbes, and *that*, is the truth, the whole truth and nothing but the truth, so help me Satan. Your husband is a serial adulterer and killer!"

"You're insane! You're insane!" repeated Alison, and yet she couldn't put the phone down.

"Oh, before I forget, he's also in a very physical relationship with guess who? Some guy called Clive Hargreaves. They've been together since they were fifteen. In fact, they're probably at it right now in the wilds of Perthshire, miles away from your heterosexual bubble. I know that you suspected something between them years ago. Well, you were spot on. Randal sweet-talked you out of your assumption. His bi-sexual behaviour is admittedly confined to Clive alone, but, oh my, what a seductive sideline! They're insatiable together. Bye then. Have a nice dinner."

Alison was speechless and appalled as she slammed down the phone.

Oh God! Tyrone's evil! Evil! *How could he lie so convincingly? It's all lies! Isn't it?*

She put her head in her hands as she felt the tears begin to prick and threaten to flow.

Randal and Lady Pennington? No! Never! She's so restrained, so… ladylike. But Clive? Oh God, I've always known he's in love with Randal, but he's gay and my man isn't! There's not a cat in hell's chance of that! Is there? And Roxanne! I've often thought she's the image of Randal, but Maxine did have the same colouring. What if Tyrone's right? Could he be? Oh, Randal, I need you to come home now. I'm so disturbed by that conversation.

Roxanne sensed Alison's distress and joined her in the hall.

"Are you all right, Mummy?" she asked, trying to get inside Alison's head.

"What? Oh, I'm fine. It's nothing. Just a hoax call," she replied, wanting to protect her from Tyrone's re-emergence.

Roxanne could see right through Alison's charade.

Tyrone! He's told her! He's told her that I'm Daddy's real child. She knows about Lady Pennington and Uncle Clive. She's distressed and doesn't know what to believe. Tyrone's probably contacted other people and caused havoc. How did I ever think I loved that savage? I hate him and he needs to be removed. Daddy has to come home right away! To put everyone off the scent.

Back at the dinner table, Alison just picked at her food then pushed the plate away.

"Are you OK, Mum?" asked Ryan, when he noticed her pale complexion and troubled expression.

"What? Oh, I'm fine. Just a tummy-ache. My lunch didn't agree with me," she lied.

"Was that Dad on the phone?"

"Oh, no. It was your grandmother," she lied.

"Hmm. I'll still keep an eye on you. You really don't look too hot."

Ryan was back home for the weekend from Oxford because he knew that she would be missing his father. He was inwardly annoyed with Randal.

Even after all these years she's still only half a person when he's away. Eternally obsessed. Pity he doesn't quite feel the same. His work always takes priority. He promised to ring her and he hasn't yet. She's upset. She thought that call was him and she's waiting with bated breath for a few warm-hearted words. You know, Dad, I do love you, but sometimes you're such a shit!

Ryan's mobile rang and he saw Tyrone was the caller.

I better take this in another room. He's not exactly the flavour of the month.

Roxanne looked up as she watched him dash out.

It's probably Tyrone. This is getting worse by the second. I'm going to contact Daddy telepathically.

Ryan climbed the stairs two at a time, entered the privacy of his bedroom and closed the door before he answered the call.

"Yes, Tyrone. It's difficult to talk. My parents aren't happy with you and it's all to do with Roxanne. You shouldn't have done what you did. Is that why you're calling?"

"Well, before I explain, I need to de-hypnotise you."

"You need to de-what?"

"Just relax, Ryan, while I do my thing."

Tyrone entered his head and deactivated the emotional blockade he had created to stop Ryan's hot love for Roxanne. He had initially performed it a while ago for two reasons.

Number one, Tyrone wanted Roxanne for himself without complications. Number two, he knew that Ryan was unaware of his blood connection with Roxanne and it would only lead to heartache for him if he knew the truth.

Neither judgment or salvation applied anymore, so Tyrone put the long-bladed, soul-stirring knife into Ryan's hidden passion and brought it back to life.

"Tell me, Ryan, is Roxanne there with you now?" he asked cunningly after he had done the deed.

"No. She's… she's downstairs," replied Ryan, as a red-hot surge of desire coursed through his veins at the mere mention of her name.

"You want to fuck her, don't you?"

"You're so out of order, Tyrone," gasped Ryan, even though it was true.

"Well, you're going to have to fight the urge, like you have all your life. You see, Ryan, she's actually the same blood as you. She's your half-sister. Maxine Hale was her mother, but Saul Curtis was not her daddy. *Your* daddy screwed his up-for-it showgirl repeatedly, one sleazy night back in 1983. Roxanne was the result. She was conceived in lust. Randy Randal or what, eh?" he mocked.

"What the hell are you saying? Are you getting back at my father because he's mad at you? You know what? I'm pretty mad at you too! You should have kept your filthy hands off Roxanne, knowing full well she's underage!" he blasted.

"Is that so? Well, I've got another little surprise for you, Ryan. Don't be so quick to defend your daddy and half-sister. Do you recall when you overheard them talking about 'the gift'? It would be eight years ago now. They also mentioned they were going to kill the starman and you went running to your mummy, frightened and upset over their alarming conversation? Remember? Huh?" he pressed.

"How do you know about that? I never told you!" exclaimed Ryan, with an ominous shiver trailing down his spinal cord.

"Oh, I know everything, Ryan. *Everything!* You see, it wasn't a game they were playing, like your daddy led you to believe when you plucked up the courage to ask him about it.

"I'm delighted to tell you that 'the gift' is real. It's a glorious benefaction. A magical, powerful dowry that enables its recipients to take over their rivals' or enemies' minds and cause their demise.

"Now, in your daddy's case, he used it, together with Roxanne, who has inherited the same endowment, to kill Maxine and Saul in order to claim her back.

"Then they used it again to rid themselves of the starman, their nickname for Carlton Flint, who also possessed the same legacy. But he used his gratuity for the good of mankind.

"Your daddy and sister, being as pitch black as umpteen Aces of Spades, couldn't hack that premise, so Carlton had to go. And what a removal it was! I have to reluctantly admit that it was enviously diabolical. Head bowed at their dark altar, to be fair.

"But now, your daddy and sister want to remove me. And do you know why, Ryan? Hello? Are you still there or have you passed out?"

Ryan had gone into shock. He could hear Tyrone's words coming at him from another dimension, so severe was his reaction. Only his thoughts remained active.

Oh God! Can this be true? Roxanne's my sister? And all that stuff about 'the gift' and the starman! I've always suspected something's not quite right with them both. But how does Tyrone know all that anyway?

"I'll tell you how I know," replied Tyrone unnervingly, as he read Ryan's riotous thoughts. "I know because I've also got 'the gift' and it's as shadowy as theirs. They've got a fierce fight on their hands because they've underestimated my powers. Your daddy is a telepathic, serial killer. He's removed numerous lives, snuffed them out without a backward glance. But all that's irrelevant now to me!"

Ryan searched for his voice and found it hovering somewhere deep inside his subconscious, but he dragged it out in fear and agitation.

"What the hell are you saying? You can't go around accusing them of such... such craziness! Where's the proof, Tyrone? Where's the proof!"

"You want proof? Watch Daddy Randal's eyes change when you challenge him about all this."

"His eyes? You mean that... that weird glint he has when he's annoyed? He's always had that. It's just his way," replied Ryan, with more conviction than he actually felt.

"That weird glint is just an esoteric aperitif. When in full flow they look like two laser beams, two flaring flashlights of destruction designed to control, dominate and remove any recipients in their deadly gaze."

"You're mad! Do you realise how insane you sound? How totally unbelievable and surreal," snapped Ryan, his heartbeat reverberating in his ears.

"Believe in the unbelievable then. It's all true because I'm the very same. I also have 'the gift' and your daddy employed me initially as his tyro. He taught me many things, but in his eyes, I failed my apprenticeship because I wouldn't go along with every piece of his advice. And now he wants to kill me because I know too much. Far too much!

"He's been playing me like an infatuated puppet on a spiritual string. He doesn't know that I know that. Oh, but he will. He so will. I've only just started my retaliation. It's the rehearsal before the box-office smash. He's a dead man, Ryan. You'll be half an orphan soon. So, expect the worse," he snarled with unadulterated hatred.

"You're insane! I thought you were my friend! You need sectioning, Tyrone! I'm going to call the police to put a restraining order on you to keep you as far away from my family as possible. Preferably Mars," hissed Ryan.

"A restraining order will do nothing to restrict my telepathic wrath. You're all dead meat. I used my own dipshit father to kill my lamebrain mother. I made him put a plastic bag over her empty head! I've still not finished with the rest of my family. They're on my psychic hit list. So, if I can do that to them, then your lot will be a doddle to deal with. I have no conscience!"

"I'm going to call my father right now! You'll regret this outburst, Tyrone! He's a very powerful man and he'll know exactly what to do with you!"

"Ha! Ha! Ha! You do that, Ryan, and watch his eyes. Oh, before I go, I just alerted your mummy to your daddy's infidelities. Note the word is plural. She's rather, shall we say, upset about it. She'll fill you in on all the details. It really shouldn't have ended this way, Ryan. I had so many grand plans but now they're all in tatters, thanks to your daddy and your half-sister. Watch your back too. I'm coming to get you all," he threatened, and then hung up the phone.

Ryan could not breathe. He felt a compression across his chest. It was so tight that he thought he was going to pass out. His heartbeat was galloping and hammering inside his ribs.

Dad needs to come home straight away! I don't care about his latest novel. We need him here! No wonder my mum looked so ill after that call. She's hiding her heartbreak and suspicion from us. Dad's the only one who can deal with this lunatic! He should come home right now with no excuses! We're all under threat!

★★★

Tyrone smiled cruelly as he poured himself a glass of wine.

This is going well. Now, who else can I alert to the dark truth? Oh, I know. Randal's double-crossed Uncle Ashley. Oh, this is such fun. I'll de-hypnotise him. That should be enough without any telephone conversation. I'll dismantle the protection that Carlton Flint so nobly afforded him to steer him away from the horrendous truth of his nephew's demonic deeds. Now where's his photo? I know, I put it in another file. Here we go then.

Ashley Forbes was actually with his brother, Edward, Randal's father, when he suddenly felt very drowsy.

"Are you OK, Ash?" asked Edward as he watched his brother's eyelids droop in mid-conversation.

"Just a bit tired, I guess."

"Well, I'd better be going now anyway. Margaret wants me to fix the kitchen cupboard. The carpenter didn't do a good job apparently," he tutted, raising his eyes.

"OK, Ted. See you soon. Love to everyone," murmured Ashley, practically asleep in his chair.

"Don't get up, I'll see myself out. Tell Julia goodbye." He smiled.

The minute Edward left, Ashley fell into a deep sleep. When he awoke, he was puzzled for the moment, but then he yawned, stretched and switched on the radio to hear one of his favourite broadcasts. His wife, Julia, was in the kitchen baking an assortment of cakes.

Then suddenly he felt very depressed. His head was like a tight band of despair and his heart was as heavy as a lump of lead.

What's the matter with me? Something's not right.

He got up to speak to Julia and he was halfway to the kitchen when the truth hit him so hard, he thought he would vomit on the carpet.

Randal killed Spencer! He willed him to jump off that motorway bridge! Carlton Flint told me and tried to help me! Oh my God! I do remember going to Carlton's house with a copy of Spencer's letter and list. That horrendous list of victims that Randal had annihilated!

That policeman who phoned me up eight years ago, just after Flint died, was right! Francine Flint had told him that her husband had helped me. I denied it. I thought someone was out there making trouble for Randal. Oh my word. Why has this come back to me now? Why did I forget for so long? Maybe I had a breakdown.

I drove back home devastated and yet… and yet I forgot! Randal was waiting for me at my house. I was so delighted to see him! Why?

Why after what I'd been told? This can't be true. My beloved nephew a murderer! A telepathic assassin!

Carlton was also gifted, but he was the essence of goodness. Carlton must have wiped away all memory of that terrible day out of compassion, eradicated Spencer's letter and list from my mind. Where's that list now? Oh, dear Lord. Carlton's dead too! Randal again?

There's only one thing for it. I have to see Randal and confront him. Ted said he's in Scotland but I'm going to ring him to come home. I need to know the truth and I pray that somehow, I've got this all wrong. All wrong. He's got to convince me. Face to face. Even at the risk of his wrath.

***

Randal was feeling relaxed and happy in Clive's uplifting company when Roxanne spoke to him telepathically.

Daddy, it's me. You need to come home now! It's urgent!

Randal stopped laughing and cocked his head to one side.

"What's the matter?" asked Clive when he saw Randal pull away.

"Shh. It's Roxanne. She's in my head now. She's upset."

Clive felt a frisson of alarm but kept quiet while Randal communicated with her.

What's the matter, pumpkin? Are you OK?

Daddy, please come home! Tyrone phoned Mummy about us. She knows about you and Maxine. Also, Lady Pennington. Not to mention Marcus and Uncle Clive. She's devastated. She doesn't know what to believe. He's very convincing and I feel he's going to contact other people whose lives have been affected by 'the gift'. He's just called Ryan and now he looks shell-shocked. I think he's de-hypnotised him. He's looking at me with real desire again. So be prepared for everyone's pain. We've got to remove Tyrone. He's insane!

What! *I'll have his head on a plate! We parted on good terms. I blocked off my wrath, so he must have listened into one of my conversations and found out how I really feel about him! I should have realised he was in my head!*

But you'd know! Even subconsciously, you'd know!

Just a minute! I know what he's done! He's gone through Clive! He's watched and listened through Clive's unsuspecting eyes and ears. That fucking piece of unadulterated faecal matter! Does he think his dangerous rants will do the trick? Expose my secrets and lies? He's barking up the wrong tittle-tattle tree!

He just wants to cause as much unrest and heartbreak as he can before he tries to remove us. He wants to bring you down to our family and friends.

Does he now? We'll see about that! I came here to unwind because of his underhand treatment of you, and his second-rate absorption of my teachings. He's dead, Roxanne! Stone dead!

I'll help you, Daddy. You can't do it on your own. I don't want you to argue with me about this. I can feel his wrath. It's very strong. More powerful than you've given him credit for. I'm not comparing or judging your dominance. I'm just telling you what I feel. I'm not a child so I'm more capable. I have to help you.

Yes, pumpkin. I agree. This will be a joint eradication.

But now you have to come home! There's a lot of people you need to reassure. Not just Mummy. There's Ryan, Dean and Uncle Ashley. Oh, and Marcus.

I'm on my way. I'll make it right with a lot of autosuggestion. Then when they're all pacified, we'll wipe that loose-tongued tyro off the face of the earth!

***

Randal returned home early with Clive into a storm of suspicion and accusation. Before he arrived, Alison had received calls for him from Dean, his Uncle Ashley and Marcus Pennington, enquiring why they could not reach him on his mobile. All of them sounded desperate and highly agitated.

She had felt an irate urgency in every request, but when she asked them if she could pass on a message, they clammed up and told her that it was only Randal who could put their minds at rest, or words to that effect.

The call that had unsettled her the most was Marcus's. She knew that he was mentally unstable, and had been since the fire and the death of his grandfather, not to mention his suicide attempt. He had never phoned up in all the years after that tragedy.

Is he disgusted with Randal over his mother? Is it remotely possible that Tyrone is telling the truth? Has he alerted Marcus to the same scandalous accusation? Oh, I'm so disturbed and upset.

Randal had phoned her previously from Scotland to say he was purposefully coming home early due to other commitments that had cropped up. She told him that Tyrone had called and that it had disturbed her.

"Randal, I desperately need to speak to you but not on the phone. When you get home, we have to talk right away," she said in a serious manner.

"Are you OK?" he replied, knowing full well that she was not.

"Just get back, Randal. It's too complicated to discuss now."

Randal wanted Clive with him to face the music. Apart from anything else, he had to convince Alison that they were just close and special friends.

The minute they walked through the door she berated him, her face pale and lined from lack of sleep.

"I've had the most nauseating phone call from Tyrone while you were away. He's accused you both of having… of a physical relationship. Not platonic but sexual! He said you've been together like that for years! Since you were both fifteen! Fifteen, for Christ's sake!" she yelled.

"He's insane, Alison! Insanely jealous of my life and family. He can't have Roxanne, so he wants to tear us all apart. It's lies.

Lies on a global scale," assured Randal convincingly. "Please tell her, Clive! Make her see how wrong he is!"

Clive cleared his throat then concocted the most award-winning fabrication of his Randal-obsessed life.

"It's not true! I admit that I'm in love with Randal, and I fancy him like crazy. Who doesn't, Alison? But that's as far as I'll ever get with him, worse luck. You're his only love. He's never strayed, and I should know. All he wants is you and the children."

"Honestly, Clive?" she wept.

"Honestly," he lied magnificently, hating himself for doing so.

Alison buried her head in Randal's shoulder as he stroked her hair and whispered words of love in her ear. At the same time, he winked at Clive with gratitude. He mouthed 'I love you' to him, and Clive's heart stalled.

"I love you, too," replied Clive, mouthing the same sentiment with guilty eyes.

"There are more accusations, Randal. They're so disturbing. Tyrone said that you've been having an affair with Lady Pennington since the first day you met her! It was that weekend, years ago, when both Clive and I were invited to Clarendon Hall. On top of that, Marcus has now phoned wanting to talk to you. He sounded livid. Why? What's going on? I want the truth! Have you ever been to bed with Fiona Pennington? I need to know!" she wept.

"Alison, don't you see? Tyrone's been phoning round my immediate circle, making trouble and planting suspicious seeds in their heads to bring me down. He's a psychopath! Plain and simple. His claims are ludicrous, designed to wound and shock. He's more to be pitied. Look, sweetheart, I'll talk to everyone and make it right. Once I explain, they'll totally understand what I'm up against. I promise to make this all go away, including Tyrone. Especially Tyrone," he soothed, his eyes glinting dangerously in the middle of the afternoon.

"There's something else. The worst accusation of all. He said... he said that Roxanne is really your blood child. That she was the result of an affair with Maxine. That she's the same as you. Telepathic and dangerous, and that you're both killers. We need to phone the police, Randal. I'm scared stiff of him." She shuddered.

Randal was practically exploding with rage. He had to summon up all his powers to hide his murderous intent.

"Just leave him to me. I'll make very sure that he won't bother us again. Law or no law. Knock it out of your head now. He's not worth the worry. Let's just be thankful we've found him out. It could have been a lot worse. He's out of Roxanne's life."

"But he could still find a way of harming her!"

"Trust me, Alison. I won't let you down! I'm going to call up Dean, Uncle Ashley and Marcus, and put their minds at rest too," he reassured her.

"Ryan's terribly upset. He also got a call from Tyrone and he's not spoken to me since. Whatever he said has knocked him for six. I can't get him to open up. He said he needs to speak to you and you alone," she sighed deeply.

"Has he gone back to Oxford? I really don't want him anywhere near that psycho!"

"But he loves being at Beaumont College. It's Tyrone who should stay away, not Ryan," she justified.

"I agree, and that's my main aim, Alison. To make him disappear for good!"

She nodded as Randal asked her to put the coffee on for him and Clive, pacifying her further to a large degree. As soon as she left them, Clive whispered his fears.

"This is some heavy shit! You're in it up to your neck! There's no hiding place. He's stolen all your moves. You've tutored him well. There'll have to be a lot of explaining to out-manoeuvre him. A hell of a lot of lying, manipulating and convincing."

"Don't you worry, Clive. I'll get round it all. You know I can do the impossible. But I'll tell you something now. When Roxanne and I have finished with that black-sheep louse, that outcast-racketeered mutation, he'll be pushing up rapscallion daisies from so deep underground that even the worms won't reach his unprincipled remains. He's simply a clear-cut case of justifiable homicide. The clearest one yet!"

9

Randal spent quite some time pacifying his victims in order of emergency. Number one on his list was his Uncle Ashley, who was out of his mind with confusion and angst. He phoned him, only to be told by his wife, Julia, that Ashley was actually driving to Weybridge to see him.

"He tried to call you numerous times, but your mobile was unattainable. Anyway, something's really bad, Randal, because when I asked him why he was so disturbed, he just buttoned his lip. Whatever it is has forced him to make the journey from here to your house. He told me that it was imperative for him to speak to you. He looked pale and unwell, so will you let me know when he arrives because I'm very anxious about him," she concluded in a troubled voice.

"Of course, I will. What time did he set off?"

"Very early this morning. He should be with you any time now."

"I've only just returned from Scotland. Clive and I were staying in a remote cottage to work on my book. My mobile was switched off most of the time but also the signal was faint. Anyway, Aunty Julia, you've got me just as concerned, but don't worry. I'll look after him and call you when he turns up. OK?"

Julia thanked him and sighed as she put down the phone. Randal cursed to himself.

Fuck! I had it all worked out. I was just going to put him back into a reduplicated form of forgetfulness. I have to modify the script. Pronto!

Ten minutes later the doorbell rang far too many times. Randal did not have to look outside to know that his uncle had arrived. Alison got there first.

"Uncle Ashley! What a surprise! Randal didn't say you were coming," she gushed.

"I bet he didn't! Is he home?" replied Ashley sternly with angry eyes.

Alison did not recognise this version of the kindly uncle who always looked dapper, welcoming and warm.

"He's been in Scotland, but he's back now. Is everything all right? Only you look rather unwell. Are you OK?" She frowned.

"Let me see him! Where is he? I'll break his bloody neck!" he exploded as he pushed his way past her in agitation and disarray, all caution thrown to the wind.

Alison gasped but then her brain clicked into gear. *It must be that evil Tyrone! He's poisoned his mind, like he did mine! Randal will sort this all out.*

"Uncle Ashley, please! Calm down! Randal will explain everything to you. Whatever you've been told, well, it's all lies. All of it!" she pleaded.

"Told? Told! Nobody has told me anything! I just remembered something I'd pushed away. Something so evil it beggars belief! So now, Alison, where's my devious, demonic nephew?" he snarled, completely out of character.

"Here I am, Uncle Ashley," appeased Randal, as he strolled casually into the hallway.

"You… you… you *murderer*! You killed my son! You killed Spencer!" yelled Ashley, red in the face with rage.

"Alison, please leave us alone because there's a lot to discuss," he said softly, as if it was just a friendly get-together.

She nodded as Randal led his enraged uncle into the large open-plan sitting room.

"*Please!* Now please take a seat, and let me explain. Do you want a drink or something to eat first? It's a very long drive from your house to mine," he enquired politely.

"A drink! Something to eat! You can wipe that false smile off your devious face for a bloody start! Let's not play games, Randal! You know why I'm here and you know what you did!"

"But I don't. I truly don't, Uncle Ash."

"Oh, you don't! Not much you don't! Just two names! Spencer and Carlton! My son, your cousin Spencer and the gifted astrologer, Carlton Flint! Ring a bell somewhere in your evil head?"

"I really haven't got a clue what you're talking about."

"Haven't you? You don't seem at all surprised by my impromptu visit! Normally you'd be full of curiosity and greatly pleased to see me!"

"I am pleased to see you, and you're right on the other count. I was expecting you."

"Oh, were you now? I doubt it! In fact, I'd go so far as to say that you're quite put out but hiding all that evil, twisted insanity that you camouflage so well. You've broken my heart in two! You killed my son, and now you've killed my love for you! My grief is twofold! Your father, my dearest brother, will be totally inconsolable. I'm so wretchedly disturbed by this whole horror story that my fear of any telepathic retaliation has not deterred me from facing you with my detestation and abhorrence of your true self," he admonished, his eyes filling with unshed tears.

Randal was genuinely, deeply saddened to see his uncle agonising and needed to think quickly on his feet to rectify the grave situation.

I can't let him suffer like this. This will be a quick but thorough hypnotic reversal.

Randal's eyes glowed and Ashley fell into a deep sleep as he spoke to his mind.

When you wake up you won't remember anything bad. You'll think you called on me out of fondness because I've not visited you for a while due to my workload. You'll tell Aunty Julia that you needed to speak about Spencer and that every now and then the grief swamps you, and I'm the one who can comfort you.

You'll never respond to any other autosuggestion in the future except mine. Anyone else will be dismissed. Your love for me is overflowing. Eternal.

Randal left him sleeping on the couch and re-joined Alison in another room.

"Randal, is he OK? Did you explain? Oh, he looks so upset. Tyrone needs locking up. He's obviously convinced him that you killed Spencer! How could he do that to a kind, unassuming gentleman like Uncle Ash? It's monstrous!" she wailed.

"It's fine. I've filled him in on the whole nasty mess. He understands and he's fallen asleep due to the long drive."

"Put a cushion behind his head, Randal. Make him comfortable. He's a very precious member of this family."

"Yes. Yes, he is," he agreed, "but then so are Ryan and Dean, who have also been affected by Tyrone's insanity. I have to speak to them both in turn."

"Of course you do. Oh, Randal, I'm so glad you're home. I don't think I would have coped if you'd been out of the country."

"Well, I'm not. You've got me larger than life itself. Give me a hug before I make some calls, not forgetting Aunty Julia, who's very worried about Uncle Ash. Apparently, he just decided to drive here without any explanation," he said, opening his arms.

Alison did not need asking twice. She fell into his embrace as always and he kissed her tenderly. He sat her down as he hypnotised her into a responsive trance.

Now my beautiful, sexy wife, I've got to wipe away Uncle Ashley's accusation from your mind. You will forget that he called me Spencer's murderer. You'll also believe that he's made a visit out of his need for solace and compassion. At the click of my fingers, you'll snap out of this hypnotic state and just go about your daily routine as if nothing disturbing has occurred today. One, two, three, clickety click.

Alison yawned and rubbed her eyes. "Oh, that's funny, Rand, I forgot what I was going to ask you," she puzzled.

"You were going to put the kettle on for Uncle Ash, and I'll have a cup of your delightful percolated coffee too. Please?" He smiled. The Randal-smile.

"Of course, I was. You know, Uncle Ash thinks the world of you. He could have easily spoken to you on the phone about missing Spencer but instead he's driven all this way to see his beloved nephew. You comfort him, Randal. It's very touching."

"I guess. I know he can't talk to my dad about it. Even though they're close, Dad still thinks that Spencer was unforgivably selfish to do what he did. I've tried to convince him that he was mentally unstable, but he still won't relent. Uncle Ash won't discuss his grief with Aunty Julia because it upsets her too much, and he can't speak to James because he's still grieving for his brother. Sad," he said reflectively.

"There's no-one on this earth like you, Randal. You've such empathy with people in need. I'm so proud to be your wife. I love you so much."

Ditto my sweet Alison. And now I've got to pacify all the others with 'the gift' and superior charm, because I have to be a demigod again in their adoring eyes.

***

Both Randal and Alison were very concerned about Ryan. He was not answering his mobile and had not responded to the several voicemails they had left for him.

"I'm going to drive down to Oxford," said Randal after checking out Ryan's riotous thoughts telepathically.

"But you could bump into Tyrone! I don't trust him one tiny bit. He's bitter, vicious and vengeful!" she exclaimed.

"He doesn't frighten me. What concerns me more is Ryan's lack of response," he pointed out.

"I'm coming with you. I'll only sit here worrying and imagining things," she fretted.

"I don't need you to. It's best I go alone. He'll clam up altogether if we both confront him, then we'll never get to the root of his silence," he accurately forecasted.

"I suppose. Still… promise you'll keep in touch, otherwise I'll be frantic. You didn't hear the tone of Tyrone's spurious rant. He sounded very convincing with a sinister, threatening edge," she recalled with a shudder, and Randal fumed.

I'll give him a sinister, threatening edge to chew on!

Randal's mobile rang and he frowned when he saw it was Dean.

"Dean's calling me. Let me talk to him at length. It's obviously about Tyrone's accusations. I'll speak to him, but don't listen in, it'll only upset you when I explain the circumstances," he suggested ingeniously, in order to throw Alison off the trail of lies.

"I'll make some coffee then. Just put Dean's mind at rest." She half-smiled.

"Yes, Dean. I was expecting your call," said Randal, preparing his fabricated script.

"I've tried to get you so many times! Are you still in Scotland? I desperately need to talk to you."

"I'm at home, but I'm off to Oxford shortly to pacify Ryan, who's also been alerted to a deluge of lies by Tyrone Pendle. I presume you're ringing about the same," he said deceitfully.

"Tyrone Pendle? You mean Ryan's friend from Beaumont College?"

"Ex-friend. You see, Dean, Tyrone's in lust with Roxanne, and she responded. He knows she's underage but took advantage of her crush on him. I won't go into it, but suffice to say he's had his dirty hands all over her. I'm livid. So I told him to vamoose in no uncertain terms. His response to the ban was to make up a barrage of villainous, brutal and dangerous stories about me to the people who matter most in my life, namely Alison, Ryan, Uncle Ashley and your good self. He even called Marcus Pennington and played on his insanity. He's ruthless. I don't know what he told you, Dean, but it was designed to make you doubt my love and affection for you and others. He's psychotic and needs locking up for his own good as well as mine."

"I've not been able to sleep since he called me. He knows everything about my past!"

"Unfortunately, Roxanne said she could have discussed private matters when she was drunk. The arsehole plied her with booze before he assaulted her. She thought she loved him and trusted him not to repeat any of their conversation. What did he tell you? Don't hold back because I need to know what callous crimes he's accused me of committing. He said the most diabolical things to Alison. She's also very disturbed by his heinous fairy tales," expounded Randal convincingly.

"Oh God, Randal, as dreadful as all this is, it's such a relief to hear your side because I've been going out of my mind with doubt and suspicion. He even had me suspecting you of the things he said. He was *that* convincing!"

"What did he say, Dean?"

"It's insane. He said you're a psychotic psychic and can control people's minds through their photographs. He accused you of killing my real father, John Sterling, and then my half-brother, Robbie. Additionally, according to him, you also hypnotised Raymond Haynes to kill his wife and then caused Nick and his two sisters to drown in the lake years ago – that day when we were both in the park. He was adamant that you see me as your creation, saved from an illegal abortion and felt it only right to murder the people who had caused me grief," he groaned.

"How surreal and ridiculous is that, Dean? I thought I had a creative imagination, but Tyrone Pendle beats me hands down. He's round the twist."

"I know, but that's only the half of it."

"What else?" sighed Randal, preparing himself for another accusatory litany.

"It's absurd, but he accused you of hypnotising Francine Flint to kill Dr Ramsey. He said that Roxanne has the same dark gift and she murdered Stella Reid and injured Carlton, who survived, but then when he was hospitalised, you mesmerised the nurse to give him a lethal dose of morphine. The police were suspicious of you and you couldn't risk that, so you made the detective throw himself under a train and induced Francine to commit suicide by jumping out of the prison window."

"He deserves the Booker Prize for innovation and inventiveness. He's certifiable."

"I know. One last thing. He said you were the author of *The Flawed Flints* and you wrote it to exacerbate Maddie's condition because you want to split us up for good."

"I can't lie to you, Dean. That's the truth. I hold my hands up to that one. I wanted you to realise the depth of her psychosis, and how it would affect you both as a partnership. I'm sorry if it caused you pain, but I felt it was necessary. Your mum knew about it as well. She's been worried sick with concern," he admitted.

"You should have told me, Randal. Anyway, you'll be pleased to hear that I've called it a day. You were right, but you didn't have to be so underhanded," he scolded.

"I'm truly sorry, but it was inevitable anyway. She's unmanageable and not for you."

"Got to go now, but I'm so relieved to hear your side. Tyrone is obviously out of his skull. Be careful, Randal. I love you."

"Love you too, and see you soon." *You're safe, Dean, but Tyrone's dead and buried.*

After talking to Dean, Randal kissed Alison goodbye then set off for Oxford. His thoughts were very active as he drove along the motorway.

I've got to repair Ryan's troubled soul. It won't take too long to appease him. After that, it's Clarendon Hall in Banbury. By the time I've finished with Marcus, the lady of the manor will have him committed again. For life!

Ryan was knocking back several glasses of beer at the students' bar with some friends when Randal walked in unannounced.

"Hey, Ryan! Isn't that your dad? He looks so cool. I wish mine dressed like him!"

Ryan's eyes narrowed as Randal made his way over. He wore a royal blue velvet suit with an open-necked denim shirt that sported an ultramarine cravat round his neck. The outfit would have looked totally absurd on another fellow contemporary, but only succeeded in enhancing Randal's stylish, charismatic aura. He smouldered as all heads turned in admiration and recognition.

"I thought I'd find you here. This was a favourite watering hole of mine and Clive's. We need to talk, so can we go somewhere less raucous?" he suggested firmly.

"I don't want to go anywhere with you," slurred Ryan, jutting out his bottom lip in a childish manner.

"I'm not asking. I'm ordering," demanded Randal, his eyes glinting dangerously in the semi-darkness of the room.

"Oh, you're ordering! Well, that's all right then! What Randal Forbes orders, he always gets! Doesn't he just? Now let's just stop for a minute so I can observe your eyes! I'll just hang on until they glow!" mocked Ryan hazardously.

Randal moved closer and whispered in his son's ear.

"Now, I'll ask you nicely one more time to come with me, otherwise I'll drag you out by your inherited red hair, in front of this very inquisitive and intrusive gathering of young reprobates. Do you understand me? I know that Tyrone has spoken to you. Our whole family is under threat from him, so I've not got time for your juvenile strops. It's imperative that we talk. Now!"

Randal's words resonated and Ryan felt a compulsion to respond.

"Tyrone's phone call has knocked me so sick that I threw up twice, and yes, Father, it's highly imperative that we talk. You've got a lot of explaining to do. I'm a fucking mess. Because of him! Because of you! Because of Roxanne!" He glared.

"Let's go," urged Randal.

"Where are we going?" asked Ryan in a flat voice, feeling suddenly sober.

"To the Botanic Gardens. It's quiet and private. Clive and I sat there many years ago when we had an issue to sort out. Funnily enough it was over your mother. Clive was pissed and he'd knocked her flying on to the floor. Accidentally, of course."

"Well, there's more than one issue to sort out, Dad. Much, much more." He grimaced.

They found the exact form that Randal had sat on with Clive in 1976 when they had discussed Clive's possessiveness and his drunken state. Randal remembered their conversation with a mixture of sentiment and regret.

So many years ago, now. We were young and carefree in comparison. He was always so melodramatic over Alison and my other relationships. I was insufferable, though, blasé and unfeeling. I didn't realise how deeply affected he was by my dalliances. I was so full of 'the gift' and its blossoming force. He took second place to everything, even though I kept him happy. Oh, the self-centredness of youth.

He lit up a cheroot and composed himself before he spoke.

"Tell me exactly what Tyrone said," he asked, straight out. "He's succeeded in disturbing everyone who means the world to me with his outright, scandalous lies."

"I don't know where to begin," replied Ryan mournfully.

"Let's take it point by point. In your own time," encouraged Randal.

Ryan took a deep, lager-lined breath. However, his recollection of that toxic conversation was crystal-clear.

"I want the truth, Dad. Is Roxanne my real sister? Tyrone said she was conceived with Maxine Hale, in a one-night, sordid stand. With you!" he accused.

"Roxanne's your sister on paper only. Your mother and I adopted her out of compassion and a mutual desire to nurture and protect her after her birth parents had both died in such tragic circumstances. Tyrone's a compulsive, dangerous liar, totally hell-bent on destroying my reputation, simply because I've kicked him into touch since he defiled Roxanne. It's his sick way of retaliating, alerting my close family to evil, cock-and-bull fabrications, designed to wound and scandalise. He's been a busy little badass bee, contacting your mother, Dean, Uncle Ashley and even the permanently damaged Marcus Pennington, with the most outrageous and libellous allegations against my character. He's insane. A first-class psycho with a sadistic and guileful streak, and if you even remotely believe him, then he's won," lied Randal convincingly.

Ryan sighed deeply and looked closely into Randal's alien eyes.

"You told me that 'the gift' and 'the starman' were all part of a game. Tyrone said it was real and that you and Roxanne are telepathic murderers who killed Maxine and Saul so that she could live with us. Also, you wanted Carlton Flint dead because he had the same powers but used them for good. You killed him because he was benevolent."

"And these things happen on a regular basis in everyday life, don't they? How could you even begin to believe such nonsensical twaddle?" asked Randal, perfecting his puzzlement beautifully.

"He was so sure. Tyrone said that he was your pupil and you were coaching him in the dark arts but now you want to kill him too because he knows so much about you."

Randal got hold of Ryan's hands and took them in his own.

"Listen to me. Tyrone's playing with your head. He's ill, really ill. He can't stand the fact that Roxanne has dumped him. In his mind he's done nothing wrong. He assaulted her, Ryan. That's a serious offence against a minor. I could report him to the police, but Roxanne won't let me. She just wants to forget that the whole thing ever happened."

"I so get that, but why did he call you a serial killer? Roxanne as well. Why would he make that up? And how did he know about that time years ago when I asked you about 'the gift' and 'the starman'? I never told him anything. It's unnerving!"

"Exactly! *He's* unnerving! Any information he had on all of us came from Roxanne. She was under the false notion that she loved him. He took advantage of that by plying her with booze to loosen her tongue. She told me she should never have confided in him about anything and that includes your misconception about 'the gift' and 'the starman', which, by the way, was a game, a very important game that helped her through her troubled childhood. I told you about it when you were ten years old. That's all it was, Ryan. An amusing distraction, an entertaining diversion away from her grief and mood swings over the loss of Maxine and Saul."

"I so want to believe you."

"Then believe. You can't possibly buy into Tyrone's ludicrous explanation."

"Why does Roxanne look the image of you if she's not related? You've always put her first, Dad. Way above me, Amber and even Oscar. Mum falls in with all her needs on your say-so. Why? There's something more. I've always felt it."

"You have to remember that Maxine had the exact same colouring as a Forbes. In fact, someone once asked me if she was my sister. Roxanne's inherited her looks, not mine. And yes, I have favoured her welfare too much. I don't mean to, but she's touched my heart. She's feisty but vulnerable. I've always felt she needed more affection than the rest of you. She's an orphan, Ryan, and I guess I just want to shelter her. I didn't mean to leave you out. I love all my children equally, it's just that she's always clingier, and I respond, rightly or wrongly, to that need. I see Maxine's face every time she speaks. It's so sad," he said convincingly.

"Not her eyes, though! She's got your eyes. You both have that same molten stare when you're annoyed. Tyrone said they flash when you're both in killer mode."

"Have you heard yourself, Ryan? Have you ever seen my eyes 'flash'? Or Roxanne's?"

"No, but I've seen them glitter with anger. Hers are the same. Slate-grey with those yellow-glinting flecks. That weird expression. It's so daunting. Like she's in my head and knows what I'm thinking."

Randal sighed dramatically before he continued fabricating.

"This is crazy talk now. The only explanation I can give you is that Maxine's eyes were green and Saul's were very dark. Roxanne's a mixture of the two of them. It's pure coincidence that they're slate-grey and flecked like mine. Granted, they are similar, but that's as far as it goes."

Ryan nodded as he absorbed Randal's version of things.

Dad seems so genuinely concerned. Surely he's not lying? Tyrone's done a good job on me. It was all autosuggestion. His words drugged me with doubt and suspicion. But Dad's come all the way out here to clear his name and show me that he cares. Look at his eyes now. They're full of consideration and compassion. He's my father, for Christ's sake! Why am I letting that little shit get to me? Because he really has. I must tell Dad what he's done and wants to do!

"He wants to kill you, Dad. He means to kill us all. He's full of hatred! I'm scared stiff. He said he caused his father to put that plastic bag over his mother's head and kill her, and that he's not finished annihilating the rest of his family. He's unsettled Mum as well. She looked devastated after his call. He said he told her about your infidelities. What the fuck does he mean, Dad? On a human level."

"On a human level? He doesn't have one, Ryan. He's three sheets to the wayward wind. Several screws loose from a crowded toolbox. He's supposed to be your friend. He's turned out to be a formidable enemy. Anyone who can fabricate such outlandish stories, designed to disturb, should not be allowed to roam free. He belongs in an asylum, well sedated."

"So, it's all lies then? All of it?"

"Every single word and punctuation mark."

"I'm so sorry for ignoring your calls. Mums, too. I've been out of my mind with suspicion and doubt. What kind of person would do that to a friend?"

"He's not your friend, Ryan. He used you to get to me. Remember, he's a budding writer and he knew I had the connections to help him sprint up the literary ladder. He's mimicked my academic footsteps and was well versed on my likes and dislikes. He flattered me and I fell for it. I saw something in him that I could nurture. He does have a gift for the written word and because his own family thought he was wasting his time, I wanted to help him prove his worth to them. They should have encouraged his ambition, but they just dismissed it. I thought that was wrong. He also wanted Roxanne. He had it all planned out. He fooled us all."

"About Roxanne. I've got a confession. You're going to freak out, but I can't hide it. I've… I've got feelings for her. I think I've always been in love with her from way back. It's eating me up because it's still wrong even though she's not blood. I can't help it. It's so strong. Don't hate me," he pleaded.

"Hate you? How could I ever hate you, Ryan? You're my firstborn. We can't always help the people we fall in love with. But it's still wrong. Roxanne's damaged and vulnerable, and it would cause untold complication. But thank you for your honesty. We'll talk about it again. In the meantime, forget Tyrone Pendle. I'll deal with him. Now come here and give your dad a hug. You're still not too old to do that," he said softly, and Ryan clung to him like a child, as he put him in a trance.

Your hot love for Roxanne will now be platonic. Your burning desire will be gone and you'll just be protective, as an older brother should be. It's for the best.

So now it's off to Clarendon Hall and it's cuckoo son and heir.

***

Marcus was in a frenzied state and his parents could not calm him down.

"I've phoned his wife, Alison, umpteen times and she just tells me he's in Scotland with his lover! His long-suffering, gay protector!" he snarled.

Fiona Pennington frowned deeply at his words and aggressive unrest.

"What on earth are you talking about, Marcus?"

"Him! Satan's partner in telepathic crime! The one who impersonates a caring, philanthropic, altruistic genius! The red-haired fiend with a personality so fragmented and split, it's as cracked as an earthquake's epicentre!" he raved.

"Now settle down, Marcus. This is doing you no good whatsoever. We really don't know what you're talking about, so please try to behave in a more undisturbed manner," pleaded his father, Miles.

"Oh well, I'll just go and take my tranquilisers, then, shall I? How many years have I been on medication? Let me think. Oh, since Halloween 1977. Not to mention the thousands of anti-depressants and anti-agitation pills. And do you want to know why? Do you want to know who caused my so-called psychosis? Do you want to know who led me down the rack-and-ruin route? Huh?"

"Marcus, please! You're not making any sense. I don't want you to be ill again, so just try to calm down," begged Fiona.

"You don't want me ill again! But do you want to know who's to blame for all my lost years? Do you? Mother dear," he mocked.

"Now you're really scaring me."

"Well, I'll tell you who. Can't you guess? It's none other than, and here comes the fanfare of trumpets, none other than Randal Edward Forbes. Yes, him! *Your fucking lover!*" yelled Marcus, and Fiona nearly passed out.

"Marcus! Your behaviour is appalling! Scandalous!" rebuked Miles. "Apologise to your mother at once!"

"Apologise? It's true, isn't it, Mummy? He's been screwing you repeatedly since the day you met him. Creeping into the marital bed behind Father's back, whether he was in or out of the hall. He knows this place like the back of his black magic hand. Just like he knows every inch of your traitorous body!"

"Right! That's it, Marcus! I'm going to phone your psychiatrist. You need help again," confirmed Miles, getting up from his chair.

"No, no, no! That's not it! Not it, at all! You need to hear the whole truth before you make any unnecessary phone calls. So, if you just sit back down and listen to me, I'd appreciate it. Please?"

Miles sighed deeply and Fiona's heart was beating so fast she thought she was going to faint. *Oh my word, he knows! How? Why now? After all these years?*

"Now settle down, children, while I tell you a story. Are you sitting comfortably? Then I'll begin." Marcus took a deep breath before he put them in the sordid picture.

"Once upon a time there were three students at Beaumont College, in Oxford. One of them was me, the second one was

Clive Hargreaves, and the third was Randal Forbes. I had a soft spot, shall we say, for Clive, but he was madly in love with Randal who led him a merry bi-sexual dance.

"One spring afternoon in 1977, Clive, Randal and his girlfriend, Alison, now his unsuspecting wife, well, they were all invited to Clarendon. I had strong feelings for Clive. Randal had the hots for Alison.

"It turned out that she wasn't enough for him because he found his way to my mother's boudoir, where he corrupted her with his special brand of highly sexed lust. After that neither of them could get enough. So, over the years he's been jet-setting backward and forward to the hall and into my mother's bed. That's right, isn't it, Mother dearest?"

Fiona was speechless with shock and shame. She opened her mouth, but nothing came out, and Miles put a different interpretation on her reaction.

"Marcus! Look what you're doing to your mother! She's horrified! Apologise immediately for your inexcusable accusation!" he barked.

"I've not finished! There's more to the story. You see, Randal is really a psychotic psychic and a serial killer. I always suspected and invited him here so that Gramps could meet him. Gramps felt he was evil, but he made a mistake in thinking an exorcism would expel the so-called demon inside him.

"Clive told me in a roundabout way that Randal was his own antichrist, so I alerted Gramps to that theory, and in the end, he backed off because I was scared of any retaliation.

"So, what did Randal do? As part of his revenge, he hypnotised me to call on gramps with a bag of tricks. Inside was a gun, some rope and a canister of kerosene. Under Randal's unholy instructions, I threatened Gramps with the gun, tied him to a chair, then sprinkled the paraffin all over the rectory and set fire to it, killing him.

"Then I ran outside with another length of rope and hanged

myself from the oak tree. All under Randal's spell on Halloween. He purposely chose that night to avenge the witches who were burned at the stake. His ultimate thrill was to do the same act to a priest.

"He wanted me dead, but because he was screwing my wayward mother, he decided to save me. But I had to pay the price. I had excruciating pain in my throat and no voice for years. He wiped my memory banks clean so I wouldn't remember anything. Every visit he has paid me of late has been designed to gloat and revel in the success of his telepathic crime.

"And *that*, dear Mother, and *that* is an accurate picture of the ever-smiling, charming charlatan you've been screwing for the past twenty-three years. He killed your father callously and gleefully, and caused my insanity. Lovely man, isn't he?" growled Marcus.

"Oh, dear God, Marcus, you're so ill again. You're breaking my heart in two. I really thought you were getting better every day. You seemed to come alive again because of… Randal. Because of his visits. And now you're accusing him of such ungodly things. It's… it's… beyond words," she wept.

"Ungodly things? That's right on the button, Mother. Ungodly things." He stared at her with angry eyes, as his father stepped in on his wife's behalf.

"Why has it taken you all these years to concoct such a story? What's happened to you? How can you dredge up such disturbing and traumatic lies? You've never mentioned this to us before. Ever. Now don't despair, I think you're ill again and it's manifested itself this time in delusion. I want to help you, son."

"I heard a voice in my head. It told me everything. At first, I thought it was my psychosis, but whoever or whatever it was alerted me to the truth. Everything came flooding back at once. All the lost years. I remembered it vividly, as though it was just yesterday. I'm not mad. You've got to believe me. And I'm not lying about Mother's infidelity either. She knows it's the truth even though she won't admit it!" he sniped pugnaciously.

Fiona hung her head for fear of Miles seeing her conscious-stricken face. She was beside herself with humiliation and guilt.

A car crunched up the gravel path and Marcus walked to the huge front windows to see who was calling.

"Well, what do you know? Guess who it is? Talk of the devil incarnate," he mocked, but his face grew ugly.

"Good Lord, it's Randal," confirmed Miles, as he looked through the window. "How fortuitous that he's called round now. We need to confront him with all this nonsense and dispel the false memories that are swirling around in your head, Marcus," he urged.

"Fortuitous? Fortuitous! Oh no, Father! He knows! He knows that I know! And that's why he's chosen to call round to see us. He's either going to hypnotise me out of my recollections or remove me altogether to a higher plane of existence, specifically, my demise."

Fiona was beside herself with fear.

Oh no! How am I going to hide my love for Randal now? What will he do when Marcus accuses him of our lifelong affair? And what about the rest of his disturbing concoction of events? I must warn him quickly. I'll greet him. I must behave normally. I simply must.

"Adams has a day off, so I'll go and let Randal in," she said casually with a heavy beating heart.

"No! I'll let him in! After all, I'm the son and heir of this estate, am I not?"

"Yes, Marcus. Yes, you are," whispered Fiona.

Marcus ran along the whole length of the corridor into the hall to greet Randal, who was stood in the doorway with a playful smile.

"Why, hello, Marcus. I was expecting Adams to open the stately door, not the next in line to the Clarendon throne.

Have you been downgraded?" He grinned treacherously with glinting eyes.

"Less of the familiar, tasteless, acerbic wit, Randal. It suits you!" retorted Marcus deliberately.

"Well, are you going to invite me into the Pennington parlour for tea and taunting? It's rather chilly in this hallway. There's a definite coldness in the air, wouldn't you say?"

"You know that I know, don't you? That's why you're here unannounced, on another maverick mission with a murderous, dark edge!"

"Why, Master Pennington, what do you mean?" he provoked.

"I remember! All of it! Every single diabolical, evil, demonic, devastating bit of it! You killed my grandfather by using me as a host body. You hanged me from the oak tree and you're still fucking my mother! You're a total evil, vile, destructive piece of satanic shit! I'm not afraid of you anymore. I'm totally immune to your threats and nefarious aura!"

"Very poetical, Marcus. Maybe you should have been a writer instead of a firelighter."

"I'm going to kill you, Randal, and I don't care if I go down for it! I've got past caring!"

"Dear, oh dear, and here's me thinking you'd actually fallen for my anti-ecclesiastical charms. Only last month you were panting to get into my Calvin Klein underwear. Apart from the enormous erection that you hid behind a cushion, your thoughts were very transparent, and ever so pornographic. But let me tell you something, Marcus. You're not a patch on your desirable, insatiable mother. She's far more up my kinky back alley. I would screw her on a daily basis if my itinerary would let me, but as you know, I'm a very busy man."

Marcus turned blood-red and lunged at Randal, wrapping his hands around his throat. Lord and Lady Pennington came into view at that very moment and were horrified by their son's violent actions.

"*Marcus!* For God's sake, what are you doing?" shouted his father, running to Randal's aid.

"Don't you worry about him; he can defend himself! He's just letting you believe that he's human!" yelled Marcus, shaking Randal's head backwards and forwards as he tried to throttle him.

Randal began to choke, but his thoughts were alive and kicking.

I'll let this carry on without a fight. They'll think he's completely gaga and I'm at his brutal mercy.

"*Marcus!* Stop this right now!" exclaimed his father, sprinting to Randal's unnecessary rescue.

Marcus would not relinquish his stranglehold. Randal was turning blue on the outside but had bodily control within. He had no other choice now but to raid Marcus's head. The Penningtons were too preoccupied with saving him to even realise anything else was transpiring.

Listen closely, Marcus. I want you to stop what you're doing. Just stand completely upright and still.

Marcus instantly let go of Randal and stood motionless on the spot regardless of his father's intervention.

"Thank God! Oh, Randal," wept Fiona, as he fell to the ground in a fake manner of collapse, rubbing his neck and throat.

As Randal wretched, he still had control over Marcus's movements.

Behind his closed lids, Randal's eyes were glowing as he pillaged his brain. Marcus repeated his script, word for word, like some hypnotised newsreader with an autocue.

"I remember everything that I did. I wanted to do it. My grandfather found out I was gay. He was going to tell you all and I had to stop him. In those days it was taboo and shameful.

"I set fire to the rectory and unintentionally killed him, but I couldn't live with my guilt, or my homosexuality, so I hanged myself. But I didn't die.

"I lied about Randal, too. He's not screwing Mother. You see, I'm so in love with him it hurts. He won't touch me. I've dropped enough hints. I made it all up because I can't have him. I said to myself that if I kill him, then it will all go away. Then I'll be free of him and the torture. I'm making sense, aren't I? I'm not mad. I'm just obsessed. You do understand, don't you? Don't you? Don't you?" he repeated, staring through vacant eyes.

"Oh, he's so ill, so terribly ill," gasped Fiona, simultaneously devastated at the recurrence of her son's psychosis and enormously relieved over his retraction of her adultery.

"Randal, let me help you," offered Miles as he bent down to his prostrate form on the floor.

He was still gagging, but the bulk of it was exaggeration. Miles pulled him up slowly and steadied him as he found his feet.

"Randal, dear chap. What can I do to make amends for all of this?" pleaded Miles.

"I'm OK," he rasped. "Just see to Marcus. He's fragile."

"He needs help, Randal. I'm so dreadfully sorry you had to witness this and be on the end of his unbalanced wrath. Fiona will take care of you. Please forgive me for leaving, but I need to be with Marcus while I make the necessary phone calls," uttered Miles apologetically.

"No problem, Miles. I totally understand the situation."

I totally understand that if you and my lady lover weren't here, then I would have killed your son on the spot. Yet, again, I've saved his unworthy skin. But this time, he'll never recover.

"Oh, Randal. We're so very sorry that he's hurt you. Forgive him. He doesn't know what he's doing. He's a very sick man," she wailed, as Randal sat down in the nearest chair.

Miles led Marcus away into another room and Fiona kneeled down in front of Randal, her hands resting on his knees.

"Darling, let me see if he's damaged your neck. It's so red. Oh, my precious love. Why didn't you phone instead of just casually turning up?"

"I was visiting Ryan in Oxford, so I thought I'd just drive over on a whim," he croaked.

"Come and see me again. I need you more than ever now," she almost begged.

"You'll never get rid of me, milady," he murmured into her ear, flicking his tongue around her lobe, and his erection began to throb. "I'll wait here with you until they readmit Marcus."

"Oh, Randal. He's so terribly ill. What am I going to do? I can't help him anymore. I'm worn out with worry and guilt."

"Guilt? Why should you feel guilty? It's not your fault that he's disturbed."

"My present guilt is all to do with us. I've been unfaithful, and although I wouldn't change one second of it, I still feel unworthy of my husband's love. Marcus actually accused me today of having a long-term affair with you. He sounded so convincing and for a moment I thought he knew. He said the most abominable things."

Randal stroked the side of her cheek with genuine deference. He cleared his throat before he carried on appeasing her.

"Now listen very carefully, milady. I intend to stay here with you for now. Leave it all to Miles because he'll make sure that Marcus is readmitted. I'm sure he'll go with him and explain everything. So that just leaves you and me in close proximity, and you know what that always does to me."

"What are you saying?"

"You know what I'm saying."

Fiona looked into Randal's burning gaze. She felt the familiar heat between her legs and her nipples hardened.

"Oh, Randal. We couldn't possibly, could we?"

"Give me your hand."

Randal guided her to the protruding bulge in the front of his trousers.

"I'm on fire for you. Unzip my fly."

"Miles will be back any minute to put us into the picture," she panted.

"I only want you to stroke it. I need to feel your touch," he groaned.

"It won't be enough. You'll be too worked up to stop. We can make love later."

"I need to come, with or without you. If you don't play with me, I'll go into another room and jerk off. In fact, I'm nearly coming now."

"Oh, my darling. I want you so badly."

"Rub it," he begged, as he reached inside his zip and pulled out his quivering penis.

Fiona could not resist as her hand glided up and down the full length of his pulsating member.

"Play with these," he moaned as he exposed his swollen testicles.

She complied with his wish, all the time looking over her shoulder in case Miles returned.

"Oh, milady. Oh, fuck, that's so good. I'm going to burst!"

Fiona cupped both hands around the oozing tip in preparation to catch his usual fountain of sperm.

"Are you coming, darling? Are you coming for me? Do I make you throb?" she teased.

"Ooh, ooh, ooh."

"Come for me, my precious. Make me forget all about my woes. Let me see your stream of love for me."

"Here it comes," he gasped, as a fountain of semen spurted five times into both of her hands and seeped through her fingers.

"Oh, my darling. How I wish you were inside me now, but we haven't time."

"Don't take your hand away. Keep rubbing. There's some more," he instructed breathlessly.

Another cascade of sperm gushed into her open palm. When it stopped, Randal reached into his pocket for a handkerchief, kissing her passionately at the same time.

"I love you so much," she whispered against his lips. "Will you stay a bit longer? I need you to comfort me."

"I'm not going anywhere, milady. When Miles accompanies Marcus to the sanitorium we'll go to bed. Don't feel guilty. Just let me take away your pain," he soothed.

Your meddlesome son will never recover and I'll be your forever lover. And then it's back to Tyrone and the most important removal of all.

10

Randal was explaining to Roxanne how he had ingeniously wangled out of all the pointing fingers and mass suspicion, when a news report came on the television that stopped him in his tracks.

"Shush, pumpkin. I just heard the name Pendle. Something's happened."

They stopped talking and concentrated.

"As reported earlier in our 'breaking news' bulletin, Tyrone Pendle is undergoing the most traumatic and testing time of his young life. His father, the multi-millionaire entrepreneur Leighton Pendle, who was in prison awaiting trial for murdering his wife, Corrine, has taken his own life by stabbing himself with a stolen kitchen knife and bleeding to death.

"Tyrone's brother, Tobias, the eldest sibling by four years, has been killed in a collision at Gallows Hill in Lancaster. He crashed into an oncoming lorry by driving recklessly. This is a tragedy with an eerie coincidence, as it occurred on the same site of execution where the so-called Pendle witches were condemned to death in 1612 for murdering ten people by alleged witchcraft.

"Tyrone's sister, Tiffany, who was recently kidnapped but

returned unharmed, was also a passenger in her brother's car. She's critically injured and not expected to survive."

The newsreader carried on, but Randal and Roxanne did not have to hear any more to know that Tyrone was totally responsible. They looked at each other resignedly.

"He's killed them, Daddy! He said he would and he has! And now he'll come after us! I know he will!" she exclaimed.

"Not if we get to him first! He's full to the brim of self-indulgence. He's a newly born egomaniac, celebrating his triumph and misplaced supremacy. We both know that feeling after 'the gift' has worked its thrashing. It's a winning game, set and match of unadulterated ecstasy. So while he's bathing in his landslide achievements, we'll catch him out before he moves on to his next master stroke," counselled Randal.

"How?"

"Let's put our heads together. Go and get that large notepad out of my filing cabinet, the one I use for drafting removal plans. I've been somewhat lax because I had to rectify the fallout of Tyrone's toxic accusations. I'm behind schedule. I'll work out a definite plan and you can throw some ideas into the hangman's hat for good measure. OK, pumpkin?"

"I'm more than ready. Should I put the percolator on? We need some strong coffee. We have to be really wide awake to get the best results."

"You do that while I chew over some homicidal hospitality for our round-the-bend friend. I'll have a piece of your mother's cherry pie. I need something sweet to take away the sour taste in my mouth. He's completely wackadoodle," mocked Randal, and Roxanne laughed regardless.

"I know. He's a nut job and we have the dubious honour of stopping him. It's going to be a difficult assignment but then that's what we were born to do."

Randal smiled widely at her as she left the room, but he was not as confident as he looked.

If wrath alone could kill him, I'd have his head on a plate right now. Clive's right. I've taught him well, far better than I gave him credit for. Behind his obsessive, deadly plans for his own family, he was still soaking up all my methods.

He's one cool, calculating rookie, with a high-octane force, but he's only twenty-one compared to my forty-two-year reign, and if I add Roxanne into the magic mix, that gives us an advantage of fifty-eight years of power. We can stop him functioning. He's not invincible.

Clive rang just as Roxanne brought in a tray with a pot of freshly made ground coffee, accompanied by two cups and Alison's fruit pie.

"Have you seen the news? It's expected but horrific," he advised.

"We're aware of it. Very aware," confirmed Randal.

"We?"

"Roxanne and me. She's with me now."

"Oh God, Randal, I'm so scared. What are you going to do?"

"We don't know yet. We're mulling over several possibilities but it's full steam ahead. There's no way out of this except complete annihilation!"

"For who? Complete annihilation for who? You and Roxanne are my whole life. I'm plagued with torment over this mess. I just want you both safe and well, and by my side as long as I live."

"And we will be, Clive. We will be. Have faith in 'the gift'."

"But your erstwhile tyro has also got the same expertise in all things dark and dutiful."

"He's had less time to perfect his act."

"Oh, I wouldn't say that. Look at what he's achieved in the space of a few weeks. He's killed his parents and brother, and now his sister's hovering between here and eternity, not to mention the avalanche of muckraking he caused for you in between. He's not going to roll over easily. I think you're underestimating him."

Randal sighed. He did not need Clive reminding him of the situation, especially with negative emotion.

"I know what you're saying, but I've waded in murderous mud before and I always came out of it smelling of rapid-fire roses. Don't have a defeatist attitude before we've even begun. Granted, it won't be a walkover, but it will be victorious," comforted Randal.

"From your mouth into whoever's up there listening in hallelujah heaven."

"We don't need any holy intervention. We're cardinal and we'll override. Trust me."

"I do. I just don't trust *him*! He's got so many tricks up his serpentine sleeve."

"And so have I, Clive. So have I. Even without Roxanne, I'm more than ready for his cloak-and-dagger tactics, his Janus-faced unprincipled version of 'the gift'."

"I'm not a religious man, Randal, but I have to tell you that I'll be getting down on my knees and praying for a miracle."

"Roxanne and I are the miracle. We've been put on this earth to perform. Even though you're my treasured protector, you still don't understand the essence of our heritage. We're born winners. In every way," he stressed.

"So far."

"Ad infinitum, Clive. Ad infinitum."

"I'll cling on to that premise. I just have to—"

"Good man! Now I have to get back to my daughter and our liquidation script. Just a minute, she wants you. Don't be long, Roxanne, time is of the essence," he stressed.

"Hi, Uncle Clive. I just want to put your mind at rest. I would have done my best to stop Daddy from any intervention if I thought our chances of victory were slight. I just know that we'll be able to halt him. We're working on it together every step of the way, so please don't worry because you'll be stuck with us for many years to come. I love you."

"And I love you both, too. Sometimes I wish I didn't, and I don't mean that badly," he sighed.

"I know, and I understand your fears."

"Just stay safe. That's all I want, Roxanne, for you both to be safe."

"We will. See you soon and stop worrying. I'll put Daddy back on."

"Now, did you hear that? My daughter's predicting an outright victory. She's confident that our joint legacy will prevail. So am I."

"I just want to hear the words that Tyrone's gone for good. I don't need to know how; I just need to know when."

"Ah, so you don't mind another telepathic removal? You're usually so against my homicidal methods. I'm glad to hear you're in tune with my reasoning, Clive. Really glad."

"It's not a matter of my opinion or approval. Can I do without this? Yes. Can I do without you? No."

"Stay calm and I'll be in touch. You'll be the first to hear of any progress, for want of a better word."

"Just keep me in the loop." *I love you so much and I always will. My beloved Randal.*

Roxanne sipped her coffee as she watched Randal jotting down several potential plots. She picked up Tyrone's photograph and felt a sweeping rancour that swamped her senses, but in the middle of her furious cogitation, an effective but dangerous solution fuelled her deadly imagination.

She studied her father, engrossed in his creative, savage script, his pen skimming the paper with intense purpose. A literary foretaste of Tyrone's annihilation. She licked her lips before she spoke. She knew that her suggestion would make him hit the roof, but she felt it was the best way forward. She cleared her throat before she spoke.

"Daddy, I've just had an idea and I think it would work. It's simple but dodgy. I want you to really consider it, and try not to lose your temper until we discuss it in depth. Please?"

Randal looked up as his pen became redundant with curiosity.

"Explain," he replied with an inquisitive but penetrating gaze.

"Don't try reading my thoughts. Let me speak," she requested, as she felt him scratching around in her head.

"Well? I'm listening."

"You know that Tyrone was sweet on me before he crossed the line and spoiled everything. Well, I could win him back easily if I block my thoughts and accept the reason why he killed his parents and brother. I'll pretend that I fully understand why he's upset with you over me. I will tell him that I hate you for it. He would be more malleable that way, not to mention weakened and open to suggestion. You could catch him out and then we'd perform a joint removal," she urged.

"Stop right there! Absolutely not! It's too risky! In fact, it's completely unsafe and I wouldn't trust him with you even if I was in the bloody room, let alone a telepathic link! So, forget it!" he chided.

"But I feel I can do it! I'm a good actress and I'd make a great spy! You know that I would!"

"I don't doubt that, but you can't underestimate the extent of his powers. Even if you fool him initially, you're still in the direct line of fire if he twigs."

"He won't get past my telepathic forcefield. You've taught me so much over the years. How to act normally when the situation is irregular. How to shape my thoughts to put people off the true track. How to flatter to deceive. All that can be applied before we stick the knife into his mortality," she enthused.

"Yes, all that can undeniably be applied to a lesser mortal, but not to another recipient of 'the gift' who is intent on destroying the pair of us. I know you mean well, pumpkin, but drop it now."

"Don't you have faith in my powers? I do, even if you don't! I'm not a kid anymore, although I saved you from grave danger when I was! Daddy, I promise you I'll be able to trick him. I'm not scared. I'm excited, truly stirred and stimulated, because I know for sure that I can do this! Don't underestimate my capability because I wouldn't even suggest this if I thought I'd fail. You have to give me the benefit of your unnecessary doubt. You simply have to!" she pleaded, her slate-grey eyes crowded with shimmering yellow glints.

Randal looked deeply into her twin gaze.

She's gone from a pocket rocket to a nuke rebuke! She's a high-pressure thresher! Just look at her beautiful face. It could melt a million hearts. But can I sanction this perilous mission of madness?

"I can hear you. You forgot to turn off your psychic antennae."

"What am I going to do with you and our identical ego? You're a lip-chip off the old electroshock block. Aren't you just?" he praised, his alien eyes full of adoration.

"Does that mean we can do it my way?"

"Let me mull it over a bit longer."

"We don't have much longer! You know we don't! Tyrone's baying for our birthright blood!"

Randal lit up a cheroot, exhaled and seemed to disappear behind a cloud of smoke.

"Just exactly what do you have in mind? I don't want his experimental, dirty hands all over you while you're soft-soaping him into a kiss and a promise," he almost snarled.

"I'll get round all that."

"All what?"

"I'll make sure he understands exactly what I want from him. And what I don't."

"I don't know, Roxanne. It's a massive, perilous undertaking and there are many other avenues to go down."

"But time is our enemy. Even more than his wrath! We can't waste it concocting possible endings. This is the most forthright path to take. We can work out a demolition plan around it."

"*If*, and I've yet to condone it, *if*, I decide to go ahead with your headstrong method, then you have to keep it all away from your Uncle Clive. Don't even mention it or make reference to it at any time. Understood?"

"Totally! I'm surprised that you even think I could! I love Uncle Clive deeply and I care about his mental health. I would never intentionally stress him out. Not like… not like…"

"Me? Not like me? Is that what you're so delicately trying to say? Rub it in, why don't you?" he admonished.

"That was way back when and then. This is now. It's a new Millennium, a present-day century, and I know you're closer to him than ever before," she affirmed.

She knows I'm going to agree with her plan. It does make sense in a perilous way. I have to trust in her legacy and together we'll make it work. He's got it coming to him. We've done it before and we'll do it again. Annihilation and victory. In that order!

Roxanne rang Tyrone's mobile. She was totally composed and ready to fake her anti-Randal stance. She did not expect Tyrone to answer right away due to all the hostile recrimination, but he did.

"Well, well, well. If it isn't the snitch-bitch with the fiery red hair. The devious daughter of the two-faced, soon-to-be-dead daddy, namely 'fly off the handle' Randal. What can I do for you?" he mocked.

"Please, Tyrone. Please don't be mad at me. I need your help," she sobbed convincingly.

"Help? You want my help! I'll help you to die, Roxanne, because that's what you deserve and that's what I intend to do to all of your feckless family, especially your baddie daddy. So, if I were you, I'd just lie low until the inevitable," he flouted.

"I don't blame you. I've really let you down. You see, I made a massive mistake and I want to put it right. Please, Tyrone, just listen to me. Just give me a chance to explain everything," she begged.

"I don't trust you, Roxanne. Do you think I'm that much of a lamebrain?"

"Again, I don't blame you, but I swear that I feel the same as you."

"About what?"

"My father."

Tyrone sucked in his breath as he scanned Roxanne's head for duplicity, but all he felt was a mutual hatred for Randal. It threw him momentarily off-balance. He cleared his throat as he felt the stirrings of genuine curiosity and renewed fascination.

"So, what happened to your undying adoration for him?"

"It died."

"Why?"

"Because he didn't believe me when I told him that I loved you. He did everything he could to split us up."

"Because you opened your big mouth!"

"No, I didn't, Tyrone. He saw it telepathically and went berserk. Then he called you rotten to everyone and terminated your apprenticeship because you wouldn't follow his teachings to the letter. He's insufferable. A perpetual control freak. Just like your father was, except with 'the gift'. I want him out of my life and I need you to help me do that," she lied magnificently.

Tyrone's heart began to pound with delight and passion.

She means it, otherwise I'd know. I've won her back without even trying.

"Tyrone? Are you still there? Can we meet up? I've missed you."

"Have you now?" he replied in Randalesque fashion.

"Very much. I know I've not been in touch, but my father rules the roost and what he says goes. Well, not anymore. With your help we can remove him and then we'll be the only two true recipients of 'the gift'. Just you and me, Tyrone. Like it was written," she said passionately.

"Like it was written. I get that. I so get that," he replied with sparking eyes.

"Good. So when can we hook up?"

"You're very eager, Roxanne. This is a complete turnaround, so you can understand if I'm a little suspicious."

"I'd be if I were you, but I assure you that the hatred and loathing that I have for my insufferable father is on par, if not more, than your own. I thought of killing him myself, but I don't know if my powers are strong enough. That's why I need your help. Besides, I want to be in on the homicidal action, to get that orgasmic buzz when our joint venture succeeds."

"Now that's like the Roxanne I fell in love with." He beamed.

"This is me, Tyrone. The *real* me, longing to be rid of the paternal chains. So have we got a deal?"

"Signed, sealed and delivered. But you have to be extra-vigilant around him otherwise he'll cotton on. You must attention-train yourself to think other things when he's nearby. Keep everything low-key and casual. Just fall in with everything he wants."

"Good advice, although I'll find it hard when I really want to break his neck!"

"Leave that side to me. I've already set the wheels in motion. I've alerted his victims. His downfall is all in hand. So, what are you doing this weekend, say, Saturday?"

"Nothing much."

"I'll drive down to Weybridge and we can meet at that hotel round the corner from your school."

"You mean The Feathers?"

"Yes, that one. I'll be there at two o'clock and I'll wait for you in reception."

"I can't thank you enough for taking me back. I love you, Tyrone, and I'll make it up to you."

"You already have. Bye for now," he replied in a thick voice, feeling aroused.

She put down the receiver after some words of affection and looked at Randal. His eyes were on fire with hatred for his foe and unconditional love for his inheritress. He was so incensed that he could not speak. She knew, so she communicated telepathically.

I didn't mean a word of it, Daddy. But he fell for it. That was the aim. My removal thoughts are totally blocked off. He hasn't got a clue what's coming to him.

Just stay focused, pumpkin. I'll be with you every step of the telepathic way.

***

Roxanne was up early Saturday morning and prepared herself for her fateful meeting with Tyrone. She looked very provocative in a pair of skin-tight jeans and a clingy purple top that emphasised the swell of her full breasts and showed a tantalising glimpse of her bare midriff.

As she applied another coat of mascara to her naturally long lashes, her slate-grey eyes glinted with anticipation of her dangerous but exciting assignment. She tossed back her long, thick, glossy red curls that framed her beautiful face and pouted in the mirror admiring the violet lipstick.

Tyrone will melt when he sees me. I've got to arouse his full passion so that he'll be unprepared for any onslaught.

Randal was already in his study. He had not slept the whole night and was incredibly tense.

I feel like I'm throwing my precious child to the lions in the Coliseum during the Roman persecutions, without the Christian factor. I don't know if I can go through with this, although we've got it all planned down to the last little detail.

"Morning, Daddy. Have you had breakfast yet?" she asked, walking into the room and interrupting his concern.

"Whoa! No way! You're not meeting him like *that*! You look like a teenage hooker! He'll ravage you and I won't be able to stick to our script! Get changed, Roxanne! I insist!" he barked, ignoring her question.

"I know what I'm doing, so calm down. I have to make myself absolutely irresistible to weaken his defences. We need him unprepared and enfeebled."

"Crap! Let me tell you, he'll be just the opposite: very assembled, fortified and stiffened in more ways than one!"

"Daddy!"

"Never mind Daddy!"

"Look, we've got a monumental removal to do. I have to stick to my rule book and go with my gut instinct. I don't need another disagreement with you about silly clothing when we have a madman on our coat tails. It's irrelevant compared to the end result, so stop playing the over-protective father. Please! I'm nearly seventeen and far, far more advanced than the average girl of my age!"

"And I'm far, far from happy with your fashion faux pas. Let's get this over and done with, once and for all," he instructed through an angry, narrow gaze.

"I don't think you should take me. There's a bus that will get me there in good time. We can't risk him seeing your car or picking up the slightest suspicious vibe."

"This just gets worse for me, Roxanne. Sacrificial lamb comes to mind," he carped.

"Tyrone's the one who'll be slaughtered. Not me. He's going to die. Today!"

Randal fumed.

I won't control my wrath if he abuses her. I'll hit him so

fucking hard that he'll be defunct prior to our script! Well before the agenda begins!

***

Roxanne arrived at her designation and saw Tyrone waiting impatiently. She walked over to join him in the hotel reception lounge. He sprang up the minute she appeared and smiled broadly as he greeted her.

"Wow! You look amazing! Far more than sweet sixteen." He salivated.

"Good to see you too," she flirted, concealing all her bad intentions.

"I've booked a table in the restaurant. Are you hungry?" he asked, his eyes trailing up and down her shapely form.

"Not really. I just want to be with you and get things straight. Can't we eat afterwards?"

"After what?" He drooled.

"You know," she intimated suggestively.

"Whatever you want. I'm all yours, Roxanne. I took the liberty of booking a room for us. I knew we'd need complete privacy, and besides, I want you all to myself. Badly," he groaned.

"Me, too. I've been dreaming about this moment. I love you, Tyrone, and my father will just have to come to terms with that, or else he'll never see me again. I also told him that if he tries to harm you, I'll intervene and add my powers to yours. From the look on his crestfallen face, I think he got the message. He loves me far too much to even try. So, we're officially an item. I made sure of it and I always get my own way in the end," she affirmed.

Tyrone's chest puffed out like a pompous toad that had record-jumped over a multiple line of floating lily pads. He led her by the hand towards the lift and up to the first floor into Room 34, the same numbered door that Randal had chosen to see Francine

Flint when he had hypnotised her to meet him at another hotel, on her own home ground, to kick-start Carlton's demise.

Tyrone had deliberately plumped for the identical room number as an ironical nod to Randal's treacherous, erotic, telepathic programme.

As soon as they were inside, he pulled Roxanne to him and kissed her passionately, his hands running up and down her beautiful young body in a desperate bid to make her his own.

"Do you know how sexy you are?" he growled thickly into her ear, as he pressed up against her, leaving her in no doubt about his strong arousal.

"Am I?" she whispered, responding brilliantly to his physical need, concealing her contempt.

He tugged at her top. She pulled it over her head and dropped it onto the floor. He was desperate to get inside her bra.

"Let's take this off. I want to see your gorgeous breasts," he moaned.

He removed it then pinched her nipples. He was breathing heavily as he rubbed the large bulge in his trousers against her. He unzipped his fly and brought out his throbbing phallus. He guided her hand towards it when a sudden, unbridled surge of power yanked him away and flung him forcefully across the room.

He shook his head as he felt momentarily dazed then looked across at her, open-mouthed.

"You bitch! Why did you do that? I should have known!" he raved.

"It wasn't me! I wouldn't!" she insisted.

"Don't give me your floozy flannel. It's your speciality!" he spat, his dark eyes alight with an unrighteous glow.

"It must be my father. He's in your head," she reasoned.

"I'd know if he was! There's no sign of him whatsoever, so this is all your own doing, Roxanne!" he accused menacingly.

"No, it's not!"

"Liar! Look, Miss Forbes, I've just made sure that my airhead of a sister has finally kicked the bucket. She should have died with Tobias in that car crash I devised! So, I tweaked your daddy's script again and got the nurse to over-inject her with morphine and then disconnect her life support to make absolutely sure! But I know your dear daddy won't congratulate me on my glorious achievement. He'll just accuse me of plagiarism! Big deal, if I nick his ideas? They work, don't they? I'm so sick of being derided and humiliated. Tiffany was part of that syndrome. Are you, Roxanne? Are you?" he pumped with flashing eyes and a grotesque facial expression, as he tucked his flaccid penis away and zipped up his fly.

"Am I what, Tyrone?"

"Are you part of that do-Tyrone-down syndrome? If you are, then I'll just have to remove you!"

"But you love me."

"Love is destitute of sight. I've just dislodged the blindfold," he sneered.

"You know what, Tyrone? That really was my father before who made you fly across the room, but now, after your pathetic turnaround and disgraceful behaviour, well…"

Roxanne's eyes glowed. Tyrone suddenly floated above the floor and was rapidly airlifted upward, until his head banged against the ceiling.

"Now Mr Pendle, *that* was definitely me! Are you enjoying the view from up there? Oh, just a minute, my father wants a little word in your unbalanced ear. He's been in the room with us all the time, courtesy of yours truly: living, loathing and breathing telepathically through me. How cool is he?" she mocked confidently.

Randal was ungovernable behind Roxanne's eyes. His fury was boiling over, positively volcanic and frenzied as he addressed the brain of his former novice.

Are you receiving me you abortive, valueless, fruitless, furtive fruitcake? Did you really think I'd disappear off the unchecked, sordid scene? Think again, shipwreck!

Tyrone's eyes were practically popping out of his head from the inordinate impact of Randal's furious thought transference.

Do you think for one squalid, solitary second that I'd let you worm your defective, poisonous presence back into my daughter's precious life? You absolute malignant, rancorous, counterfeit, double-dealing non-starter!

I detest you to such a degree that you make my former hatred for Carlton Flint amiable! And now, I'm going to sever your filthy, perverted hands that have left their tainted touch on Roxanne's beautiful body. You whoremonger!

Randal pulled out of Roxanne's head and focused on the full-length photographic image of his ex-tyro. He picked up the razor blade on his desktop and slashed Tyrone's wrists with great precision, pressing so hard that he split the glossy paper.

Tyrone screamed as he felt the full voodoo effect, blood pouring down the joints uniting his hands to his arms. Roxanne's own hold on him was merciless as he remained in mid-air, glued to the ceiling by his hair.

"I'll kill you both!" he screeched as he struggled to free himself from his terrifying, telepathic trap.

His incandescent eyes bore into Roxanne's and she felt her head jerk backwards with the powerful force. It threw her completely off-balance as Tyrone dropped to the floor, breaking her hold over his floating state.

He was losing blood rapidly from both slit wrists but was spurred on by pure hatred and revenge. He grabbed her, pushed her over and pinned her to the ground with his full weight, covering her in red gore.

"Now who's in charge? I'm going to kill the host body, namely yours, and then daddy dearest won't be able to see me! Will he now?" he spat.

"Oh yes, he will, cretin! He's not in my head anymore. He's in your photograph!" she squealed.

Randal's fury went up another six notches. His head felt on the verge of violent detonation. He punched Tyrone's image repeatedly in his abdomen, and the raging action demolished its recipient as he rolled off Roxanne in agony, doubling up from the extreme pain.

Stop thumping him now. Leave him to me, Daddy. Leave him to me!

Roxanne stared at the ultra-heavy paperweight on the desk nearby. It began to rise up and move steadily towards her target. Tyrone sat up the minute his pain ceased and twisted his head round to face her.

"I slipped up, you bitch! I came unprepared! I should have brought a photo of daddy Randal with me!"

"And *that*, Tyrone, is one of the many reasons why he terminated your apprenticeship! Because you just handpicked the parts out of his tutorials to suit your murderous needs and you didn't pay full attention to all of the snags that might occur when faced with an unexpected attack! The first major rule is *always* carrying an image of your rival in your wallet. But no! Tyrone knows best. You thought you'd manipulate me into some simpering, virginal patsy. No way! And now it's your turn to die!"

The white, ornate paperweight, in the shape of a slick Lotus Elan, hovered in the air and then motored along an invisible thread of motivation in Tyrone's direction. Roxanne ingeniously guided it while administrating a further lecture on his unsuitability as Randal's tyro.

"I was under the false assumption that you were a worthy successor of 'the gift'. I fell in love with the idea. I thought you could replace my father after he'd gone. I must have been drunk. You could never, ever come a fraction close to his majesty. He's omnipotent. You're just excrement!"

"You dirty little whore! You're in love with your own father! Does he feel the same way, I wonder? Are you already having a repulsive, incestuous relationship? Do you imagine him all over you when I touch you? Slut!" he defamed.

"You're disgusting, Tyrone! Truly nauseating. You belong in a padded cell with chains wrapped around your straightjacket. You're shameful. Just detestable!"

"Oh, well now. The lady protests too much, methinks! I use the word 'lady' very loosely, you understand?"

"Don't move, Tyrone. Stay exactly where you are."

"And why's that, my little incestuous hussy?"

"Because I want to savour the moment."

"What moment, bitch?"

"This one."

The glass-car ornament struck the back of his head with great force. He slumped forward, losing consciousness instantly, and lay on the caramel-coloured carpet which was soaked in blood stains from his slashed wrists.

Roxanne walked over to him to make sure he had no pulse. She went back to the desk and sat down on a plush cream leather chair, as she called to Randal telepathically.

Daddy, can you hear me? I've killed him.

I hear you and I'm blazing!

I know you are, but now he's out of our lives. He can't torment us anymore.

That maybe so, but I wanted to kill him, Roxanne. I feel short-changed. He got away with that filthy, verbal bile and his perverted passion.

It doesn't matter who removed him. He's gone for good.

"Are you quite sure about that?" mocked Tyrone behind her, wrapping his blooded fingers around her throat with superhuman strength, regardless of his catastrophic injuries, and she began to choke as his stranglehold tightened.

Daddy, help me!

Randal's eyes glowed with radioactive intensity. It was a deadly emission. It resembled the radiant energy of formed particles caused by the disintegration of atomic nuclei. So blinding was his enraged vision that Tyrone's head became instantly and violently invaded.

He let go of Roxanne as his fingers caught fire. Randal had set Tyrone's photograph alight with his cheroot lighter, moving it along every digit of his blood-streaked hands. Tyrone screamed as his skin began to blister and blacken, the smell of burning flesh permeating the air, as Randal was relentless in his vengeful, furious punishment, which was as deadly and effective as him being present in the room.

He continued to raid Tyrone's mind until it was incapable of rational thought, let alone retaliation. His brain felt like a soggy, limp, septic sponge. Every cell was contaminated with telepathic venom: a cerebral invasion so powerful that it obliterated his spinal cord and whole central nervous system, until he lay completely motionless on the floor, his vacant eyes staring into nowhere.

Roxanne's breathing was erratic as if there was an obstruction lodged in her larynx, caused by Tyrone's former suffocating grip.

Now listen to me, pumpkin. Just sit back while I heal you.

I can heal myself, I think.

Don't even try.

Randal's soothing, healing ritual took effect with effortless ease. It was the least he could do for his precious inheritress.

How's that? Better now?

Much better.

Good. Now, this is what I want you to do. Phone reception and ask for the manager of the hotel. Sound unrestrained and frantic.

I will.

Tell him that Tyrone Pendle forced himself upon you and ripped off your clothes. He… he exposed himself and when you wouldn't play ball, he tried to kill you and acted completely insane. He slashed his wrists and set fire to his fingers, to freak you out. Then he tried to strangle and rape you. You had no choice but to hit him with that paperweight as a means of defence.

I understand.

Rip your top and look as dishevelled as you possibly can. Are you covered in his blood?

Yes. Especially round my neck and breasts.

Randal groaned, still full of hatred for his dead foe.

Put your bra back on but not your top. This is killing me, pumpkin. If I had a flamethrower, I'd incinerate him!

No need. He's gone for good.

Randal pulled himself together.

After you've spoken to reception, go into the corridor and ring my mobile. Act hysterical. Let people hear what you say. Beg me to come and get you.

I will.

Good girl. I'll be with you very shortly. Oh, pumpkin?

Yes, Daddy?

I'm so proud of you. So very proud. I love you.

Roxanne beamed. It was all worth it to hear him praise her efforts. Her heart sang. She loved him beyond words. But he knew that.

And that's all she wanted from life. Randal's unconditional love. His plaudits and devotion. For eternity.

EPILOGUE

Ryan was with a crowd of fellow students in the refectory at Beaumont College. Tyrone Pendle was the sole topic of conversation.

"My God, Ryan! Your sister was so lucky to escape! How is she? It must have affected her badly. He was a complete basket case! I always thought he was an oddity!"

"She's had to be fatalistic, I guess. I mean, at first, we couldn't calm her down. Only Dad was able to do that eventually. I think she wants everything and everyone to go away now – too much publicity. The police have questioned her quite a few times. It's hard for her to talk about it. Me, too," he admitted, putting an end to the discussion.

Ryan got up and walked away, but they all understood. He phoned Randal for the umpteenth time.

"Hi, Dad. How's Roxanne doing?"

"She's OK. She's on the mend. Try not to worry, Ryan. It's all under control now," reassured Randal.

"How can it ever be under control? It's my fault entirely. I introduced him to you all. Why didn't I realise that he was insane? She could have died! Oh, God, Dad! She could have died!"

"She didn't, and you're not to blame. I readily accepted him into our family circle, as a friend. Even I couldn't see his dark side," he lied validly.

"But—"

"But nothing. We'll get through this. We have before and we will again. It's not your fault that he was deranged. You didn't cause it; his psychosis did. Now stop beating yourself up. Your mum and I want you to take some time off and come home. OK?"

"I need to. I want to be with you, especially Roxanne."

"At times like this we have to be undivided."

"Yes, Dad. Expect me today. I've had enough of the gossip and analysis. It seems the whole world wants to talk about Tyrone Pendle and his cursed family. I'm so sick of it all."

"Of course you are. Now, get your stuff together and drive safely home to the family who love you the most. Hmm?"

"Thanks, Dad. You're the best. I love you," he said softly.

"See you soon then, son. Bye. Love you, too."

See you soon, my hoodwinked firstborn. I do love and care about all my lesser mortal children. I still have to protect them from homicidal fallout. In my own inimitable way.

***

Edward and Margaret Forbes were full of concern and remorse.

"I feel so guilty. I had such a go at Randal about Roxanne being his favourite daughter, especially after Amber complained she felt left out. Well, it seems that she's become very protective of Roxanne since the horrific incident and they are now very close," confessed Margaret.

"Indeed. It appears that way to me. It's certainly cemented them together. When I spoke to Roxanne yesterday, she sounded so pleased and grateful that I'd rang her," admitted Edward.

"Ryan's also very caring. He still feels guilty about introducing her to that lunatic. He said that Roxanne has been wonderful to him considering her ordeal. She makes him feel less culpable and puts his troubled mind at rest with her selfless compassion. You know something, Edward? I think we got it all wrong. Randal was right. She was just looking for a harbour in an orphan-storm and touched his heart in the process. It's about time we showed her some affection and respect."

"Oh, absolutely! Adopted or not, she's one of us now. A Forbes. Another beautiful granddaughter."

"She's seventeen this weekend. Alison's asked us to the party. I think it's more than just a birthday celebration. It's an act of thankfulness for her survival. It's a wonder that her mental health is still intact. She's had so much trauma in her young life," sighed Margaret.

"Much too much. Losing both parents as a child is life-changing. Let's face it, they didn't pass away from illness. They both died in tragic circumstances. Maxine committed suicide and Saul was violently murdered. We've known this all along and should have been more understanding of her plight, instead of admonishing our son for smothering her with love. It's just that Ryan, Amber and Oscar seemed so pushed out. I guess we didn't see the whole picture," deducted Edward.

"We didn't. Considering we've spent our whole working lives teaching children and preparing them for their journeys into the world at large, we were very negligent and heedless with Roxanne. Well, that's all going to change from now on," she said resolutely.

"Let's take time out and make her feel really wanted. Invite her down with Amber, next weekend. We simply must make amends. We won't be here forever and she needs grandparents. We've never afforded her that essential input."

"Oh, you're so right, Edward. I'll give her a ring now. Go and put the kettle on, and we'll have tea and apple pie." She smiled.

Margaret phoned and Randal answered.

"Hello, darling. I want to speak to Roxanne. She's in my thoughts and prayers every day. Randal, I was wrong. So was your father. We have to make it up to her."

"She'll love that. That's all she's ever wanted. A family. I'll go and get her. Thanks a lot, Mum."

It's taken a near-death experience for my pumpkin to be loved by all. What a fantastic result! A jubilant removal, then acceptance status! Rock on, Roxanne! The world's waiting for you!

***

Randal and Roxanne were bathing in good wishes and misplaced commiseration, but as sincere and well meaning as they all were, not one of them came a fraction close to the deep, abiding love and relief felt by Clive. He was delirious with deliverance.

I never thought I'd be so ecstatic over the success of this latest cut-throat murder. The imagery, sorcery and butchery lived up to an award-winning Hammer horror production. Yet, I'm on cloud nine, ten and eleven.

He's safe and she's saved! Tyrone's gone for good! Randal and Roxanne have turned me into an assassin by association because I was willing him to die, so that the love of my life, and his precious daughter, would blossom and grow. And if that makes me evil too, then I'm guilty as charged, your honour!

Clive's mobile rang. It was Randal.

"Hello, you. Your delight is winging its way through my receptive airways. I can hear your gratitude and sense your unfettered joy. It's catching, Clive. I feel much the same," he said warmly.

"You've no idea how much I love you both. I'm only human."

"You, my dearest most cherished friend and protector, are superhuman. Your love, loyalty and devotion take my breath away. We'll be together forever more, as we always have been. Is that clear?"

"Clear."

"Now, get yourself down here. You're like family to me and we need to stick together. Alison wants a word," said Randal, handing his mobile over to her.

"Hi, Clive. We're having a birthday party for Roxanne this weekend. She wants to celebrate her seventeenth and we need you here with us all. We love you, Clive. Roxanne thinks the world of you. Please come and stay over."

"Just try and stop me because you'll fail for sure." He choked, the tears of happiness cascading down his freckled cheeks.

"I'm going to give your mum and dad a ring now, and invite them as well. It will be so nice for all of us to get together, like the old days," she said nostalgically.

"Ah, yes, those old days. Where did they go, Alison? I blinked and forty-two years disappeared."

"Don't remind me. I'm five years older than you and Randal. Remember? You could say that he's my eternal toy boy," she joked.

"I guess you could call him that." *Not so much your toy boy as my eternal joy boy.*

"See you on Saturday. Oh, Clive, please come whenever you want; before then if you wish. You really are family to us. You're the brother that Randal never had."

"I'll come on Friday instead. Thanks, Alison," he concluded.

The brother that Randal never had, eh? I'll come on Friday all right. Saturday and Sunday as well. With him!

***

Dean was looking forward to Roxanne's party. He was just finishing some paperwork for the latest Astral TV drama when there was a timid knock at the studio door.

"Come in," he requested, still concentrating on the job in hand.

The door opened. He looked up and did a double take.

"Maddie! What are you doing here? Does your... your psychiatrist know you're out? I thought you were still under supervision." He frowned.

"You mean am I still sectioned? I've not escaped, Dean. I'm recovering well as an out-patient, especially now that I've got something amazing to live for," she declared.

"What do you mean? Are you suggesting that we get back together again? I don't want to give you false hope. I care about you very much, but you need professional help and I'm not equipped to give that to you on a full-time basis. I'm so sorry," he said with compassion.

"I understand that, but things are very different now. I don't expect you to run into my arms. That's not why I'm here. There's someone I want you to meet. Someone very special. He's changed my life for the better."

"Oh, I see. I'm delighted for you, Maddie. Is he with you now?"

"He's waiting outside."

"Well, bring him in."

She nodded and left the room. Dean was puzzled and somewhat unnerved.

God, I hope she's really OK. Last time she came at me with a bloody knife. One minute calm and then boom*!*

Maddie returned and Dean's jaw dropped wide open.

"Dean, this is Carlton. He's four months old today. He's your son and I've named him after my dad, so I registered him with my maiden name. I don't want anything from you, but it's only right that you should know that you're his actual father, even though your surname isn't on the birth certificate."

"Oh my God, Maddie! Are you sure?"

"That he's yours? One hundred per cent certain. There's

been nobody since you. Do you want to hold him?" she asked, bringing him over in his carry cot.

"I'm stunned. He looks so like Carlton. The same features and colouring." He gulped.

Randal's going to freak out. My whole family will. I think I should take a paternity test. God!

Maddie's baby kicked hard underneath the blanket. His little fists were grasping the air around them. His tiny, rosebud mouth curled upward in a knowing smile.

He opened his eyes and looked at Dean. They began to glow with electric-blue vision. Exceptionally alert. So vibrant. Almost holy. Just like his late grandfather's.

And now he had exactly the same name. It would never die. It would just live on.

Carlton Flint.

About the Author

Fran Raya currently lives in Manchester. Her career has been predominantly in music since the 1970s, both in the UK and abroad, originally as a singer-songwriter but now in later years purely as a songwriter who places original songs with other artists. Fran is a member of The Guild of International Songwriters and Composers (GISC) and has been featured in their quarterly magazines. She has performed throughout Europe as she used to be based in Denmark and was the support act for Eric Clapton on his Scandinavian tours in the 1980s. She has also published poetry in numerous anthologies and as a result was awarded her own book, Thoughts of the Poet.

For writing and publishing news, or
recommendations of new titles to read,
sign up to the Book Guild newsletter: